HANNAH GREGORY WAS NOT WHAT SHE SEEMED.

But then, neither was he.

His lips curled into a harsh smile. "The dancing lesson is over, Miss Gregory. You will be so good as to remember your place."

Flushing deeply, she stepped out of his arms so quickly that she crashed into the divan behind her and toppled backward onto its cushions.

As she flailed about for a helpless moment, Julian caught a glimpse of her bare legs. With a muttered curse he reached down and jerked her to her feet.

"You need not trouble yourself—" she began heatedly, only to break off with a startled squeak as he brought his lips to hers.

The Dastardly Duke

Eileen Putman

A SIGNET BOOK

SIGNET
Published by the Penguin Group
Penguin Putnam Inc., 375 Hudson Street,
New York, New York 10014, U.S.A.
Penguin Books Ltd, 27 Wrights Lane,
London W8 5TZ, England
Penguin Books Australia Ltd,
Ringwood, Victoria, Australia
Penguin Books Canada Ltd, 10 Alcorn Avenue,
Toronto, Ontario, Canada M4V 3B2
Penguin Books (N.Z.) Ltd, 182-190 Wairau Road,
Auckland 10, New Zealand

Penguin Books Ltd, Registered Offices:
Harmondsworth, Middlesex, England

First published by Signet, an imprint of Dutton Signet,
a member of Penguin Putnam Inc.

First Printing, January, 1998
10 9 8 7 6 5 4 3 2 1

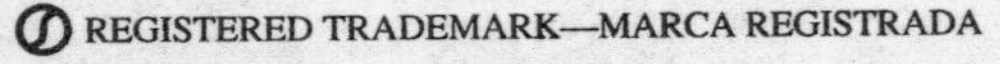

Printed in the United States of America

Prologue

A reformed rake led a miserable existence.

Regarding the half-filled brandy bottle with a mixture of longing and dread, Julian LeFevre vowed never again to sit through one of Lady Harwood's musicales without the fortification of spirits coursing through his veins.

Sobriety—and reform in general—was painfully boring.

Julian winced at the memory of the tedious evening he had endured. Lately, all his evenings had been tedious. Since resolving to face his future squarely, without the numbing distractions of dissipation and debauchery, he had not enjoyed one moment of his drastically altered lifestyle.

Respectability held no allure. This hair shirt he had manfully donned only left him itching to be rid of it. Quiet evenings made him restless, like a suit of clothes that did not fit him properly.

Life had lost its spice. Lady Harwood's vapid punch had not soothed him, and the only women he had encountered were the few pallid debutantes willing to overlook his reputation in exchange for elevation to the rank of duchess.

Virtue most assuredly was *not* its own reward.

Anyway, no one believed he had truly changed. Despite his excruciatingly civilized demeanor, watchful mamas still hovered protectively over their chicks when he was near.

The betting books had given him a month to return to his former ways. Julian doubted he would make it two weeks. Boredom held no solace. The gaming hells beckoned still. The sirens of the night sang as seductively as ever. Certain thirsts were unquenchable, it seemed.

Glowering at the brandy bottle, hating its seductive promises of forgetfulness, Julian told himself he had done his best. He had accepted all respectable invitations, avoided his usual excesses, donned his best society manners, and kept a civil tongue. But it was no use.

He was a bastard at heart.

The inner demons that demanded he reorder his dissolute life and face the dilemma of his lineage would not be silenced by good behavior—just as they had not been assuaged by debauchery. Neither sin nor virtue had resolved the uncertainty that tormented him. A dukedom and his immortal soul hung in the balance, and he did not know how to save either one.

With a jaundiced eye, Julian regarded the family Bible that lay open before him. The pages recording the births and deaths of generations of heirs to the dukedom had been obliterated, a defect he had long ago discovered. Tonight he had been desperate enough to hope he had overlooked something that might finally reveal whether he was living a lie.

But there was nothing, only some of his moralizing aunt's sermons that someone had tucked inside the cover of the least-read book in the house.

A loud thump sounded from the shelf above him. Without the sturdy old Bible as a bookend, the books that had stood next to it toppled over. Julian slammed the heavy tome shut and heaved it up to its place on the shelf, out of sight and memory. It was a perfect bookend. But then, a family Bible ought to be good for something.

His mouth curled into a bitter smile. All hesitation gone, he reached for the bottle.

Chapter One

"Devil take it, Julian! Your sister has refused me three times."

Frowning at the glaring sunlight that invaded his study with Sir Charles Tremaine's abrupt arrival, Julian regarded his friend with a less-than-sympathetic eye. His head ached like the devil from the worthless solace he had sought last night in his brandy, and his brain felt as thick as a wad of cotton.

"Lost your touch with the ladies, have you, Charles?" he drawled as Charles flopped glumly into a claret leather wing chair.

The baronet grimaced. "She is holding out for an earl, I am sure of it."

Unable to fathom how any man could allow a woman to reduce him to such a state, Julian shook his head—an unwise move that produced a blinding spasm of pain. "Your problem is that you are too eager," he muttered. "Women never want anything unless they think they cannot have it."

"And *your* problem is that you do not have the vaguest idea what it is like for us lesser mortals," Charles grumped. "The fact is, a duke's daughter may wed as high as she chooses. Why should your sister bother with a mere baronet whose pockets are to let?"

With a grunt of impatience, Julian rose and moved to a small table to pour out two glasses from a crystal decanter that had beckoned him all morning. "Drown your sorrows in this," he commanded. "And while you are at it, reflect upon the fact that your financial shortcomings cannot matter one whit to a woman who has thirty thousand pounds a year in pin money. Lucy has never cared about pedigree."

"I suppose when one dwells in the lofty altitudes of a dukedom, one need not concern oneself with how the *ton* will view a match with an impoverished baronet." Charles sighed.

Julian's mouth curled contemptuously. "No one has ever dared to meddle in our affairs. They will not start now."

"You but prove my point. Why, look at you! You wear Weston's finest—without padding, of course—with the effortless assurance of royalty. Your cravat is tied so intricately no one could possibly mimic it. And those boots are from St. James's Street, or I am King George."

Julian glanced down at his burnished black leather Hussars and shrugged. He had never bothered about fashion, leaving such matters to his valet. "So?"

Charles made a sound of disgust. "Despite the rakehell's reputation you have so richly earned, nothing can erase that magnificent ducal shadow you cast. Do you think the *ton* would tolerate your behavior otherwise?"

Tossing off his drink in a single gulp, Julian scowled. "If society chooses to look at a sow's ear and call it a silk purse, that is not my concern."

"You underestimate society," Charles responded. "Breeding will out. And you, my friend, are bred to a fare-thee-well. The list of your titles would fill a ballroom: 'His Grace, the Duke of Claridge. The Most Honorable the Marquess of Ramsey. The Right Honorable the Earl of—'"

"Cut line, Tremaine," Julian snapped, "before I cut out that glib tongue of yours."

"Nevertheless, your pedigree—"

"Might be worthless."

Charles frowned. "Not *that* again."

With a muttered curse, Julian set down his glass. "Admit it, Charles: you can no more swear to my right to this position than you can fly to the moon."

The baronet looked away. "You make too much of the deathbed utterances of a vengeful old man."

"And you make too much of a title," Julian returned scornfully. "Anybody with hubris and intelligence can manipulate the *ton*. Those biddies at Almack's are too vain to look beyond the end of their noses. Wave a bit of glitter at them and they are caught. Why, I could take someone from the streets and pass her off as a duchess."

An intrigued expression crossed Charles's face. "A bet?" he asked softly, eyes suddenly alight with anticipation.

Julian pushed back the thick shock of black hair destined to fall onto his forehead no matter what his valet did to tame it. "Why not?" he returned in a bored voice.

"Someone from the streets, you say?"

"Or the gutter." Julian shrugged. "It makes no matter."

"And the wager?"

"Anything you wish. I care not."

Charles took a deep breath. "I will have your sister, then, if it is all the same to you."

An incredulous bark of laughter was Julian's response. "Winning a bet with me will scarcely bring Lucy around."

Charles did not smile. "An elopement might."

"Idiot!" Julian glared at him. "I cannot allow you to elope with my sister."

"I should not do so without your permission, of course," Charles rejoined, his gaze bleak. "But I am convinced that if we could only share one night of passion, she would never have eyes for another man."

"Not even a reprobate would collaborate in his sister's seduction." Julian's brows met ominously and his voice held a dangerous edge.

"You misunderstand," the baronet hastily assured him. "My intentions are entirely honorable. But Lucy's court is large, and she is pleased to have her fun. By Jove, I will not wait forever."

Such a declaration from the normally phlegmatic Charles prompted Julian to roll his eyes. "Do you honestly expect me to look the other way while you married my sister over the anvil and ruined her reputation?"

"A duke's daughter is impervious to ruin," Charles reminded him.

Slowly, a spark of interest kindled within Julian's deep-set eyes, eroding the permanent look of boredom that had fallen over his features lately.

"You are mad," he said quietly.

"Not at all," Charles assured him. "But the odds against your turning some street wench into a paragon of respectability give me reason to risk the highest stakes."

For the first time in weeks, Julian felt the boredom leave him.

"Done."

Charles blinked. "What?"

"I said I will take you on," Julian said calmly. "Your matched bays against my sister's hand. You pick the wench I am to transform. My only condition is that she must be young and passably pretty."

"You have that much confidence in your ability?"

Bottomless, dark eyes filled with scorn. "I have that much confidence in society's stupidity. Do you think I would risk Lucy's reputation otherwise?"

"You would risk whatever serves your purpose. But you need not worry about Lucy. She will be in good hands—mine, eventually." Charles smiled, his mood considerably lightened by the prospect.

"Your lack of confidence in my abilities wounds me." Sardonic humor radiated from Julian's gaze. "How shall you go about picking the formless lump of clay I am to mold into one of the season's Originals?"

A cunning look crept over Charles's features. "I know just the place. The Lock Hospital."

"What!" Julian stared in disbelief. "You would saddle me with a syphilitic whore?"

"Not at all," Charles said blandly. "Some of the, ah, patients are quite healthy, I understand, just down on their luck. I wager that the perfect candidate for you reposes within those walls."

Julian's brows arched heavenward, but his harshly planed features looked anything but angelic. "I will say this, Tremaine—you know how to hedge your bets."

Charles cast his friend a baleful look. "A man in love can be desperate."

"Balderdash." Julian's gaze grew coolly assessing. "By the way, Charles."

The baronet eyed him warily. "Yes?"

"You will take no steps to win my sister before I have had my chance with the woman. I will need time to pull this off." At Charles's mulish gaze, he added, "I assume you do not wish to let Lucy get wind of our little wager."

His friend paled. "Certainly not."

Julian's lips curled. "Then I expect you will do your best to smooth the way for our lump of clay."

"What?" Charles frowned.

"I want no sabotage. My protégée will succeed or fail on her own merits. You will not by so much as a raised eyebrow hint to anyone that she is not the proper young lady I will make her appear to be."

"Very well. But you have forgotten one thing. Any young lady introduced as your protégée cannot help but have certain . . . rather lurid assumptions made about her character from the outset."

"How kind of you to point that out. And now, let us go and choose the poor young woman whose dismal fortunes are about to take a turn for the better."

"Disease is God's punishment of sinners," declared the Reverend James T. McGougal.

Gravely stroking his chin, as if considering the minister's words, Charles allowed the statement to stand without comment. Julian possessed no such tact, however.

He regarded the man with the embedded cynicism of one of Satan's own angels. "Presiding over a building of sick whores must bring you great delight, then," he said idly, "for surely it is rare to witness such tangible proof of the Creator's justice."

As Charles erupted in a sudden fit of coughing, Reverend McGougal looked uncertain.

"I only meant that you must not expect too much of this young woman, Your Grace," the minister explained, eyeing Julian nervously. "Her character was formed long ago, I am afraid."

"We understand completely," Charles managed. "You must not concern yourself with our expectations."

A hint of suspicion flashed over the minister's features. "You will not use her ill? I release her to you only upon your word that you will not abuse her, nor return her to the streets.

Our goal is to change the animal-like behavior of these girls, not to encourage it."

"Locking them up in cages is perfectly consistent with your philosophy, of course," Julian drawled.

"They are not cages." Reverend McGougal reddened. "The bars on their rooms are for their own protection."

Charles eyed Julian reproachfully. "You must not regard the duke this afternoon," he told the minister. "He has been a trifle ill himself lately."

"God's punishment, no doubt," Julian muttered.

Hastily, Charles shepherded the minister away from Julian. "I can assure you that we will treat the young woman with respect."

Julian arched a brow. "And in any case, my donation to your hospital should be sufficient to assuage your doubts."

The minister flushed. "You have been most kind, Your Grace."

"Then may we get on with it?" Julian asked in a silky tone that bore a distinct note of impatience.

"I have already sent for the girl." Reverend McGougal mopped his brow. "I should mention, perhaps, that while Hannah is one of the few women here who meet your age and, ah, other qualifications, she has one or two drawbacks."

"Drawbacks?" Julian frowned.

"I hope the Lady Lucille will find her acceptable nevertheless," the minister quickly added. "The young woman is quite intelligent and possesses a hardy constitution." He cleared his throat. "She is also quiet. Very quiet. And unassuming. One could not say that about many of our other patients."

By this time, Julian was thoroughly weary of Reverend McGougal. Nor was the hospital a particularly pleasant place. Its dingy gray walls imparted an oppressive air of gloom and decay. The knowledge that most of the inmates were suffering from incurable illnesses contributed to the atmosphere of hopelessness. Julian had seen one tight-lipped nurse and a slovenly orderly, but otherwise, the Lock Hospital appeared to have little in the way of staff.

Vulgar propositions came from some of the patients who watched them through cells off the corridor to McGougal's office. Women with pockmarked faces, toothless grins, and wild eyes reached through the iron bars, their blistered hands extended in a plea for freedom that acknowledged the futility of their plight. Julian had no doubt that McGougal spoke the truth when he insisted that few of the women could pass muster outside of these walls. He only hoped that the woman McGougal had in mind bore no resemblance to these tormented souls.

As the sound of creaking hinges indicated the opening of the door to McGougal's office, Julian turned warily.

A young woman in tattered clothing stood at the threshold. She nodded briefly as the minister introduced them, but said nothing. Her eyes searched the faces of each person in the room.

Julian did not bother to hide his distaste for the ragged scarf that covered her hair and the formless dress that looked to be some larger woman's castoff. But while her skin bore an unnatural pallor, it appeared otherwise healthy. And her light gray eyes were clear and earnest, as if a lucid intelligence resided behind them. She clutched her hands tightly, without the frantic wringing and constant nervous movement he had seen in the other women.

It was difficult to take her measure, but with a little cleaning up and a new wardrobe, she might do for his purposes. Reverend McGougal began to explain matters to her, and relief swept her features as the minister told her she was to leave the hospital. It was quickly replaced by doubt when the minister informed her that she was to be turned over to these two gentlemen.

Julian eyed her speculatively. Most women in her position could not care less about the minister's fervent assurances that she was going to a respectable household, but she seemed to hang on McGougal's every word.

Finally, she nodded her understanding. Her gaze flew to Julian and did not waver as she spoke in a clear, soft voice. "What would be my position in your home, Your Grace?"

Her gray eyes sought his with unusual intensity. Turning away from her oddly unsettling scrutiny, Julian spoke more to the wall than to her. "If all goes well, Miss . . ." He tried to remember her name, but could not. "If all goes well," he repeated, "you will be employed as my sister's"—he searched for an appropriate word—"assistant."

Reverend McGougal cleared his throat. "It is important to look at Hannah when you speak, Your Grace."

Surprised, Julian turned. The girl was staring at him without comprehension. He frowned at McGougal. "What are you talking about?"

"Hannah is excellent at reading lips, but you must afford her the opportunity to do so," the minister replied uneasily.

"Reading lips?" Julian stared at the woman as comprehension began to dawn. "Do you mean to say the girl is *deaf*?"

No doubt envisioning the evaporation of Julian's donation, Reverend McGougal nodded in resignation. The woman seemed not at all discomfited, however. She shot him a self-possessed smile.

"Yes, Your Grace," she confirmed with more than a shade of defiance. "As deaf as a post."

Chapter Two

"You must take me for a fool!" Julian impaled his friend with a murderous gaze.

Charles shifted uneasily. "I did not know about this young woman's . . . deficiency. I swear it." He paused. "But you did say I could choose the candidate. Despite her infirmity, she is young and passably pretty, the only conditions you laid down. I believe you must accept her."

"What!" Julian's incredulous bark was almost a roar. "You said nothing about handing me a deaf mute to work with!"

"Obviously, Miss Gregory is not mute," the Reverend McGougal interjected. "She is in fact exceedingly well-spoken. You see, she was not born deaf—"

Julian rounded on the man. "What the devil difference does that make?" he demanded.

"A great deal," Reverend McGougal quickly assured him, taking a hasty step backward. "The doctors say language develops from birth, so that if hearing is lost later in life, the person usually retains normal speaking skills . . ."

Julian ignored the minister and returned his attention to Charles. "Our bet made no mention of a deaf whore," he growled.

Reverend McGougal gasped. Even Charles winced at Julian's pithy choice of words. Nevertheless, the baronet stood his ground. "It is Providence, not I, who has presented you with this lump of clay," he insisted. "For these stakes, the bet must be something of a challenge—do you not agree?"

"Bet? Stakes? Lump of clay?" Confusion swept Reverend McGougal's face.

"A low blow, Tremaine," Julian snarled. "Not sporting in the least."

Charles nodded in mournful acknowledgment. "A man in love is desperate, Julian. Perhaps one day you will find that out."

Trickery he might abide, but a lecture on love was too much. "The woman is unacceptable!" Julian thundered. "I call upon your good faith as a gentleman to release me from our agreement."

"As your friend, I would dearly love to oblige," Charles assured him calmly. "As a man who hopes to be your future relative, however, I can only applaud what Providence has seen fit to drop into my lap."

"The devil take it!" Julian advanced on him like an avenging angel.

"Gentlemen!" cried the Reverend McGougal, quickly juxtaposing himself between the two men. "There is no need to come to blows."

"No, indeed," Charles agreed gravely, stepping adroitly out of Julian's reach.

Because everyone was speaking, and not to her, Hannah could not make sense of the rapidly moving lips that must have filled Reverend McGougal's tiny office with a cacophony of voices. No special brilliance was needed to discern the Duke of Claridge's displeasure, however. If his words were lost to her, the angry glint in those coal-black eyes was not.

A deaf woman was clearly not what he had in mind. Hannah could scarcely blame him. Someone in a duke's employ must be above reproach. It would not do to be . . . different, a laughingstock.

Anger fed by a familiar sense of isolation swept through her. Why must everyone assume her to be an imbecile simply because she could not hear?

"You cannot require my presence any longer, gentlemen," she said with as much dignity as she could muster, hoping she had made herself heard above the clamor.

Instantly, the men stilled. Indeed, they looked momentarily stunned, as if she were a puppet who had startled them by possessing a voice of her own.

Pride stiffened her spine. Despite her tattered clothing, despite the dreadful state of her life, she would not linger to be discarded like so much useless garbage. With her head held high, Hannah whirled toward the door, dismayed to find an unaccustomed wetness in her eyes.

"Wait."

At least that is what she imagined he said, for the vibrations that shot through her as the duke grasped her arm bore the force of a sharply uttered command.

Slowly, she turned to meet a gaze that could have sliced a man to ribbons. Dark eyes, hinting at some grim torment amid the anger, held hers. For the first time Hannah allowed herself to study him at length.

Above that cruel slash of a mouth, harsh lines of dissipation had carved stark cynicism and weary age into a face that probably had not more than thirty years. His sharp granite features betrayed no trace of softness. A scar on one cheek looked to be of recent vintage, and she wondered how he had come by it. *Doing the devil's work,* an inner voice answered.

And indeed, the Duke of Claridge resembled nothing so much as that infamous dark angel. His carelessly tousled hair formed a halo of midnight around that uncompromising visage, and his eyes were seas of unrelenting black. His broad shoulders and solidly muscled frame easily dominated the room, and he radiated physical strength. He had a soldier's bearing—proud and tall—but there was a tension about him, an aura of unpredictability suggesting that a soldier's discipline had eluded him. Having witnessed that brief display of his temper, she had no desire to see more of it. The duke was a dangerous man.

Hannah felt rather than saw the sudden awkwardness that came over him as he responded to her scrutiny.

"Look," he began, speaking slowly and with forced patience, as one might address a dim-witted child. "Your infirmity is regrettable and obviously not of your own making, but . . ."

"On the contrary," Hannah interrupted, rejecting his misguided pity. "I was completely to blame. I fell out of a tree when I was seventeen and have been unable to hear ever since."

The duke frowned. "A tree? At *seventeen*?"

"Yes," she confirmed, eyeing him defiantly. "I was a veritable hoyden. A subsequent life of deafness is a fitting punishment for engaging in such unladylike activities, do you not agree?"

He did not immediately reply. Doubt clouded his gaze, as if he was uncertain whether or not she was making sport of him. His silence fueled her reckless anger.

"Being a tiresome burden, I was tossed out of the house—on my ear, you might say," she continued, wildly pleased at her little pun. "I found myself walking the streets of London, where some interesting women were kind enough to introduce me to their way of life and provide a roof over my head."

She reached for the doorknob. "As for how I managed to find myself in this place, that is another story that would doubtless bore you. Anyway, women like me do not give of their time without recompense, so I do believe I shall not waste any more of it."

Her huff of an exit from Reverend McGougal's office halted abruptly, however, as one large hand came down upon her shoulder. Bracing herself for another display of the duke's temper, she turned toward him.

To her surprise, a strange smile played at the corners of that cruel mouth. An unsettling glimmer that might have been amusement flickered in those bottomless black eyes, but his brows furrowed forbiddingly. It was an odd quality, this stern mirth, as if laughter were so utterly foreign to him that he must restrain it like an enemy within.

Hannah frowned. A man with unlimited food, clothing, wealth, and consequence should know how to laugh. But that was the least of her concerns at the moment.

"I beg your pardon," she said coolly and made to push by him. He only tightened his grip on her shoulders. Then he put one hand under her chin to tilt it upward, forcing her to look directly into his face.

The force of that relentless black gaze immobilized her more than any physical restraint. But although he eyed her intently, his words seemed to be for his friend.

"I have changed my mind." Unsettling seas churned in that midnight gaze. "She will do."

* * *

"I do not understand, Julian. Who is this young woman and why do I need her company?"

Lady Lucille Pembroke, daughter of the late Duke of Claridge and half sister to the present duke, regarded her brother from clear blue eyes whose acute perceptiveness was not diminished by the radiant feminine charms that had ignited the ardor of dozens of eager suitors this season.

Julian had known that getting around Lucy would be a challenge. It was not that she lacked a kind nature and willingness to help others. Far from it; Lucy was gifted with an altruism utterly foreign to him. But she was also an independent sort who had inherited their father's mulish streak, and her wit was as sharp as steel. Lucy would not be mollified by some lame story about his protégée's origins. Moreover, despite the fact that they had not grown up together, Lucy had come to know him rather well.

"I shall not be bamboozled into taking one of your women into the house," she added with mock sternness.

Rather *too* well, Julian reflected wryly. "Have I ever done such a thing?" he asked with studied innocence.

Lucy cocked her head. "As I recall, it was only last summer that I returned to town unexpectedly and found the house occupied by a rather odd assortment of . . . creatures."

The memory of her unexpected invasion of one of his lost weeks of debauchery brought a scowl to his face. "If you had been considerate enough to send word ahead"—he spoke sternly to cover his discomfort—"you would have been spared a scene entirely inappropriate for a young lady of your youth and breeding."

"And miss the opportunity of seeing my brother surrounded by a bevy of wondrously colorful beauties?" Lucy shot him a teasing smile. "No, indeed. Thanks to you, Julian, I realize how woefully inadequate was the information about the world that my poor, embarrassed governess tried to impart."

Julian grimaced. "I suppose your precociousness must be laid at my door. But for all that, you are only eighteen. You need guidance. And a better example of proper behavior than I can offer."

"No one exemplifies propriety better than Aunt Eleanor." His sister sighed heavily. "Have I thanked you recently for sending her to me?"

Julian shrugged. "There was no one else. Someone must see to your season."

"And you know very little about escorting well-bred young ladies," Lucy put in mischievously. "But Aunt Eleanor has the disposition of a persimmon, Julian. You cannot pretend that you enjoy having her ensconced in the house like a queen."

It was true. His father's elder sister had made herself about as pleasant as the plague. Yet it was time Lucy made her come-out, and the only appropriate relative for the task was the dowager Countess of Huffington.

A high-stickler of the worst sort, Aunt Eleanor had rubbed Lucy the wrong way from the start. She was fond of quoting from her own sermons or some other moral authority, making her presence most tedious. The first month of the season the two women had battled over almost every aspect of Lucy's appearance. With her wispy blond hair and delicate features, his sister had an angelic countenance but no fondness for the demure pastels his aunt insisted were proper for a young lady. Despite the disputes, Lucy had taken to the relentless parties like a fish to water, probably because her own exuberant and outgoing nature thrived on being around people of all sorts.

That part of her had undoubtedly come from Lucy's mother, whom he had not known, as she had died birthing a stillborn son just before the duke reluctantly brought Julian into the family bosom. Julian himself had inherited no social skills that he knew of—only his father's disdain for the elaborate rituals that guarded society's portals from any hint of impropriety. But that was another matter. Turning his attention to Lucy's complaint, he saw a way to use her dissatisfaction for his own ends.

"That is precisely why I thought you would enjoy the company of a young woman nearer your own age," Julian said smoothly. "Miss"—he racked his brain for the woman's name and hoped the one that popped into his head was correct—"Miss Gregory is most interesting."

"Oh?" Her blue eyes clouded with suspicion. "Interesting enough to be your latest mistress?"

Julian arched a brow. "One of these days, you are going to regret that lively tongue of yours. She is nothing to me other than a chance to provide you with relief from Aunt Eleanor's company—and," he added as inspiration suddenly struck, "a chance to assist a friend."

"A friend? Who might that be?"

"Tremaine." Julian took satisfaction in laying some of this mess at Charles's door. If it made more difficulties for his friend's suit, so be it. Charles had not exactly dealt from the top of the deck in this wager.

Lucy frowned. "What has Charles to do with this?"

More than you know, Julian wanted to reply, but he merely pretended to inspect the sleeve of his jacket. "She is one of his distant relations," he lied. "Her family could not afford to give her a season—and neither could Charles," he could not resist adding, "so I agreed to take her on, on your behalf. I felt sure you would not turn away a needy young lady who, but for the accident of her lack of fortune, would have already made her come-out and be dancing alongside you this very night."

The words rolled easily off his tongue, with the intended effect.

"Well," Lucy began uncertainly, "if she is a relative of Charles's, I suppose she is quite acceptable. How kind of him to think of helping a distant connection."

Too late, Julian saw that his improvised tale had given Lucy a new appreciation of Charles's sterling qualities. "She will need coaching, I am afraid," he added, intent on taking some of the bloom off that particular rose. "She is not accustomed to society and has no notion of how to go on."

Lucy tilted her head consideringly. "My own age, you say?"

Julian hesitated. Women like Miss Gregory undoubtedly aged rather rapidly. Still, the woman had not looked much above twenty. "She may be a year or two older. But do not take her age for experience," he warned. At least not the sort of experience society valued. "We will both have to work to help her fit in."

"*We?*" Lucy eyed him suspiciously. "I do not believe I have ever known you to take an interest in any woman who was not your—"

"Why must you think that I have any ulterior motive?" Julian scowled.

"Because you invariably do," she replied cheerfully.

If he had possessed a conscience, it might have bothered him, but Julian had no difficulty meeting Lucy's gaze and assuring her straight-facedly of his impartiality as to the fate of Miss Hannah Gregory. "My only interest is in helping an unfortunate member of Tremaine's family. The young woman is deaf, you see."

Lucy blinked. "*Deaf?* Oh, dear, Julian. How can you expect that she will be able to attend parties and dance and converse with the gentlemen?"

"I said she is deaf, not feebleminded. She reads lips and is otherwise as normal as any other young lady."

Other than being a prostitute, Julian mentally amended. Not for the first time he wondered whether he was mad to take such a woman on.

Pushing the thought from his head, he regarded his sister without guile. "Do you intend to allow her unfortunate disability to stand in the way of your acceptance?"

Lucy colored. "I should not like to think of myself as subject to unreasonable prejudices, but there are others who will have difficulty accepting Miss Gregory. Including Aunt Eleanor, I imagine."

"All the more reason for you to stand as Miss Gregory's supporter." Julian gave her an encouraging look.

"Yes . . . of course," Lucy said slowly, smiling. "Indeed, I believe Miss Gregory and I shall be great friends."

Julian nodded gravely. "That is precisely what I had hoped."

Chapter Three

"A relative of *mine*?" Aghast, Charles stared at him.

Idly Julian watched the view out the window, where the denizens were subjecting his coach and four to great scrutiny. It was not often that such a fine vehicle made its way through this part of town. "Cheer up, Charles. This knowledge that you are aiding a poor relation caused your estimation to soar in Lucy's eyes."

"Truly?" The baronet frowned uncertainly.

"Most assuredly."

Charles looked dubious. "But if I cooperate in your lies, I would be working against my own interests."

"Not at all," Julian replied in a bored tone. "You need merely refrain from contradicting my assertions regarding Miss Gregory's background. You did promise not to sabotage my effort, if you recall."

"Why do I have the feeling I am outgunned?" Charles crossed his arms and sighed.

"Oh, come, Charles," Julian said scornfully. "The odds are very much on your side. *I* am the one who must turn a deaf whore into a paragon of ladylike behavior."

But Charles sank into a glum reverie that did not dissipate until the carriage stopped outside the gloomy and forbidding Lock Hospital. "Miss Gregory seems rather genteel to be in such a place, does she not?"

Julian's lips curled. "You know as well as I that the cleverest of her breed are skilled at conveying the notion they are better than they are. It is precisely that quality in her that gives my scheme any hope of succeeding."

Charles fell silent as an attendant let them past the sharp iron gates that kept the world out and the women in. "Come on," Julian urged as they strode into the building. "I daresay your poor relative is eager to be off."

"Do you think she will go along with your story?"

"A woman in her position will do anything as long as it comes with a bit of gold," Julian replied with a smirk as the door to Reverend McGougal's dingy office opened.

Hannah Gregory was sitting with the minister, her hands crossed gracefully in her lap. She wore a plain blue walking dress that Julian had sent ahead, along with a straw bonnet and plain gray gloves.

Plain suited her, Julian decided, pleasantly surprised at how much she looked the part of a poor but respectable young lady come to town to acquire some polish and find a husband. Perhaps his task would not be so difficult after all. There was no coarseness about her. Indeed, she looked thoroughly out of place in this godforsaken hospital.

But as greetings were exchanged, Miss Gregory displayed no particular gratitude at the prospect of being rescued from this hellish place. Instead, she remained stiffly in her chair, unsmiling.

"I must insist that you tell me precisely what my duties will be, Your Grace," she said.

Annoyed by the challenge in her voice, Julian fixed her with a cool gaze. "I have already explained that you will be assisting my sister. Do not be concerned," he added dryly. "The position pays quite well."

The somber eyes studied his face intently. "But what, precisely, am I to assist her with?" she persisted. "The household, her correspondence, her wardrobe?"

He waved a dismissive hand. "We will discuss that later."

She did not look away. "I fear it must be now, or I will not be able to leave with you after all."

Julian's eyes narrowed. "What did you say?"

The ominous tone in his voice prompted Reverend McGougal's hasty intervention. "Although Hannah realizes how fortunate she and the hospital are to have your patronage," he assured Julian, "she has some concerns about going to live in the household of an unmarried peer." He gave Julian an ingratiating smile. "Perhaps you can reassure her that there will be no improprieties."

"No improprieties!" Julian echoed, glaring at the woman in stunned disbelief. "Does she think she is the queen herself instead of a whore with no better fate than meeting a syphilitic's death in a madhouse?"

The minister paled. Miss Gregory gasped. Slowly, she rose to face him. "I have every right to question your motives," she said in a trembling voice. No tears spilled from her eyes, however, to his great relief. He detested women who cried to get their way.

Indeed, though her eyes shimmered with moisture, there was a decidedly mulish glint in those gray depths. "Only a fool would move into the home of a notorious libertine without receiving some assurances that she will remain unmolested," she stated firmly.

Julian arched a brow. "I gather you have learned a bit about me since last we spoke."

A flush sprang to her cheeks. "Your reputation is well known. Even within these walls—*especially* within these walls."

That information surprised him. To be sure, his reputation was widespread among the *ton*, but he had not imagined himself so notorious as to come to the attention of the class of women that plied the streets. Somehow, the thought unsettled him. He regarded her coldly.

"I do not frequent prostitutes. If you are entertaining any hopes along those lines, I would advise you to forget it. Your presence in my household is for another purpose entirely."

Daggers shot from her eyes, but if thoughts could kill, he would have cocked up his toes long ago. Julian returned her murderous gaze with cool contempt.

Nervously, Reverend McGougal rubbed his hands together. He looked from Julian to his charge. "Now, Hannah. Let us not offend His Grace. As you can see, everything is on the up and up. This is a wonderful opportunity, a godsend. Why, the other girls would dearly love to be in your shoes."

"Would they?" She tilted her head.

"How can you look at those new clothes of yours and doubt it?" Reverend McGougal replied reproachfully. "His Grace has been most generous, and his sister must be the soul of piety to offer to take one such as you to her bosom. Whatever tasks she sets for you can never begin to repay such generosity."

"Nevertheless," she replied stubbornly, "I should like to know what will be expected of me."

Charles tried to stifle his laughter. "Your lump of clay is rather determined," he observed.

Miss Gregory remained motionless, unaware that Charles had spoken. Looking into her intent, unsmiling features, Julian tried to remember what about the woman had persuaded him to accept her on the basis of that first meeting. Was it that spirit he had seen—which on second inspection now appeared to be decidedly inconvenient rebelliousness?

Why the devil had he taken that ridiculous bet anyway? He had no hankering for Charles's matched bays, which was the only decent team his friend owned. He could buy a splendid pair for himself anytime he wished.

To be sure, the wager offered a diverting distraction from confronting the dilemma of his birth. And Miss Gregory certainly presented an intriguing challenge. But there was something else at work here, he realized as he stared into her defiant features. If the *ton* could be fooled into accepting a whore as a lady, then whore or lady, bastard or duke—what did it matter? The blood that ran in his veins—and hers—was as good as those whose right to their titles would never be challenged.

In passing Hannah Gregory off as a lady, he would prove that breeding was not a measure of worth. In an odd way he did not care to fully understand, succeeding with this wench would restore some of the manhood his father had stolen with his dying breath.

"Miss Gregory," he began, as her gaze bored into his, "my sister is a spirited young woman. The only other female in our household is our aunt. Lucy needs a companion near her own age."

"But why me?" She eyed him distrustfully. "There must be many women who would love such a position. I cannot imagine why you would wish to have your sister befriend a person of my situation and background."

She had a point, of course. "My sister is a bit *too* spirited," he improvised, seizing on a sudden idea. "I fear she will do something rash."

"You do?" Charles frowned.

Julian shrugged. "Lucy has a wild side to her nature. She is especially curious about certain . . . matters that are not appropriate for a young lady."

Charles gave him a speaking look, as if to say that Lucy's exposure to any inappropriate behavior could be laid squarely at Julian's door. Julian ignored him.

"I fear it is only a matter of time before she indulges her curiosity and ruins her reputation," he added mournfully.

Reverend McGougal made a sorrowful, tsk-tsking sound.

"I can think of no one better suited to recognize the warning signs than a woman whose pandering to the delights of the flesh brought her to a sorry pass," Julian finished, quite pleased at his logic.

"I see." Miss Gregory's voice was brittle. "I am to serve an example of how *not* to be."

"Oh, she will not know of your true circumstances," Julian assured her.

Miss Gregory frowned. "I am afraid I do not understand. You wish me to serve as an example of how not to go on, and yet you do not plan to tell her who I am?"

"Precisely," Julian replied, as a loudly clearing throat told him that Charles thought he had woven an impossible web of lies. "You will be brought into the household as Sir Charles's poor relation whom we are assisting in making her come-out."

She eyed him in astonishment. "I must have mistaken your words. I thought you said that I was to make my come-out."

Julian nodded. "As is my sister. You will be able to monitor her behavior and provide a credible foil to any wild actions that might pop into her head."

"But, surely, your aunt can provide any guidance your sister requires," Miss Gregory said, bewildered.

"Our aunt is a curmudgeon," Julian replied bluntly, knowing that in this, at least, he spoke the truth. "Whatever Aunt Eleanor decrees, Lucy is sure to do the opposite. My sister is something of a rebel."

"Oh, unwise tempestuousness of youth," Reverend McGougal murmured.

"Despite your . . . occupation, Miss Gregory"—Julian continued, reining in his distaste for the minister's platitudes—"you seem to have a sober nature. I expect you will provide a steadying influence on my sister."

In the corner of the room, Charles sat red-faced, though whether from suppressed laughter or outrage, Julian could not tell. He suspected it was the former. Both of them knew that while Lucy and Aunt Eleanor had indeed clashed, there was no one possessed of more common sense than Lucy. Julian did not for a moment think that Lucy's spirited nature would lead her into committing any unwise act. But his tale was having its intended effect. Reverend McGougal nodded his approval.

"Just think, Hannah, dear, you will have the opportunity of redeeming yourself by your good works. It is the fervent hope of every fallen soul."

Miss Gregory frowned. "There is something about this, Reverend, that does not seem quite right."

"Did I mention that I will pay you five hundred pounds?" Julian added pleasantly.

"My word!" Reverend McGougal gasped. Miss Gregory eyed him blankly. Julian wondered whether she had understood.

"Five hundred pounds," he said slowly.

Vaguely, she nodded. Her face bore a troubled expression.

Julian had expected the mention of such a sum to erase all doubt from her face. "Five hundred pounds," he repeated, even more slowly. Perhaps Miss Gregory's skills at lipreading did not extend to numbers.

"I am not an imbecile," she said sharply. "I understand that you mean to pay me five hundred pounds to pretend to be someone I am not in order to keep your sister from coming to harm because of what you would have me believe is her wild nature. You wish me to lie to her in hopes the means will justify the end result."

"Now, Hannah," Reverend McGougal said coaxingly, "you do not think I would urge you to do anything immoral?"

"Forgive me, Reverend, if I remain incredulous that the duke thinks it fitting and sensible to hire one such as me to guard his sister. That he is prepared to pay such an exorbitant sum merely fuels my suspicions that he has some ulterior motive."

As Charles made a strangled sound, Julian whirled on the hapless minister. "You assured me that this woman had a biddable disposition," he said accusingly.

"Compared to some of the other patients, she is docile indeed," McGougal began, but Julian made a sound of disgust and the minister quickly retreated into silence. Julian turned to discover Miss Gregory regarding him grimly.

"I have seen the world, Your Grace," she said. "It is not a place where miracles occur. When a man offers a woman a great deal of money for something, he is invariably not driven by altruism."

His patience for this game vanished. "What does it matter?" His gaze was as hard as stone. "You need the money, do you not? Women like you always do."

Suddenly all the life was gone from those gray eyes. Defeat suffused her features. She sank into a chair.

"Yes," she said in a dull voice. "Oh, yes."

Julian swept her a mocking bow. "Then shall we be off, Miss Gregory—now that we understand each other?" He offered her his arm.

But she was not looking at him and did not know he had spoken. She stared straight ahead, seemingly lost in the inspection of a spot of dirt on the wall. Gently, Reverend McGougal touched her elbow to get her attention. She looked up and met Julian's derisive gaze.

Without another word, she rose and took his arm.

"If things do not work out, you will always have a home here, Hannah," the minister assured her.

But she had her back to him and missed the words.

They did not go directly to Julian's magnificent town house on Berkeley Square, where eight previous Dukes of Claridge had lived when in London and where Lucy was even now readying herself for the evening's parties. Instead, they made a quick stop at Lucy's dressmaker, where a footman picked up a small trunk before the carriage turned up the Oxford Road and headed west.

"Where in blazes are we going?" Charles demanded, as the carriage rounded the park and kept on going.

Julian eyed him in surprise. "My hunting box. Surely you did not think I would simply thrust her into the social whirl without benefit of tutoring?"

"What you do with her is your own concern," Charles responded with asperity. "You can let me off right here, thank you." He tapped on the carriage roof to get the coachman's attention.

Julian eyed him blankly. "But I need your assistance."

"It is one thing to refrain from contradicting your lies, and quite another to actively work against my own interests," Charles declared. "I draw the line in helping tutor your protégée. You are on your own now."

As the carriage slowed, he opened the door and leaped out. Catching sight of Miss Gregory's startled expression, he tipped his hat to her and walked off down the street.

"Damn it, Charles!" Julian shouted after him. "I have no intention of spending time alone with the woman."

"Pity," his friend called over his shoulder. "I would have thought that was just your style."

Hannah stared miserably at the increasingly dense landscape that whirled past outside the carriage window. She had missed the substance of the exchange between the duke and his friend, and His Grace had been in such a black mood since then that she had dared not question him about Sir Charles's sudden departure.

As best she could gather, they were traveling through the countryside with a trunk of new clothes and absolutely no thought of meeting the duke's sister. Hannah wondered if the duke even had a sister, or whether this were not some twisted plot to kidnap her.

But why would anyone wish to kidnap her? She had nothing of worth to offer for ransom—not money, nor beauty, nor military secrets. A disturbing thought seized her. Gossip had it that the Duke of Claridge had a wondrously hedonistic appetite. What if his tastes were strange, as was reputed to be the case with some of the wealthiest noblemen? The women who had befriended her had told her about such men—men aroused by the unusual, men who took pleasure in debasing the flesh of the infirm or deformed.

What if—dear Lord!—the duke was a man inclined to such tastes? What if her deafness, of all things, was a spark to his unnatural desires?

Did he mean to hold her hostage, to use her until she cried for mercy? Hannah knew that men could be cruel, and the man who stared broodingly out the window looked cruel indeed. His eyes were dark, bottomless pools of mirthless cynicism; the frank sensuality of his wide, slashing mouth fueled their dangerous air. The jagged scar on his cheek bespoke violence, and that unruly black hair crowned him with a wild, untamed look. As they drove ever deeper into the forest, Hannah thought of a satyr, waiting to wreak his will on her in some unholy woodland bower.

Panic seized her. What could she do to save herself?

Just then, his hand touched her arm. She shrank against the seat.

"Stop!" she cried. "Do not touch me!"

He seemed puzzled. "I merely wanted to speak to you. That is how it is done, is it not?"

Hannah realized that he had only imitated the way he had seen Reverend McGougal get her attention when he wished to talk to her. She colored, greatly embarrassed at having let her imagination run wild.

"Yes," she confirmed in a small voice. "That is how it is done."

Those dark eyes studied her for a disconcerting moment. "I thought you would wish to know where we are going," he said slowly, obviously trying to enunciate every word so that she would understand.

Carefully, Hannah nodded.

"We are traveling to some property I own in the country a few miles from London," he continued. "There is a hunting box that will afford us some privacy."

"Privacy?" Nervously she adjusted her bonnet.

"Yes. I mean for us to spend a few days there before I take you to my sister."

"A few days?" Alarm knifed through her. She could think of only one interpretation to the fact that he meant to be alone with her in a secluded hunting box.

"Well, perhaps it will not take that long," he conceded with a careless shrug.

Hannah stiffened. "Yes, who knows?" she flung at him. "Perhaps you will tire of me before very little time has passed."

Once again, the duke stared at her as if she had lost her mind. Then his brow cleared. His mouth quirked upward into something that might have been a smile if it had not been so tinged with contempt.

"As I have said, Miss Gregory, prostitutes are not to my tastes. You need not fear that I will insist on your services as payment for rescuing you from that place."

Hannah bristled, but he merely continued: "I simply wish to make certain you are prepared to meet my sister. Lucy understands that you have lived away from society, but she would be shocked if I presented her with someone utterly ignorant as to polite behavior. We will spend the next few days coaching you, Miss Gregory—not engaged in the lascivious pursuits to which you are accustomed."

His unflattering assumptions about her character left her speechless. He seemed not to notice her revulsion and turned his attention to the small stone house that appeared as the carriage rolled to a stop.

No lantern brightened its windows. No bustling servants hurried to greet them. Indeed, there was no sign of any activity. The place was truly empty. Hannah could feel the coachman's knowing eyes upon her as he waited for her to descend the carriage steps. He did not tarry but hopped back onto the vehicle, which promptly pulled away.

She and the horrid Duke of Claridge were utterly alone.

Chapter Four

In three years, Hannah had grown accustomed to the silence. The carriage wheels that no longer squealed, the horses' hooves that struck the ground soundlessly, the whinnying that produced only a hot and silent stream from the nostrils of those gentle beasts.

The world around her had lost its voice.

At first, when her infirmity was thought to be only temporary, Hannah took pleasure in the fact that she no longer had to listen to the giggles and biting comments of her sophisticated cousins, who were ever so pleased to be the offspring of the earl himself rather than the impoverished orphaned daughter of his younger brother. Her aunt's constant bemoaning of the herculean task of turning a country hoyden into a presentable young lady was finally lost to her, and Hannah did not mourn that loss.

But when her hearing did not return, as even the doctors had expected it would, the bitter solitude of loss hit home. Hannah could not accept the cruel permanence of the deafness that had resulted one sunny spring afternoon, when budding trees awakening to the sparrow's song seemed to plead for her kindred spirit to join in that song from the highest branch overlooking a verdant valley.

Acceptance had come gradually, reluctantly. And even now, it was not complete. The heart of a rebel still beat in her breast, the heart of a young girl who would not be denied the joy of spring, no matter how hoydenish it was to climb a tree and soar recklessly among its branches.

Her heart still held the sparrow's voice. Her ears still remembered the nuanced huskiness of her mother's ancient clavichord and the musical skill that had been her parent's only legacy. Even amid the silence, she yearned for the beauty of sound.

But the silence she had come to know differed from the palpable stillness that now fell over her and the duke in that stone cottage. It was as if a muffled drum had started somewhere, its beat growing ever louder with each thump of her suddenly thundering heart. And though her other senses had heightened over the years to compensate for her deafness, their acuteness could not account for the sudden tingling of her skin or the stifling breathlessness in her chest.

Did he feel it too? Surely not. A man who had made his contempt so plain would not be drawn to the likes of her. She kept her gaze down as he carried her trunk into a little alcove, but the cottage was small and his nearness loomed like an omnipresent shadow. She did her best to seem nonchalant, but his presence crushed her like a vise.

Out of the corner of her eye, she caught the movement of his hand. He was trying to catch her attention and did not want to set her off again by touching her arm. Or perhaps, since he loathed prostitutes, he merely found touching her repulsive. Slowly, she lifted her gaze.

"Miss Gregory," he began.

Hannah wished she could hear his voice. A man with such a dark and stormy countenance would have a voice to match. Low, deep, and resonant, it would hold undertones of restrained emotion—anger or perhaps even passion. More likely the former, she thought, studying the dark eyes that regarded her with more than a little impatience.

Belatedly, she realized that he had been speaking and that she had been staring—not at that wide, sensuous mouth, but at the enigmatic sparks in those midnight eyes.

"I am sorry," Hannah said, flushing. "If you would be so kind as to repeat . . ." She trailed off. His eyes rolled heavenward, as if asking for patience.

"I said I greatly regret that Sir Charles elected not to accompany us." He spoke slowly, as if she were an idiot unused to civilized speech. "It was certainly not my wish to have us thrown together in such enforced intimacy. I am resolved to make the best of it, however."

"How admirable," Hannah muttered, unable to suppress a surge of irritation.

The duke eyed her coldly. "Let us agree on one thing, Miss Gregory: I am your employer. You will treat me with proper respect or I shall toss you back into that sea of disreputable filth where a woman like you belongs."

Hannah paled. The Lock Hospital had not been a pleasant place. Though the cries and wailing that so unsettled the staff and visitors fell unheard upon her ears, she could see the other women's suffering, almost feel their pain. She did what she could to ease their discomfort, but many of them had had their minds affected and were simply beyond help. Their helplessness and hers—not the bars or the dirt or the staff's hostility—had tormented her.

If the duke sent her back, Reverend McGougal would be angry at losing his donation. Perhaps he would turn her out, for he was not at heart a generous man. She would have to return to the Covent Garden boardinghouse where she had spent a year trying to survive by relying on skills not unlike those of a hunted animal. Mrs. Simmons, her previous landlady, had made it clear that she expected Hannah to be like the other girls and do more to earn her keep than cook and clean. She had never known when the woman's husband would sneak up on her, his grimy hands darting out to grab her. She had no privacy, no respect.

That sort of life was the best a woman like her could hope for; as bad as it had been, there were far worse fates—she had seen them firsthand. Whatever plans the duke had for her could scarcely be worse. Though much about this situation did not make sense, the farther she traveled from the Lock Hospital the less that seemed to matter.

And then there was the money. Five hundred pounds was a great deal, almost precisely Dr. Itard's fee, in fact. When the duke had uttered that sum, the die had been cast.

"I apologize," she said quietly. "I shall endeavor to be more respectful."

Scowling, he gestured to the little alcove where he had placed the trunk. "That is to be your room. I regret that there is not more privacy to offer, but I do not imagine you are accustomed to it in any event."

Hannah shook her head.

"I do not know how long we will remain here," he continued. "Sir Charles and I will present you to my sister as soon as possible. How soon is up to you."

"What is it that you expect of me here?" Hannah said with studied politeness.

But even her docileness seemed to provoke him. He scowled. "I thought I had made that plain in the carriage. We must give you a background, history, a past, a respectable life that will raise no eyebrows. My sister will help with your introduction to society, but we must present her with decent raw material. I have told her not to expect too much, so she will be prepared to make some allowances . . ."

"How fortunate," Hannah murmured, fighting a rising temper. He had spoken as if she were some sort of scruffy animal one did not normally allow in the house.

He eyed her skeptically. "She will be expecting someone who merely needs a little polish—not a woman from the dregs of London with no notion of respectability."

That was too much. Hannah tilted her head defiantly.

"Passing me off as respectable must challenge even your formidable skills."

His brows drew together. "Miss Gregory, you have a harpy's tongue."

Though his criticism stung, Hannah knew she was being difficult. She must try to remember that this was her only honorable opportunity to collect Dr. Itard's fee. With some effort, she willed her anger away. "I suppose my manner of speech is something we must work on as well," she offered meekly.

"Ladies do not employ sarcasm, Miss Gregory. Let that be the first lesson you learn."

"Yes, Your Grace." But resentment simmered within her, and when Hannah executed a perfect curtsy to show him that she knew the ways of a lady as well as anyone, he regarded her with suspicion.

"How is it that you can inject sarcasm even into a curtsy?"

She colored. "I will try to do better," she said, sighing. "But you should know that I have never had a biddable disposition."

The duke muttered something that was lost to her as he turned and strode from the house.

* * *

The wood on the pile looked to be newly chopped, depriving him of even that excuse to work off his seething temper. Eyeing the ax longingly, Julian cursed his servants' efficiency.

Though manual labor was not part of a duke's duties, he still remembered the calluses that growing up as a virtual orphan in Sommersby Castle had given him. As Lady Sommersby's nephew, his presence had been tolerated by the late earl, but no quarter given. Julian had been expected to earn his keep, and hauling wood for the castle's insatiable chimneys had been only part of the exhausting labor that had given him muscles as strong and solid as any fully grown man's.

What he would not give to savor the mindless predictability of steady chopping and the comforting smoothness of the ax handle in his hands now. Fool that he was, he had actually assumed that a deaf woman dependent on Reverend McGougal's charity would be malleable.

Miss Gregory was no accepting young woman undyingly grateful for her salvation. Even though he knew she must needs stare to read lips, it was impossible to miss the challenge in that unflinching gaze. All in all, she was about as biddable as a crocodile. And he was stuck with her for as long as it took to give her a prayer of pretending to be a lady.

Otherwise, he supposed she was a decent candidate for respectability. In that plain gown, her figure looked fine enough, without the coarseness or voluptuousness of others in her trade. Her grooming was inoffensive, even a bit severe. He had never cared for women who hid their hair under caps and bonnets as if it were something to be ashamed of. A woman's hair was never more glorious than when flowing loose over her bare shoulders in all its seductive splendor. He could not even guess the color of this woman's hair, so rigorously did she discipline it under that straw bonnet.

Julian knew that Charles thought he could not keep his hands off any female for more than an hour, but Miss Gregory was not to his tastes. Accustomed as he was to taking his pleasure where he found it, Julian had never cared for the mercenary nature of the pleasures one purchased from whores. He preferred to employ the seductive skills honed to perfection over the years. He knew that women were drawn to him and was pleased to reward their adoration with his considerable talents. He did not care to examine the reasons he chose to validate his seductive skills again and again.

Yes, the only hand he would lay on Miss Gregory was the firm one needed to school an untamed filly to the bit. As long as he took care to remember that the filly was likely as not to bite, he would be prepared.

Eyeing the stone house that had never before seemed so confining, Julian allowed a cynical smile to hover at the corner of his mouth. At least there was nothing boring about the task ahead.

"My sister will not expect you to possess an elegant wardrobe, only a respectable one. I have taken the liberty of procuring a few simple frocks that will suit you. You will oblige me by trying them on."

Hannah swallowed the biting retort that hovered at the tip of her tongue and obligingly retreated to her little alcove to obey the duke's imperial edict. The man was truly insufferable, apparently assuming he had purchased the right to order her about as if she were his slave. At least he stepped outside to afford her some privacy.

Fatigue filled her. Her last night at the hospital had been a sleepless one, as the prospect of leaving with the duke had kept her awake and worried. Since their arrival hours ago, he had done nothing but bark orders. Now it was nearly dusk. She wished for nothing so much as a nap and a decent meal, but he would view any request for a break as a sign of weakness. That, she would never show him.

Hannah shrugged into the first of the dresses from the little trunk. Since she had never had the luxury of a maid, she was accustomed to doing for herself and managed the task quite easily.

Surprisingly, the duke's tastes seemed to match her own. The bottle-green walking dress bore none of the elaborate decorations she had always abhorred in the fashions her aunt had tried to force upon her. It was a simple frock of serviceable broadcloth that would keep her warm and unrumpled in town. There was a lilac morning dress in airy muslin, a plain dimity gown in a muted print, and a simple cotton calico in a tiny blue-and-white check.

As she modeled the dresses, the duke nodded his approval, no doubt congratulating himself on his skill at guessing her size, for they all fit perfectly. Hannah supposed that he was more than familiar with ladies' fashions, but even though his taste was excellent, it was utterly humiliating to be regarded as chattel for him to dress as he wished.

He seemed surprised at the ease with which she wore the gowns. Perhaps he figured she did not know how to arrange the fichu of her morning dress so that it covered her neck and shoulders modestly. Since he undoubtedly assumed that modesty was unknown to a woman of her background, it pleased her to confound his expectations.

But when she picked up the only evening attire he had bought her, Hannah groaned in dismay. It was a high-waisted gown made of a delicate batiste and cut rather low in front. Nearly two dozen tiny buttons in the back were necessary to create the figure-hugging neckline and to make certain it remained in place.

Hannah knew she would never manage the dress alone, but she was not about to ask the duke for assistance. The thought of having his fingers fiddling with all those buttons against her bare back mortified her. Hannah placed the batiste gown back in the trunk and put on the plain blue dress she had worn upon leaving the hospital.

When she called to let him know that she was presentable once more, he came back into the cottage.

"What about the other?" he demanded, eyeing the blue dress in surprise. "The evening gown?"

Hannah lifted her chin mulishly. "It needs a maid to get it on properly. As there is not one about, you will have to wait to see it another time." She could not prevent a flush from staining her cheeks.

"I am perfectly capable of assisting you—" he insisted, then broke off as she reddened. He smirked. "I collect that you would have me believe modesty prevents you from allowing such a thing, but that will not wash, Miss Gregory. I have never met a modest whore." He laughed at his own joke, but his expression bore no true mirth.

It was too much.

Hannah whirled away so that whatever other hateful things he said would be lost to her. She had no idea whether he was still speaking when she strode past him out of the house, rage and humiliation driving her feet over the little stone path and deep into the thick, dark woods.

Chapter Five

Not only was the woman stubborn, she possessed a strangely delicate sensibility for a prostitute. Now he would have to go beating the woods for her, when all he really wanted to do was retire to a corner and lose the day's difficulties in a decent bottle of wine.

Wearily, Julian stared out the door. Night was descending. The forest would soon be an impenetrable thicket of darkness. His hot-tempered protégée had picked a devil of a time to take herself off.

As he lit a torch, his temper flared as well. Just his luck to end up with a prudish whore—did she take him for a fool to believe in such nonsense? Angrily, he stomped down the path toward the woods. The woman had no business putting on airs.

Then again, he mused as his breathing settled into a steady rhythm, he would have to accustom himself to pretending she was no slut from the streets but an impoverished and delicately bred country miss. If he did not treat her like a lady, Lucy and his aunt would be sure to detect something amiss.

As Julian pushed aside a laurel branch and stepped into the woods, he realized darkness had taken hold rather faster than he had figured. The torch pushed back the encroaching blackness, but it illuminated no chastened female waiting patiently next to a tree for rescue. He gritted his teeth. Not only was the woman not biddable, she possessed appalling judgment. Dashing alone into a dark wood at night was certain trouble. He ought to let her wander about until she was thoroughly lost and contrite.

But even as the thought formed, a shaft of uneasiness shot through him. He did not like to think of the nocturnal creatures that prowled these woods in search of just such easy prey as an irrational and deaf female might offer. She would not hear a lynx or a bobcat or any of the feral cats that claimed the forest when darkness descended. A wild boar could charge through the bushes at her and she would never know until the last.

All thought of teaching her a lesson vanished in the gruesome images that sprang to mind. At first he increased his pace to a trot. Then he began to run.

"Miss Gregory!" he shouted, knowing she could not hear but hoping the sound would scare off any predators.

The growth around the path grew thicker, more ominous. He had brought no weapon; the torch would have to serve. In his haste, he paid little attention to his footing. He tripped over a fallen log and let out a string of curses. As he groped for his balance, the torch fell to the ground, rolled into the bushes, and went out.

Night engulfed him. Black humor coaxed a bitter laugh from his gut at the irony of the situation. Here they were, bastard duke and prudish whore, both lost in the forest, their respective stations in life utterly insignificant.

He sat on the stout log and began to listen intently to the noises in the deep wood.

Hannah's anger had quickly changed to chagrin and then to fear as she realized the extent of her foolishness. By the time her temper had cooled, she had no idea how far she had plunged into the forest.

None of the trees whose craggy shapes swayed in the darkness or the cloying bushes whose clinging branches caressed her seemed remotely familiar. As the night closed around her like a silent shroud, Hannah realized she was hopelessly lost.

Do not panic, she told herself sternly. The horrid duke would soon find her and no doubt chastise her severely for putting him through the trouble of coming after her.

But when the moments stretched into minutes and then into the better part of an hour, Hannah began to wonder whether he would come for her after all. Perhaps he had decided she offered too much trouble to suit his purposes. Perhaps he had resolved to find another woman to insinuate into his sister's company. Perhaps his careless cruelty was just what she deserved for not controlling her temper more carefully. The Duke of Claridge had been her last, best chance. Why had she not shown more restraint?

Recriminations did not distract her sufficiently to keep the fear at bay, however. The branches and thorns that caught at her dress recalled the malevolent hands that had reached out for her so many times in her life. The silent grasping forest had come as alive as those evil hands.

She had not eaten today. Excitement at her changed circumstances had kept her going, and fear now stepped in to serve that purpose. But how long could she continue? Already, the crushing fatigue taunted her, along with a strange sensation that echoed in her head—almost, she would have said, like a sound.

Hannah put her hands to her ears. As she did, she caught sight of something bright that might have been a light or a firefly or the yellow eyes of some unknown beast. In the next instant, it vanished.

Dare she move toward the spot where that glimmer of light had been? Or did some creature lie waiting for her to walk straight into its talons?

Mired in indecision, Hannah stood still, enduring the thundering within her head and the fear in her heart. Her breathing raced out of control. Around her, the ever-present silence gave no hint of what awaited.

A nearby branch shook. It shook again, more violently. Then something lunged at her, catching her fast around the shoulders. Hannah shrieked—not knowing whether she had gotten the sound past her lips or whether, indeed, there was any purpose in doing so.

Like a rabbit in a trap, she was caught. And, like any self-respecting creature facing the prospect of becoming a predator's next meal, she struggled for all she was worth.

Despite her slender form, Hannah Gregory was no weak female. When she put her heart and soul into the struggle for freedom, she made small inroads.

Enough so that Julian—who was trying to turn her around so that she could recognize him—sustained a momentarily debilitating kick in the shin and a painful bite on his forearm.

"God's teeth!" Abruptly he brought her to the ground with a tackle that left her writhing in the dirt and looking wildly around like a frightened animal. He realized that she still did not know who he was.

Instantly he brought his face to hers so that she could see his features. Slowly, the wildness in her calmed, although her dazed look remained.

"Y-Your Grace?" she asked hesitantly.

"What is left of me," Julian confirmed.

She squinted up at him through the darkness. "I cannot see you distinctly. I . . . I cannot catch your words." Her breathless voice had a strangely haunting quality. Ridiculous as it was, a sudden heat flared within him.

Then she smiled and took his breath away. Her lips parted to reveal straight white teeth that gleamed like pearls in the darkness. The damp of the night gave her mouth and cheeks a luminous sheen akin to the fine marble of those Greek statues that were all the rage. As she lay smiling up at him, Julian realized it was the first time she had displayed pleasure in his presence. He willed away the little thrill that shot through him.

No doubt her smile stemmed from the expectation that he would lead her to safety. Grimly, Julian stared at the impenetrable forest around them. Escaping this deep wood tonight was an uncertain prospect at best. Yet he could not stay here, hovering inches above her as she eyed him like a rescuing knight.

"Come," he barked, jerking her to her feet.

She did not object to the rough treatment. Instead, she merely brushed off her skirts and regarded him expectantly. He could not abide that hopeful expression.

"Miss Gregory," he growled, "I think you should know that I do not have any idea how to get out of here."

The dark was too thick between them. She gave no indication that she had understood.

Julian tried again. "It will be simple enough in the morning, but if we tried to find our way out now we might get hopelessly lost. I suggest we seek shelter in a stalwart tree and make ourselves at home until dawn."

She simply stood there with that expectant air.

Julian disciplined himself to patience. "We are better off staying in one place until dawn," he said, speaking slowly and distinctly. "Then we can see where we are going—" He broke off.

Good God. She was swaying like a reed in the wind. Instinctively, he put out his arms. In the next moment she tumbled into them.

"What the . . ."

Her lashes fluttered shut.

Holding her like a rag doll, Julian could not help but wonder whether this was some new trickery. In a scant few hours, she had shown him so many different aspects of her temperament that he scarcely knew what to make of this one.

On the chance that she was truly ill, however, he decided that now he had no choice but to try to get them out of this cursed forest. Lifting her to his chest, he registered a moment of surprise at how light was his burden. Carefully, he began to make his way along the path toward what he hoped was the forest's edge.

Brambles tore at his face, but he shielded her when he could. Without a torch, he could see almost nothing. Several times he stumbled, but he quickly adjusted his balance to avoid falling with his delicate burden.

Delicate burden? Julian shook his head in amazement. Miss Gregory was about as delicate as steel. She fought like a hellion and possessed a barbed tongue that was itself a formidable weapon. Despite her deafness, he had long ceased thinking of her as infirm.

And yet, in his arms she was as light as a feather. Her form was thin as a leaf but decidedly feminine. She might have been any woman he carried in the dark of night—except that he had always known what to do with *those* women. This one had him stymied.

"Put me down."

Julian felt rather than heard the words as her warm breath graced his face, and he looked down to find Miss Gregory's unnervingly direct gaze mere inches from his. But instead of releasing her, he pulled her protectively to his chest to avoid a large branch.

She began to twist and turn in his arms.

"I demand that you put me down!" she cried, struggling so furiously that Julian was tempted to drop her on the path and leave her there. Instead, he forced himself to set her carefully on her feet. She swayed momentarily, then took a deep breath. "I am fine now."

"Then perhaps you would care to take over the task of leading us to safety," he snapped, all patience gone. The woman was as prickly as briars.

Again, that black, uncomprehending stare. With a muttered curse, Julian strode ahead, pulling her after him. The sooner they got out of this forest, the better.

"Your Grace!" she protested. He did not answer. The only words that came to mind were a tirade about what a nuisance she was.

Then she stumbled. Her hand pulled desperately on his. He turned. And saw that her eyes were wide with fear.

Guilt ripped through him. He tried to imagine what it must be like to be dragged pell-mell through the unfamiliar black woods, unable to hear the whipping of the branches or the cry of the night birds or even the solid thud of their feet on the dirt path.

Frightening.

"Are you all right?" he asked, bringing his face close so that she could understand. Slowly, she nodded.

With a gentleness that surprised him, he took her hand. Schooling his pace to hers, he began to lead her more slowly. Soon the path began to widen.

When they emerged from the thick curtain of forest and saw the stone cottage ahead, Julian sighed in relief. Somehow he had managed to bring them home—or what passed for home on a hellish night like this.

Inside, he settled her into a chair and moved quickly to the hearth to stir the embers to life. She did not say a word as he tromped past her to bring in some large logs. But when the hearth was at last blazing with light and warmth, he heard her expel a deep sigh.

"Thank you for bringing me out of the forest," she said. "It was . . . it was childish of me to go charging off. My temper got the better of me."

Julian turned. The tirade that had sprung to mind in the woods somehow now eluded him. Instead, as he stared into those somber gray eyes, he found himself removing a blanket from the nearby divan and handing it to her.

A look of surprise swept over her face. "Th-thank you," she stammered, gratefully tucking the blanket around her.

"How long has it been since you have eaten?" he demanded.

"I am not sure. Yesterday, I think."

Julian walked to the small larder his servants kept well-stocked. Without a word, he prepared a plate of cheese, bread, and cured ham.

"Eat this," he commanded as he set the food in front of her then turned to tend the fire again.

After a time, he risked a glance and saw that she was hungrily finishing what he had given her. He returned to the pantry and opened a bottle of wine, which he poured into two glasses.

"Do you often faint like that?" he said, handing her a glass and drinking deeply from his own.

She did not reply. Julian knew she had understood, for she was staring intently at his face.

"I asked whether you were given to fainting spells," he repeated impatiently.

"Once in a great while, I experience a dizziness," she said slowly, as if reluctant to confess this small weakness. "It seems to go along with a terrible ringing in my ears."

"Ringing?"

"More like a clanging or crashing sound, actually."

Julian frowned. "Have you ever been examined by a doctor?"

"Dozens of them. They can offer no explanation."

Julian tried to avoid imagining how a woman of Miss Gregory's meager means had managed to pay dozens of doctors for their skills.

"When we get to London, I will have you examined by my physician," he declared gruffly.

"No." She took a sip of wine. "You have hired me for a job, and I will do it to the best of my ability. But I will not incur any monetary obligation that I cannot discharge."

Julian stared at her in exasperation. "A quack's fees are hardly worth sneezing at."

"I will grant that they must be insignificant to you, Your Grace," she returned. "They are not to me. I will not be in your debt."

"I have already said that you will not be asked to tender your services as payment for anything," Julian snapped. Her haughty stubbornness irked him. One would think she had not readily serviced scores of men.

"Yes. You have said that." She took another sip of wine. "Thank you for your considerateness."

Even a "thank-you" from her lips became a condemnation. "Never mind," Julian said wearily. "I believe we have had enough of each other's company for tonight. We will continue our work tomorrow."

Wistfully, he eyed the solitary bed in the small alcove that held her trunk. He had slept upon it many nights and knew it to be exceedingly comfortable. He also knew it sported fresh linens, for his servants were most efficient.

"I trust you will find the bed satisfactory," he said. "I will sleep on the divan." Where his feet would hang off and he would be unable to roll over without tumbling onto the floor. "I regret I cannot offer you anything more private, but—"

"As you have said, I am not accustomed to privacy," Miss Gregory finished, meeting his gaze.

Julian snatched up the blanket. "I shall see to things outside." He stomped out to afford her all the privacy any missish whore could want.

By the time he returned, all was dark inside, save for the dying blaze in the hearth. He stirred the fire and added another log to keep it going through the night. Then he removed his boots, lay down on the divan, and covered himself with the blanket.

Belatedly, he recalled his resolve to treat her more like a lady. "I apologize for my words this evening," he called awkwardly across the room. "I should not have referred to you as a who—as a loose woman."

Unaccustomed to making apologies, Julian decided that would have to do. "I wish you good night, Miss Gregory," he added stiffly.

Feeling oddly virtuous, he pulled the blanket over him. Later, as he began to drift into sleep, he realized that she could not have heard a single word of his noble apology.

Chapter Six

"We must devise a fitting background for you," the duke said, drumming his fingers on the table.

Hannah bit into one of the fresh biscuits that had appeared at the cottage door this morning as if by magic. His servants came and went with such stealth that she supposed he must be accustomed to entertaining females without intrusion. The thought of being viewed as one of his women brought a flush to her face.

"Your Grace," she began, "there is a great deal about this arrangement that I do not understand."

He looked up in irritation. "It is not necessary for you to understand. For five hundred pounds, surely you can simply cooperate."

"It is my right to ask *some* questions," she persisted.

"And my right not to answer them," he replied curtly.

Hannah bit back a retort. His arrogance made it hard to keep a civil tongue, but he was right about the importance of the money to her. She would try not to incur his displeasure—though it would not be easy, for the duke was a moody sort. Last night, for instance, he had seemed almost solicitous, but this morning there was no trace of softness in him. If anything, the sunlight only underscored his ferocity by illuminating that jagged scar and the impenetrable bleakness of those dark eyes.

She wondered about the circumstances in which he earned that badge of violence. Had it resulted from a dispute over a woman? Impugned honor? A slanderous remark? The duke did not strike her as a man who cared enough about such things to fight for them. He must have been challenged, then. Sabers at dawn.

Had he won? Hannah could not imagine him losing. Beneath that civilized ducal costume lay a very uncivilized power—dormant now, perhaps, but Hannah had no illusions: the duke was not a man to be crossed. That cruel mouth and brooding eyes radiated cool contempt for anyone foolish enough to confront him.

She wondered why the duke seemed so embittered and whether that harsh face ever relaxed its watchful cynicism. Certainly not when he regarded her, as he was doing now, with suspicion and distaste—as if he expected her either to steal everything in sight or throw herself on him like some tawdry seductress.

As if a man like that could be seduced. Hannah suspected he was thoroughly immune to feminine wiles and regarded women as necessary evils to be used and discarded. He was reputed to have a notorious appetite for pleasure and none whatsoever for lingering in female company once that appetite had been satisfied.

Had disappointment in love sent him on the road to dissipation? But no. The duke would never allow a woman to affect his actions. Whatever pain radiated from that bleak gaze started somewhere deep inside him. He needed no other person to make him miserable; he managed well enough himself.

"Charles had an uncle somewhere," he said absently. "Something of a recluse, I believe. We will make you his daughter."

"Will not people wonder why I am staying with you and Lady Lucille instead of Sir Charles?" Hannah frowned. "Ought not Sir Charles himself instruct me as to his family background? Why is he not here?" The duke scowled. Too late, she remembered her vow not to provoke him.

"Charles has decided that his interests do not coincide precisely with mine," he said coolly. "As for the other, surely you know that an unmarried lady does not share a roof with an unmarried gentleman. Or perhaps you do not know," he added with a speculative gaze.

"I am sharing this cottage with you," she pointed out. "What if that should become known?"

"It will not. Even my servants do not know who is here with me. They have been instructed to leave food at the door twice a day and make themselves quite scarce at all other times. My orders are always followed precisely."

"I see." Hannah supposed the duke's servants were accustomed to the strangeness of those orders. "Well, then, perhaps we should return to the question of my identity. Did you say that Sir Charles's uncle is deceased?"

"Let us assume so."

Hannah thought him remarkably cavalier about the matter. "But what if he is not?" she persisted. "What if this uncle should suddenly present himself in town? We should be found out!"

"Less than two months remain of the season," the duke said, looking bored. "I daresay that Charles's reclusive uncle, if he lives, will not take it into his head to visit London during the height of the season when he has not done so in decades."

"You seem remarkably confident of that."

"Enough questions." He stroked his chin. "Charles's father was not a rich man, and his younger brother would have had even fewer resources. Therefore, you would have been raised in near-poverty—in the country, let us say."

"The country," Hannah repeated slowly, suddenly feeling inexpressibly sad. "That would have been lovely."

Rolling hills, clear streams, and proud trees had dotted her father's small property. They had kindled a yearning deep inside her for the stability they represented but which her father could never provide.

"I have always been fond of nature," she said, smiling at the memory. "It is as if a part of me is connected somehow to . . ."

"Perhaps," he continued, lost in concentration, "your father would have lost his meager inheritance . . ."

"In a card game," Hannah supplied softly. "He would have lost everything in a card game."

The duke regarded her approvingly. "I believe you may have a talent for this sort of thing."

Hannah did not reply.

"Then your father died," he said slowly. "Perhaps he would have been so mortified at losing what little funds he could pass onto you that he would have—"

"Taken his own life," Hannah finished dully.

"Excellent!" He beamed. "He was a coward—unable to face the consequences of his reckless behavior. His death left you an orphan, and you would have had to seek out other relatives. You lived with them for a time, but the situation grew difficult."

"Most difficult." Hannah shuddered.

"You lost your hearing . . ." He furrowed his brow. "You say you fell out of a tree?"

She nodded.

"We shall not dwell on the tree-climbing incident, so as not to horrify my aunt." He paused. "Naturally, after you became deaf, you viewed yourself as a burden and generously departed—"

"Not at all." Hannah eyed him indignantly. "*They* viewed me as a burden and turned me out. I was delighted to go. I held them in no regard, nor they me."

He frowned. "We must endow you with a noble nature, Miss Gregory, or no one will understand why you have reached the age of twenty . . ."

"Twenty-one."

"Twenty-one, then. No one will understand why you reached that advanced age without imposing upon Charles to help you find a husband."

"Perhaps I never thought one necessary," she replied.

"Every woman needs a husband."

"I see." She paused. "Do you feel yourself in need of a wife, Your Grace?"

Cold ice glittered in his gaze. "I do not intend to marry."

Hannah wondered why one of society's most notorious bachelors had no desire to wed. Perhaps he did not care to abandon his wild ways. But there were many women—like her cousins—willing to overlook a husband's excesses in exchange for becoming a duchess and having a fortune at their disposal. Looking at his rigid features, Hannah knew better than to pursue the topic. Still, his high-handed manner irked her.

"Rather than be a burden to your relatives," he continued after a moment, "you retired to a small cottage to live independently, perhaps supporting yourself by teaching poor children or taking in laundry, or—"

"Selling myself in the streets?" she offered helpfully, schooling her expression to innocence.

His hand moved so quickly that Hannah felt the wind in its wake. She flinched, expecting a blow, but his fist merely slammed down on the table in front of her.

"Spare me your tasteless attempts at levity, Miss Gregory."

"I assure you, there is nothing amusing about the world that a prostitute inhabits," she retorted.

His jaw clenched. "I will not tolerate insolence," he said as his fists slowly uncurled. "You will mark my words closely and commit this background to memory."

Hannah did not say a word. He studied her for a moment. "You retired to the country for a time, but loneliness finally led you to write your cousin Charles to inquire as to whether he could assist you in finding a husband."

"Loneliness," she echoed. Yes, she had plenty of experience with that.

"Regrettably," the duke continued, "Charles was not possessed of sufficient funds to sponsor your come-out but offered to prevail upon the family of his dearest friend to do so. You, of course, were overjoyed."

"Overjoyed."

He eyed her with suspicion. "I trust I do not have to remind you that sarcasm is unbecoming in a young lady."

"No."

"Charles and I personally came for you—hmm, where can we put your country home?"

"Cheshire." Hannah brightened at the memory of crystalline skies and purple mountains silhouetted against the horizon.

"Too far away," he said dismissively. "We shall put you close to town. Kent, perhaps. Or Essex. Yes, Charles and I fetched you one afternoon from Essex."

"But will Sir Charles go along with your tale?" Hannah did not know what to think of the baronet. He appeared to be the duke's friend, but she had also seen the two men argue heatedly. There was something wary in Sir Charles's gaze.

"It is in his interest to do so," he replied curtly. "Let us move on to other matters." He gave her an assessing gaze. "I forbid you to wear mobcaps in the future. That one is ugly."

She opened her mouth to tell him exactly what she thought of his order, but he was already onto another topic. "Your table manners are surprisingly adequate, so we will dispense with those and take up dancing. Do you have the slightest notion how to dance?"

Hannah flushed. Was he deliberately holding her up for ridicule? "Let us just say the music eludes me," she replied pointedly.

His face was a blank. Then his mouth curved into that familiar sardonic smile. "Never say you intend to let a small defect like deafness prevent you from joining in society's little amusements?"

"You are hideous." The words were out before Hannah could stop them, but strangely, no answering anger blazed in his eyes. Instead, he merely extended his hand as if he fully expected her to take it.

Was this man the soul of cruelty? She could not dance in a fancy ballroom. She would be ridiculed if she even tried. She had learned a few dances before she lost her hearing, but that was years ago, when she could hear an orchestra and appreciate the way a violin's plaintive tone swelled like a cry on the wind.

Did he have to remind her that Mozart and Haydn would never again bring her delight? Did he have to taunt her with memories of Beethoven's searching restlessness and the torment that mirrored her own?

He meant to humiliate her, to vanquish her self-respect, the thing at the core of her being that had sustained her during the time with her hateful relatives and the subsequent years of silence and degradation.

"Come," he commanded, his gaze brooking no refusal. "I will teach you to dance."

With tears of hopeless anger burning in her eyes, Hannah took his hand.

For one moment, Julian had forgotten that she could not hear. She was simply a difficult woman who had made it her mission to infuriate him. Her lack of hearing in no way stemmed her sharp tongue, nor dampened the angry sparks from her uncompromising gray eyes. She carried herself with pride, even though she must have had precious little of that left at this point in her life. He had never met a woman so determined to meet the world on her terms.

Inquiring about her dancing skills had been tactless, but at the time he had been imagining her in that flowing batiste gown, moving gracefully to the music of a waltz.

Music she could not hear, of course.

Julian felt like a fool. How in the world would he teach her a Scottish reel or the complex tempos of the new quadrille? Lucy was right: she would not be able to do the things other women did.

Yet her lithe form was meant for the waltz. Her hand fit lightly into his, her elegantly tapered fingers curled naturally around his own. Though her skin was roughened, there was something delicate about the shape of her hand, something almost regal in the way it rested in his palm.

Perhaps this was possible, after all.

The three-quarter beat was simplicity itself. She would feel the moves as he guided her in his arms. She had only to follow his lead. The thought of being able to partner her in a dance pleased him. Society would be charmed. Charles would be apoplectic.

"Look at me." Julian touched her chin. Slowly, she raised her gaze. He chose not to see the shimmering moisture there. "Let us not quarrel. With a little work, I believe you will find the waltz not at all beyond you."

Before she could reply, Julian swept her into his arms. He hummed the music to himself as he moved her around the floor. At first she tried to follow his lead. Then, abruptly, she pushed him away.

"I will not let you put me on display like this," she said, blushing furiously. "Everyone will be staring at me."

"There is nothing to be ashamed of," Julian said charitably. "You stepped on my toes a few times, but that is to be expected from a beginner—"

"Stop it!" She stamped her foot and made as if to flee, but there was nowhere to go in the tiny cottage.

Dejected, she sank into a chair. Tears of mortification rolled down her cheeks. "I cannot dance, and both of us know it. I am not like the other women. I am *deaf.* I cannot pretend otherwise. If there is any kindness in you, you will not parade me across the dance floor like a . . . a trained animal."

"Some of us rise every day and pretend to be something we are not," he said coolly. "You have an infirmity, it is true, but you also have the intelligence to see that your defects have only the power you grant them." Now where had that bit of wisdom come from? How easily it had rolled off his tongue, as if mastering one's demons was child's play.

"You talk as if I have but to assume that I am entitled to be treated as any other woman and it will be done," she retorted. "It is not so easy as that."

Damn her perceptivity! "And yet, you do it remarkably well," he snapped. "I have never met a more high-handed wh"—he caught himself—"young woman."

She stilled. Her solemn gray eyes searched his face. Finally she sighed. "I should like to try again."

Julian held out his arms. After a moment's hesitation, she stood and walked into them. He began to waltz her around the little room. Unfortunately, however, there was more stumbling than waltzing.

"*One*-two-three. *One*-two-three," Julian barked, but she was looking at her feet and did not notice. She held herself so stiffly that she had not a prayer of catching the beat from him.

As she stepped on his feet for the fifth time, Julian halted the painful exercise. "You are making this difficult."

She eyed him uncertainly. "I am doing my best."

"You seem to think you must learn some intricate trick, like that trained animal you accuse me of trying to make you into. All you need do is relax."

"Relax?" Her lips parted on the words and remained so, as if the concept stunned her.

Exasperated, Julian pulled her close. When she tried to push him away, he merely held her tighter. "Stop struggling," he ordered. "Put your hand in mine and pretend as though you have not a bone in your body. Lean into me, if you must. Let me do the work for both of us."

Her impossibly intent eyes regarded him carefully, then closed in concentration. She took a deep breath. He felt her relax into him. Her hand grew supple and her breathing became even and slow.

Slowly, he drew her into the dance. She did not tense or stumble, nor did she resist his force but rather leaned into it like a leaf that flew wherever the wind willed. A few strands of hair had come loose from under that hideous cap she wore. They tickled his nose as he whirled her around. Her body fit his amazingly well, he noticed. Now she was moving perfectly with him. He marveled at her powers of concentration. His, on the other hand, had gone disturbingly awry.

Suddenly and inexplicably, he stepped too deeply into the figures. She would have fallen had not he pulled her tight. In that moment, as her slight form pressed against him from his chest to his knees, Julian decided that the dancing lesson had continued long enough.

But where his mind was willing, his body was not. Somehow, his arms would not obey his brain's command. Instead of setting her away from him, he held her tightly within the circle of his arms.

Her eyes fluttered open and regarded him in confusion. He was struck by how many different shades of gray they contained.

Their gazes held. Staring into those mesmerizing gray depths, he could not think of a single thing to say.

Then he remembered who it was he held in his arms—a woman whose body was only a tool to be used when expedient. No matter that she looked the picture of untried innocence, no matter that her deafness made her seem achingly vulnerable—Hannah Gregory was not what she seemed.

But then, neither was he.

His lips curled into a harsh smile. "The lesson is over, Miss Gregory. You will be so good as to remember your place."

Flushing deeply, she stepped out of his arms so quickly that she crashed into the divan behind her and toppled backward onto its cushions.

As she flailed about for a helpless moment, Julian caught a glimpse of her bare legs. With a muttered curse, he reached down and jerked her to her feet.

"You need not trouble yourself—" she began heatedly, only to break off with a startled squeak as he brought his lips to hers.

Chapter Seven

A pulsating resonance shot from the place where the duke's lips touched hers down to the pit of her stomach, where it took up residence like a thousand fluttering butterflies. Their wings beat out a song that rivaled any she had known before silence became her way of life.

With a sigh, Hannah leaned into that strong, solid chest. Slowly his arms came around her. She felt safe, as she had in the woods when he had braved the dark dangers of the night to return her to safety.

But that heady song within her breast also resonated with a danger more ominous than anything in the forest that night. As his lips grew more insistent, Hannah felt as dizzy and helpless as a lamb, unable to resist that pulsating force which held her in its thrall. She knew she ought to be afraid, but that exhilarating song within her pushed all fear away.

Abruptly, the duke severed the kiss and took a quick step backward.

"What is it?" she murmured in alarm, steadying herself against the divan.

A contemptuous sneer settled over the sensuous lips that had moments ago met hers. "I would advise you to abandon your attempt at seduction, Miss Gregory. It will not work. I have no taste for prostitutes, as I believe I have already explained."

Hannah eyed him incredulously. "It was *you*, sir, who kissed me!"

"Only after you treated me to that display."

"*Display?*" She blinked.

He scowled. "Falling with helpless abandon . . . exposing your bare flesh like a practiced trollop. Clever, but ultimately ineffective." He regarded her as if she were a loathsome specimen of insect. "I am not one of your jug-bitten, gullible customers."

For one long moment, Hannah stared at him in disbelief. Then fury filled the places where those little butterflies had fluttered happily. "You think that I tried to—to—" She broke off helplessly.

Hannah whirled away from him. She had no idea whether he was speaking, so she raised her voice to make herself heard over his just in case.

"I have no intention of wasting whatever feminine wiles I possess on the likes of you!" She glared back at him over her shoulder.

His face was a picture of ducal disdain. "There is no need to shout. *I* am not deaf."

"No," Hannah agreed sweetly, turning to face him squarely. "You are merely thickheaded or a liar. I have not yet decided which."

"What?" He stilled.

"*You* kissed me, Your Grace. Only an idiot would deny the truth—or someone accustomed to lying to himself or to others. Yes, I believe that is what you are," Hannah finished, pleased at her insight. "A liar."

Instantly, she walked away so that whatever mean-spirited retort he had would be lost to her. There being nowhere else to go in the small cottage, she busied herself with straightening the larder, although its shelves were already neatly stocked and arranged. That was what came with having scores of servants to take care of such things, she thought resentfully. The man had probably never known a moment of want in his entire coddled life.

Then the thought occurred to her that perhaps one ought not speak so to a man possessed of the devil's own temper. They were alone in this cottage, after all. There was no one to stop him from doing whatever he wished with her. Once again, her temper had clouded her judgment. Perhaps even now he was contemplating wringing her neck.

Warily, Hannah peeked around the pantry corner.

He had not moved. A strange stillness enveloped his rigid form. Then she saw that his lips were moving slightly. She could not make out the words.

As she ventured closer, he took no notice of her. Waves of torment filled his dark eyes as he stared straight ahead, muttering to himself.

Now she could make out the words. One word, that is. Over and over, he repeated it.

"Liar. Liar. Liar."

Dear Lord. The Duke of Claridge was quite mad.

"*Only an idiot would deny the truth—or someone accustomed to lying . . . That is what you are. A liar.*"

The truth at last. She had made him see quite clearly what he had tried to forget with his fine French brandy, what he had tried to obscure with his doomed attempt at respectability. Without any definite proof of his parents' marriage, he was living a lie. And he would live this lie until honor or conscience demanded otherwise.

And that was the rub. For he possessed neither honor nor conscience sufficient to relinquish his title and thereby brand his mother a whore.

Bitterly, Julian's mouth curled with hatred for the man whose blood ran in his veins. Octavius Pembroke had never done anything that did not accrue to his own self-interest. Having inherited a dukedom but no wealth to support it, his father desperately needed a fortune. Going through estate papers after his father's death, Julian had discovered dozens of loans Octavius had been obliged to seek from his wealthy sister, Lady Huffington. Helene LeFevre, daughter of a wealthy French comte, must have seemed a perfect solution to his financial problems. To cement the alliance, Octavius had doubtless seduced her. But when her parents lost their lives and property in the Terror, he had no need for a penniless, pregnant wife.

And none for his son. After Helene's death, the task of raising Julian fell to her sister, Lady Sommersby. Only after the rich wife Octavius finally secured died birthing a stillborn son did he come for Julian and acknowledge him as his heir.

Julian did not delude himself. The fact that his father gave him a dukedom was no proof of legitimacy. Octavius would have done anything to control his wealth through his own seed—even if it chafed to make a bastard his equal. And it must have chafed. Hate had lain in that paternal gaze.

Julian had long tried to understand its roots. Perhaps Octavius had realized Julian had no particular loyalty to the cold, harsh stranger who claimed him much too late. Perhaps, facing imminent death, Octavius had seen the futility of trying to control his fortune from the grave.

Whatever the cause, his father had detested him. And so, on his deathbed, he had inflicted an everlasting blow.

"Will you like being 'Your Grace,'?" his father had rasped in a voice that, like the rest of him, was ravaged by disease. "Your mother would be pleased—she always wanted to be a duchess." A sinister smile briefly enlivened his shriveled features.

The words raised the hairs along the back of Julian's neck. Until then, he had not thought to doubt his legitimacy. His mother *had* been a duchess, had she not? He assumed that it was her declining health that prevented Octavius from fetching them from France. After her death, Julian told himself that his father did not come because he was overcome with grief.

A horrible suspicion had entered Julian's mind.

"I do not understand, sir," he said carefully.

His father's sunken features filled with contempt. "Did you never wonder why you were sent to be raised at Sommersby, boy?"

Oh, yes. He had wondered that a thousand times. Countless nights he had lain awake in that old musty castle trying to guess why his father had not come for him. Not that he minded his aunt, Lady Sommersby, whose dark beauty reminded him of his mother. But she had had no children of her own; life in that ancient castle had been unremittingly lonely for a boy of six.

Another raspy laugh erupted from the figure in the bed. "You were an errant branch of the tree, boy. Perhaps you are not even mine. Your mother was the flirtatious sort, if you catch my meaning."

"Now, *son*"—his tongue spit out the word like a curse—"soon you shall have it all—my name, wealth, position. Guard them well." The bitterness in his tone had brayed louder than trumpets.

An errant branch of the tree. Julian had stood there on the cusp of manhood, burning with a thousand fearful questions. His father breathed his last that very afternoon, taking the answers with him.

The pieces had begun to fit shortly afterward. The horrible suspicion had hardened to chilling certainty. He had been given his mother's surname instead of his father's. Lady Sommersby had always grown curiously silent whenever the subject of the duke came up. No birthday greetings ever came to the castle from his father. Julian never even met his sire until he was fifteen and Octavius appeared at the castle to claim him.

The excuses Julian had made over the years to explain Octavius's behavior fell apart. He realized that his father was a cold and unfeeling cur who would never grieve for anyone, much less a woman he had seduced. Even around Lucy, the charming sprite of a daughter whose mother had brought him such wealth, Octavius displayed little warmth. Octavius Pembroke loved no one, least of all his son.

Charles was the only one Julian had told about that deathbed scene. His friend had loyally pooh-poohed the prospect that anything Octavius had said was to be trusted.

"The old duke was a scoundrel—not to put too fine a point on it," Charles had declared roundly, and Julian had raised a glass with him and put the matter aside.

Only it had not gone away, not in the wasted years in which he tried to forget and the recent months in which he had sought to learn once and for all if he was a bastard. He had searched everywhere for his parents' marriage papers—the family Bible, the little French village where his mother died, even the tunnels under Sommersby Castle where he had played as a boy. He had found nothing to indicate he was a fraud. But nothing to disprove it, nothing to give him the reassurance he craved.

"Liar."

With that one word, she had unknowingly summed up his world of self-deception.

Buttoned up in that high-necked traveling dress, Miss Gregory was the picture of ladylike rectitude as she perched stiffly on the seat across from him. Julian could not imagine how he had allowed himself to be moved by the sight of her legs poking out from her staid blue frock, how he had fallen prey to a moment of lust, how that kiss had scared him sufficiently to put an abrupt end to their secluded time in his hunting box.

When the spires of London came into view, Julian almost breathed a sigh of relief. Now there would be something to do besides avoid meeting his protégée's intense gray eyes. He had never been so glad to see Charles as when his friend hopped into the coach in front of his bachelor's rooms and they set off for Claridge House.

Charles did not seem at all happy, however.

"Damn it, Julian. I do not like lying to Lucy." He crossed his arms and expelled a sigh of disgust.

"You should have thought about that earlier," Julian said calmly.

"What if she should find out?"

"She will not. Miss Gregory is fairly presentable, as you can see, and her story is guaranteed to generate sympathy in Lucy's breast and perhaps even my curmudgeonly aunt's. They will make allowances for any defects in manners and turn her out in proper style. No one will guess she is not what she seems. I will win our little wager handily."

"I do not want to do this."

Julian stretched out his legs and yawned. "It is too late for second thoughts. If you expose our little masquerade, I will be forced to confess that it was your idea. Lucy will not think kindly of you for that. I am afraid you will just have to wait and see whether Miss Gregory and I can pull this off. If society refuses to accept her, victory is yours. If it does, you will have to win your bride by other means."

Charles glowered. "Patience, in other words?"

"And virtue," Julian replied blandly. "Though I am not sufficiently familiar with either quality to judge, I have heard that some women find them quite appealing."

"You have obviously never been in love."

Amused in spite of himself, Julian shot his friend a sidelong glance. "I am heart-whole and glad of it."

"Even after spending three days with your protégée?" Charles arched a meaningful brow.

Julian's gaze went to Miss Gregory, who was studying the view out the window, unaware of the conversation occurring around her. "Give a man some credit, Tremaine."

Charles eyed Julian uncertainly. "Very well," he said in resignation. "What is this story that I, as Miss Gregory's distant relative, am expected to confirm?"

"Not so distant, actually," Julian corrected. "I have made her your cousin—the only child of your father's younger brother, who put a period to his existence after losing what little funds he had in a gambling spree."

"My *uncle*?" Charles echoed, aghast.

Julian nodded. "It is quite a clever tale. After she became deaf, she thought to spare relatives any additional burden and went to live alone—"

"*You have killed off Uncle Erasmus?*"

Julian arched a brow. "I assumed he was already dead."

"The man is as healthy as a horse," Charles sputtered. "A fine pickle this is. If he presents himself in town do you plan to introduce him to his long-lost 'daughter'? By Jove, we are all going to be found out!"

"I doubt that."

"He is a recluse, to be sure, and keeps to the country, but—"

"Ah, then we have nothing to worry about," Julian replied. "The odds of your Uncle Erasmus discovering our little ruse are negligible."

Charles drew himself up straight. "It is not 'our' little ruse."

"Oh, but it is," Julian returned smoothly. "Here we are," he added as the coach rolled to a stop in front of Claridge House. "As usual, my servants are ready to accommodate us. I trust we are all ready?"

Charles stared morosely at the impressive stone town house that rose like a grande dame above the lesser houses around it, the line of servants waiting to see to their every need, and the beautiful female who tripped gaily down the steps to greet them.

"Lucy," Charles murmured with the tone of a condemned man as the vision of loveliness broke out in answering smiles.

Julian turned to Hannah, who sat perfectly still, her hands crossed primly in her lap. She appeared the picture of assurance, until he stole a look into her gray eyes. They were filled with uncertainty.

"Not you, too," he admonished. "Come, now, Miss Gregory. Attitude is everything—especially in the matter of fooling the world. Shall we begin?"

With a self-assured smile, he extended his arm. She regarded him with considerable distaste.

"I think, Your Grace," she said at last, "that my 'cousin' should be the one to escort me to your sister. It would not do to have anyone form an untoward impression about my relationship with you."

Julian glowered as she descended from the carriage and took Charles's arm, leaving him quite alone in the carriage.

"No," he muttered, eyes narrowing at her retreating figure. "It would not do at all."

Chapter Eight

The lady in puce with a matching gauze demi-turban stared at Hannah as if she were a queerish museum exhibit. With a frankly appalled expression, the woman raised a jeweled lorgnette and subjected her to unnerving scrutiny. Hannah realized that this must be Lady Huffington, the duke's formidable aunt.

Hannah's graceful curtsy betrayed no signs of her inner misgivings, but she held the woman's censorious gaze rather longer than was strictly necessary, which caused the countess to arch her thin eyebrows in reproof.

In contrast, the duke's sister, Lady Lucille, wore a friendly smile. She chattered so rapidly that Hannah could not even begin to make out the words.

Though Hannah held her head high, she felt small and insignificant in this grand house. The duke expected her to move about these folk as if she had every right to do so, but the gulf between her station and theirs was so large it would take a ship of the line to cross it. Nothing underscored the ducal grandeur so much as the startling sculptures flanking the main stairway—twin gold-leafed sphinxes that seemed to be staring right back at her.

Conducting the introductions with perfect aplomb, the duke did not convey by so much as a shrug that she was different from any other invited guest. If he was not precisely overflowing with warmth toward her, neither did he display the coldness he had shown after that disastrous kiss. Hannah did not understand how he could kiss her fervently one moment, rain condemnation upon her the next, then ignore her completely as he had done during the carriage ride here. She had comforted herself with the thought that he probably held little charity for any woman. That notion was dispelled, however, by the affectionate kiss with which he greeted his sister.

Dejected, Hannah held back as the others moved into the large parlor on the ground floor. She was not ready to face this grand assemblage. The duke must have read her mind, for a firm hand at the small of her back gave her a gentle but definite push. He turned her around.

"Attitude, Miss Gregory," he admonished. "And please do not act as if you have never seen a respectable home." Hannah could almost imagine his arrogant, no-nonsense tone.

"But I have never encountered anything this grand," Hannah protested, eyeing the enormous marble staircase that soared upward in kingly fashion. He quickly moved to obscure her view of anything else but him.

"No, I imagine the air in Covent Garden is not so rarefied, but I did not take you for a coward."

"Nor am I one," she returned indignantly. "But did you see the manner in which your aunt stared at me? I believe she must suspect—"

"Aunt Eleanor would disdain the king himself. She is suspicious, judgmental, and as unsympathetic as any jailer you will meet in Newgate when you arrive there someday. I suspect her cold heart turned to stone long ago."

His comment about Newgate affected her less than the image of his aunt turning her censorious glare on the king. Sheer nervousness made Hannah giggle. The vaulted ceiling must have amplified the sound, for in the next instant the stern-faced servant who had attended Lady Huffington arrived in the foyer to say that the countess wished to have the sherry poured and requested him to ask that they not tarry further. Glowering, he left them.

"That was Higgins, my aunt's majordomo," the duke explained, his lips curling in sardonic amusement. "His goal is to make life miserable for those with the bad luck to displease his employer—that is to say, everyone Aunt Eleanor encounters."

The duke stared after Higgins with an expression that made Hannah thankful she was not in that man's shoes. "His presence here prompted my own butler to give notice," he continued darkly. "The only reason I have not had him drawn and quartered is that my aunt plans to return with him to her home when the season is over. I do not know how Yorkshire endures the both of them."

Hannah could not imagine that the duke would suffer anyone he did not find tolerable, but perhaps he had his reasons. The subject vanished from her mind, however, as he eyed her expectantly. The time for delay had passed. Hannah took a deep breath and moved toward the parlor, feeling much like a condemned prisoner.

"That is the way." To her surprise, his eyes gleamed with something that might have been encouragement.

He extended his arm, as if she were any lady he had the pleasure of escorting to meeting his family. Gingerly, Hannah touched his sleeve. He promptly covered her hand with his, as if he suspected she might flee unless he had a hold on her. She was dismayed at the decidedly masculine warmth that penetrated the soft kid of her new gloves.

And even more dismayed as those mischievous butterflies returned to her stomach.

"We shall not find any decent young man to overlook her glaring deficiency." Lady Huffington wrinkled her nose with distaste, studying Hannah as if she were a piece of week-old fish.

Marshaling her temper, Hannah told herself that the countess had only spoken the truth. No man wanted a deaf wife. Still, she had no wish to be judged so harshly by a woman she did not even know. She hoped that good manners would prompt someone to change the subject, but before anyone else could speak, the countess held up the lorgnette and fixed her with a dour gaze.

"If she had a dowry, that would be helpful, of course. But since she has nothing, I fail to see why we must create a spectacle by introducing her to society as if she were any other female." Then Lady Huffington yawned.

Hannah blinked. Had anyone else thought the woman's pronouncement excessively rude? Sir Charles, for one, appeared speechless, but he had been excessively tongue-tied since their arrival. Lady Lucille was frowning. The duke merely studied both Hannah and his aunt with an unreadable gaze. The intimidating Higgins stood stiffly in the corner, like a statue whose dour lines had been etched by a sculptor with no skill at subtlety.

If she had truly been Sir Charles's cousin and had entered this house desperate to win acceptance and find a husband, Hannah probably would have burst into tears at such a harsh, unfeeling treatment.

But at twenty-one, she had seen far more of the world and its cruelty than Lady Huffington could possibly cast her way. More importantly, she had survived.

"Do you not think," she said, leveling a gaze at the countess, "that only those people with inferior minds will regard me as exceptional?"

Lady Huffington, in the act of fiddling with the side knot of her turban, froze.

"Though some persist in viewing deafness as indicative of a deficiency of the brain," Hannah continued, "in my experience it is only the most ignorant who do so. Others are sufficiently intelligent to discover that I am rather like any other female." She slanted a look at the duke, whose brows arched skyward.

"In point of fact, I read lips quite well," she added, returning her gaze to his aunt. "My understanding is not at all diminished."

Now they were all staring at her. Lady Lucille wore a smile that broadened as her friendly eyes met Hannah's. The duke's lips twitched, and Sir Charles's intrigued gaze shot from Hannah to the duke and back again.

Lady Huffington was red-faced. "My sherry," she commanded weakly.

Higgins hurried to oblige as the countess rapidly fanned herself. She took a long sip, closed her eyes, and quickly downed the rest of the amber liquid. Then her eyes shot open and she regarded Hannah sternly.

"Perhaps deafness is God's punishment for your sharp tongue, Miss—"

"Gregory," Hannah supplied with a decidedly martial air. The countess's comment put her in mind of Reverend McGougal's chafing axioms. Her blood began to boil anew.

"The Scripture teaches us that God will punish the wicked for their iniquity," Lady Huffington continued, her face a portrait of superior scorn.

"And the proud for their arrogance," Hannah added softly.

With a gasp, the countess put her hand to her breast, looking as if she might faint from shock. Shame filled Hannah. Her wretched temper had gotten the better of her again. She had returned insult for insult, when she knew she ought to have been more humble, more . . . ladylike.

Hannah saw the duke rise, and it was all she could do to avoid cringing as she imagined his rage.

But as he approached, his attention was averted. Sir Charles had also risen and was speaking. Hannah tried to catch the baronet's words.

". . . to take my leave, but perhaps the ladies would care to take a turn with me in the garden first." Sir Charles addressed them all, but it was Lady Lucille whose gaze he held.

The duke's sister smiled. "That would be lovely." She regarded Hannah, and her eyes held nothing but friendliness. "Miss Gregory, would you care to come?"

"With pleasure." Hannah fairly jumped from her chair in her haste to escape the confines of the parlor.

"Lady Huffington?" Sir Charles queried politely, but the countess waved them weakly away and seized the fresh glass of sherry Higgins brought her.

Lady Lucille took Sir Charles's arm. Gallantly he offered the other to Hannah. As she was about to take it, however, the duke deftly substituted his own. They walked through the door that led to the garden, but when Hannah would have followed Lady Lucille and Sir Charles down a serpentine path, he drew her aside.

"Must you act as if you have the manners of a street wench?" He looked furious.

"Your aunt . . ." Hannah protested lamely.

"Was insufferable. But a young lady of gentle breeding would not have traded insults with an old biddy beyond hope of reform."

"I thought I was quite restrained."

"Indeed." His mouth twisted curiously. "I suppose in other circumstances, you would have had her at fisticuffs."

Hannah pressed her lips together, knowing that the duke was right. She had been unforgivably rude to Lady Huffington and certainly owed the countess an apology. But part of her rebelled.

"What would you have had me do? Sit there and suffer her insults as if I did not understand them? I am not stupid, and I refuse to act as if I am."

Within the stern depths of his black gaze, something softened. "You are rather touchy on the subject of your deafness, are you not?"

Hannah lifted her chin defiantly. "With all due respect, Your Grace, you have the understanding of a turnip. You cannot know what it is like to be the only one in a room unable to hear."

"A turnip," he repeated, frowning.

"I am sorry . . . I did not mean . . ." Hannah's voice trailed off as those enigmatic eyes held hers.

"I do not know what it is like to be deaf," he said, studying her. "But I do know that if you show your enemy your weak spot, he will make the most of it."

Suddenly she felt deflated, like a balloon whose flight was halted by an artfully thrown pellet. "I have behaved disgracefully, have I not?" She sighed. "I do not know what to say."

"Why do you not simply apologize?" His gaze held a mixture of pique and amusement.

"I am sorry." She stared at the ground, feeling miserable.

He touched her chin and brought it up so that she had to look at him. "I have never seen anyone stand up to my aunt in such a fashion."

"I said I was sorry," Hannah said unhappily, pulling away. "If you are expecting me to grovel . . ."

"No." He caught her arm, preventing her flight. "I am not expecting that."

"Then what do you want?" she cried in frustration, eyeing the firm hand that held her captive. "I have acknowledged my appalling behavior. I promise to apologize to your aunt. What is the point of keeping me here, making me feel like a chastised child?"

"Is that how I make you feel? Like a child?"

Looking into that black gaze, Hannah felt a confusion more womanly than childlike. Almost, she felt desired, though she had never experienced desire before. To be sure, she had in the past been the object of lechery, of lust that did not recognize the person she was inside. But she had never been desired in the way that she felt now, looking into the Duke of Claridge's dark eyes and recalling that moment he brought the waltz to a close and their lips together in that magnificent kiss.

Would he have kissed her if he had not desired her? She knew part of him wished her at Jericho. But perhaps another part of him held her in some regard. Was it possible?

Hannah shook her head. Who was she to think that this lofty peer held any regard for her—especially since he believed the worse about her?

"You have not answered my question."

"Very well, Your Grace," Hannah replied wearily. "You do not make me feel like a child. You make me feel like a complete and utter idiot."

She turned and walked toward the house. She could feel the duke's gaze boring into her back, watching with amused contempt as she realized she had absolutely no idea how to find her way around his home. Fortunately, she was spared the humiliation of returning to him to ask for directions by the sudden appearance of Lady Huffington's majordomo.

With all the haughtiness of a duchess, Hannah acknowledged his presence with a slight inclination of her head. "I wish to go to my room now, Higgins. Please have someone direct me."

Higgins looked taken aback, but the command in Hannah's voice evidently produced an instinctive reaction. "Yes, miss. Right away."

Barely stifling a nervous giggle, Hannah followed him into the house.

Out of the corner of her eye, Hannah caught a movement. The door of her bedchamber opened. Hesitantly, Lady Lucille peered in. "I am sorry to intrude. I knocked and then remembered that—" She broke off, flushing.

"It is all right." Hannah rose from the small vanity where she had been staring unhappily into the mirror and wondering whether she could ever face the duke or his family again. "Come in."

". . . so glad . . . another female . . . Aunt Eleanor . . . such fun . . ." Lady Lucille twirled around the room, her clear blue eyes sparkling.

Hannah could pick up only a few words. "I fear I must ask you to slow down," she said at last.

"Oh, how stupid of me! And you must call me Lucy." She came to a stop directly in front of Hannah. "What a trying afternoon you have had! Allow me to apologize for Aunt Eleanor's rudeness. I hope you will not reconsider your decision to visit us."

Hannah knew she must have misunderstood. The duke's sister was making it appear as if she were actually a welcome guest despite her appalling behavior. "Lady Lucille," she began, her cheeks burning in shame.

" 'Tis Lucy," she corrected. Her smile brought twin dimples to her flawless cheeks. "'Else I will be forced to call you Miss Gregory, and I have no intention of doing so. After all, you are Charles's cousin. That is practically like a member of the family!"

Hannah swallowed her guilt. "That is very kind of you, but it is I who owe you and your aunt an apology."

Lucy tilted her head consideringly. "I suppose you must go through the motions for form's sake, but do not feel badly. I used to take Aunt Eleanor on when she first came here, but it was not worth the constant battling." Lucy smiled. "Now, I pretend as if I am deaf and go on about my—" She broke off, stricken. "Oh! I am sorry."

"I did not take offense." Hannah smiled. "The duke has accused me of being touchy about my deafness, but I assure you I am not."

Lucy frowned. "Julian said *that?*"

"Immediately after upbraiding me for my behavior, and he was right to do so." Hannah paused. "Though I made it worse by calling him a turnip, and—"

"You called Julian a *turnip?*" Lucy's eyes filled with awe. "I have never know anyone to speak so—"

"And live to tell the tale?" Hannah interjected. "Yes, I can imagine that one would do well to avoid displeasing your brother. Unfortunately, I fear I have a rather reckless temper." She sighed.

Thoughtfully, Lucy pursed her lips. "How is it that you and Julian are at odds, when he and Charles are such good friends?"

Hannah flushed. She would give the game away if she was not careful. "I suppose we took an instant dislike to each other. I have heard of such things happening."

"Oh, I hope not. Julian is such a dear."

Dear? That contemptuous, haughty man? Well, perhaps even a tyrant could seem tame when seen through his sister's charitable eyes. Hannah murmured something noncommittal, but Lady Lucille had crossed the room and was staring out the window.

". . . needs a wife . . . you would not believe all those creatures he cavorts with . . . poor unhappy man."

Hannah frowned. Though she missed many of the words, it was clear that Lady Lucille's view of the duke differed greatly from her own. She walked over to the window. Lady Lucille was looking down at the front drive, where Sir Charles was entering his carriage. That put Hannah in mind of the role she was to play. She cleared her throat.

"Sir Charles . . . Charles and I are grateful for you hospitality," she said awkwardly.

Lucy whirled around. ". . . not at all . . . wonderful idea . . . make the rounds together." She halted, then spoke more slowly. "And, of course, we will find you a husband," she assured Hannah. "You must not pay Aunt Eleanor any mind. I am sure the suitors will flock to your side."

For the first time Hannah wondered if Lady Lucille possessed all of her faculties. There was absolutely nothing about her own appearance to draw a second look. Lady Lucille, on the other hand, was an exquisite beauty. Her hair shone like spun gold, and her blue eyes bore the clear serenity of Cheshire skies.

"I can well imagine they flock to your side, Lucy, but I am not expecting—"

"Oh, 'tis easy, Hannah," she interrupted. "You are smart and direct. The truly interesting men do not enjoy women without a thought in their heads. Aunt Eleanor says that I must learn to be docile and agreeable, but I think it is much more interesting to say what one thinks. It is amazing how many men agree."

Privately, Hannah thought that most men would agree with anything Lucy said. "Is there any one man who has taken your fancy?" she asked.

Lucy shook her head. "Aunt Eleanor says I must soon fix my attention or risk being scorned as a relentless flirt, but I am enjoying my fun. Why must a woman be limited by the expectations others have for her?"

Why indeed? Hannah thought. But she saw the source of the duke's fears for his sister. Though she could hardly imagine this delightful young woman doing anything truly rash, perhaps Lucy did have a reckless streak. "I suppose one must be mindful of flirting unwisely," she ventured.

"Oh, I am not a flirt," Lucy said. "I would marry if I found the right man. But I have not, and so I suppose I shall be an ape leader when all is said and done."

"Surely not." Hannah eyed her incredulously.

"Perhaps I should not tell this to you," she added, blushing, "but Charles has proposed to me three times. Of course he was only being polite. Julian probably confided his worry that I will be a dreary old spinster, and Charles was trying to be kind."

"I do not think that men propose marriage out of kindness," Hannah said dubiously.

"Perhaps not in general, but Charles has been Julian's best friend for ages. He is like a . . . well, like another brother to me. And I am like his sister. We had quite a laugh over it the last time he proposed."

Hannah could not imagine such a thing, but she kept her own counsel. It was quite possible that Sir Charles was smitten with Lucy but did not know how to get over the barrier of their friendship. She wondered if Lucy's feelings were engaged, and decided that even if they were, she had not admitted it to herself.

"I can think of worse things than marrying a good friend," Hannah said carefully.

With sudden dejection, Lucy flounced into a chair. "I do not want a friend. I want passion—a man who cannot live without me, who offers a love that will stand the test of time."

Hannah suppressed a sigh. The duke's sister truly lived in a fairy-tale world. "I am sure some friendships have caught fire," she offered.

"Perhaps," Lucy replied. "But if something is right, should it not be right from the outset? If there is to be passion, should it not turn one's head from the very start?" She laughed. "I want to be swept off my feet, Hannah. And soon."

Oh, dear, Hannah thought. Lucy was in greater danger than even the duke thought.

Chapter Nine

"Yes, Higgins. What is it?"

Though Julian's tone was curt, he welcomed the interruption, even from his aunt's minion. Hoping to find some meaningful clue he might have overlooked, he had begun to examine Aunt Eleanor's sermons that had been inserted into the family Bible. But he had no heart for the tedious task; his mind was mulling last night's troubling dream.

"Lady Huffington is not coming down today, Your Grace. She has a headache." Higgins's pursed mouth strongly hinted of reproach. Julian knew the man blamed him for Aunt Eleanor's megrims over the set-to with Miss Gregory.

Because Aunt Eleanor preferred the peace of Yorkshire to the noisy discomforts of London, Julian had never spent much time in her burdensome presence. Thus, he had only lately discovered the degree to which she was prepared to go in her bullying. If her truculent temper did not succeed in getting her way, she was wont to develop some dreadful illness that had the household catering to her every whim. Her current stay had pushed the limits of his temper.

Julian held out little hope for the success of Miss Gregory's apology. His aunt would either reduce her to tears or, more likely, reignite Miss Gregory's own considerable temper and spark another tiff. Aunt Eleanor would doubtless then go into a decline that would make her unavailable as a chaperon—and render Miss Gregory's come-out impossible.

Somehow he had to gain his aunt's cooperation, but he had no idea how to overcome her entrenched contentiousness. In the time he had known her, his bitter, snappish aunt had disdained a pleasant word when a sharp one would do.

Julian studied Higgins thoughtfully. If personal experience was any guide, people who thrived on making others miserable invariably were miserable themselves. He did not know why Aunt Eleanor was miserable, but if anyone knew how to get around her, it was this man—her household servant, secretary, and business adviser. Higgins had been in her employ for ages.

"Tell me, Higgins," he said, making a tent of his hands, "how long have you worked for my aunt?"

Was it his imagination, or did the man suddenly stand a little taller? "Fifteen years, Your Grace. Since before Lord Huffington's unfortunate demise a decade ago."

Julian had never known Lord Huffington, but if it was his death that had soured Aunt Eleanor's disposition, surely she had had time to adjust to his loss. On the other hand, if their marriage had been a miserable one, she had long ago put in a respectable period of mourning and should be enjoying her freedom. Either way, widowhood did not appear to explain her misery.

"You would be accounted something of an expert on Lady Huffington, would you not?" Julian prodded.

This time it was not his imagination—Higgins blushed beetred, rather incongruous in a man of his years. "I would never presume to claim such a thing—"

"But you know her rather well," Julian persisted. "You serve her in a number of capacities—do you not?"

"Yes, Your Grace," Higgins replied in a clipped voice. Julian stifled his impatience. Higgins would not willingly divulge any of his aunt's secrets. He was as prickly as his aunt and as faithful to her as any lapdog.

Perhaps that was the key.

"For all my aunt's . . . idiosyncrasies, you have stayed with her all these years," Julian offered pleasantly.

Higgins stiffened. "Lady Huffington is an excellent and generous employer."

No one who prized truth would describe his aunt as generous, yet Higgins gave no sign of realizing that he had uttered a bold-faced lie.

"Then perhaps," Julian continued in a silky tone, "you can help bring out this 'generous' nature."

Stunned, Higgins dropped his jaw. Then, disciplining himself, he recovered and regarded Julian warily.

Julian rose and walked slowly around him, like a panther circling hits prey. "Since you are acquainted with my aunt's better nature, I can think of no one more equipped to encourage her to help the unfortunate Miss Gregory."

"Help *that* woman?" Higgins looked appalled.

"'That woman' is a guest in my house." Julian's gaze narrowed. "A relative of my dearest friend."

Higgins colored. "Yes, Your Grace."

"She is also afflicted with an infirmity that none of us would wish to have. Surely some allowances must be made?"

"It is not my position to say."

"But it is your position to advise my aunt," Julian pointed out coolly. "I imagine you wish to avoid having her party to another scene that might damage her health."

Higgins frowned, trying in vain to discern the message Julian was sending his way. Like his employer, Higgins appeared to have no talent for subtlety.

"Let me be plain." Julian's tone held a note of warning. "Miss Gregory is not leaving us, so you may disabuse my aunt of that hope. If an accommodation is not reached between Miss Gregory and Aunt Eleanor, I will not answer for the consequences to my aunt's health."

Higgins paled. "You are threatening your own aunt?" he asked in amazement.

"Not at all. Merely pointing out that as Miss Gregory's disposition appears every bit as difficult as my aunt's, future fireworks must be expected, and they will surely wreak havoc on Aunt Eleanor's delicate constitution."

Higgins could not conceal his outrage. "You would sacrifice Lady Huffington's health to mollify one insolent young female who has no sense of her proper place?"

Julian hid a smile of satisfaction. He had guessed right. Strange as it seemed, his aunt had somehow endeared herself to Higgins, for beneath the man's stiff, unbending exterior beat a loyal and protective nature. It was time for the coup de grâce.

"My aunt and I have never made any pretense of great affection for each other. Indeed, I believe she holds you in higher regard than me. Her health is in your hands, Higgins, not mine."

Higgins went very still.

"You will use your influence to bring my aunt around to an amicable view of Miss Gregory," Julian commanded.

"That—that is quite impossible," Higgins stammered.

"Not at all," Julian returned. "I have a great deal of faith in you, Higgins."

"I do not see how I can—"

"You have not lasted all this time in her employ without learning how to give Lady Huffington what she needs," Julian said bluntly.

To his surprise, deep unhappiness swept Higgins's features.

"I have not handed you a difficult task," Julian reassured him. "You need only help Lady Huffington understand that it is unworthy of her to play the shrew. Appeal to that generosity in her about which you so gallantly speak."

"I would not know how to begin," Higgins said softly.

"Nonsense," Julian declared. "Any man who can handle Aunt Eleanor for fifteen years has a considerable bag of tricks at his disposal." Or was short a sheet himself, he mentally added.

Blushing like a new bride, Higgins barely managed his customary bow before he turned and walked silently from the room. Julian grinned. Who would have guessed that Higgins had a soft spot for the old biddy? Perhaps he would bring Aunt Eleanor around after all.

Alone once more, Julian tried to return to the papers at hand. But he could not concentrate, for images of last night's dream intruded.

In the dream, Hannah Gregory had come to him, speaking in that softly modulated tone she used. She wore that prim bonnet and the plain blue walking dress he had bought her. He had looked into those somber gray eyes and seen a message there: Uncertainty. Hope.

With the practiced words and pretty phrases of a skilled seducer, he had soothed away her doubts. Then he had untied the strings of her bonnet and removed it. As her hair tumbled down around her shoulders, he let it fall through his fingers, reveling in its velvety feel against his skin.

Even as he lay her down into the feather softness of his bed, he knew he was taking advantage of her weakness. But that realization had not stopped him from taking his pleasure with her, for shoring his masculine confidence with her conquest.

If you show your enemy your weak spot, he will make the most of it.

Julian was well acquainted with his own flaws. Bastard or no, he possessed a driving need to validate himself. Her flaw was more interesting: deafness had apparently left her unable to believe in her own desirability. Why else would she hide under those ugly mobcaps and shapeless dresses? It was odd that a woman used to bartering her flesh would have such a weakness. Yet she had accused him of making her feel like a child one moment and a fool the next—two images that belied the self-confidence with which she pretended to face the world.

In the dream, he had soothed her with pretty words and seductive phrases. When he had awakened this morning, he was as aroused as a raw youth. It had taken him some minutes to steady his breathing and all morning to shake the feeling that he had done something reprehensible.

Julian could not remember when his conscience had stricken him over a woman, much less over a harmless dream.

Was the dream harmless? Or had it shown him the way to win the war of wills with his protégée? Julian considered the possibilities.

Risking his sister's chastity and his aunt's health for a secret wager was shameful enough, though presumably no real harm would be done because he would win the bet. Playing to Miss Gregory's weak spot by seducing her as balm for his wounded manhood would be truly dastardly.

Julian's eyes narrowed thoughtfully. Could a man truly seduce such a jaded creature as a whore, a woman accustomed to being a man's plaything?

Now *that* would be quite a victory.

The last place Julian wished to be was at the mantuamaker's overseeing the commissioning of ball gowns. But with Aunt

Eleanor stubbornly refusing to leave her room, someone had to escort Miss Gregory and Lucy and prevent his sister from running amok in her enthusiasm.

True to his calculations, Lucy had taken Miss Gregory under her wing. Only the best gowns would do for her new friend and they must be had right away. Lucy had not stopped chattering all morning, although judging from Miss Gregory's baffled expression, she missed a great many of the words Lucy flung her way.

As the seamstress brought out yet another pattern book, Julian frowned. "I see no need to fill the whole of Claridge House with Miss Gregory's gowns."

His sister paused in the act of fingering a bolt of cloth. "Since the season is nearly half over she will not need so much, perhaps," she conceded. "But Hannah looks so lovely in these colors, I want to have something from each of them made up for her."

"And I would like to get home before nuncheon," was Julian's clipped reply.

To her credit, Miss Gregory looked exceedingly uncomfortable. "There is no need for all of this, Lucy. I have some perfectly fine gowns that will do very well."

"You have one evening gown, a morning dress, and two rather ordinary walking dresses," Lucy retorted. "That is nothing for a young lady making her debut."

Miss Gregory caught his eyes, and the silent appeal in her gaze surprised him. Most women of her stripe would have relished the receipt of such a stylish wardrobe as his sister was happily commissioning.

"Oh, look, Julian!" Lucy exclaimed. "Does not pink become her? It goes so nicely with her eyes."

Reluctantly, Julian studied the swath of pink silk the seamstress had draped over Miss Gregory's shoulder. It brought out the unusual gray of Miss Gregory's eyes to rather appealing effect.

When he made no reply, the seamstress quickly substituted another bolt, this one a deep shade of violet that gave Miss Gregory's complexion an intriguing glow. Or perhaps it was his scrutiny that brought the flush to her cheeks, for abruptly she stepped down from the little platform on which she had been standing.

"Can we stop for today?" she said. "I am rather fatigued." She did not meet his gaze.

"Oh, do forgive me, Hannah," Lucy trilled. "How selfish of me to keep you standing up there like a trussed goose. I must confess I cannot decide between the last two colors, so I will have Madame Celeste make up something in both of them, if that is acceptable?" She cocked her head, waiting for her friend's objection. When none was given, she smiled and said, "Good."

But Miss Gregory had not been looking at Lucy and did not know her permission had been sought. Julian suspected his sister knew very well what she had done; his suspicions were confirmed when she gave the order to the modiste and guided Miss Gregory out the door before the confused young woman detected what had transpired.

Julian shook his head. "Imp," he said, unable to suppress a smile.

"Not at all," Lucy protested. "Surely you do not begrudge the money, brother dear? I am certain you have spent far more setting up some light-o-love."

"You know nothing about such things," he admonished, appalled.

"Not firsthand, of course," she agreed. "But I do know that men like to see ladies dressed in beautiful clothing, and you are a man—even if Miss Gregory has failed to notice."

Julian frowned. "What?"

"Does it chafe so very much to hear that?" Lucy regarded him pityingly. "Poor Julian. Then perhaps there is hope after all."

"Hope for what? What the devil are you talking about?" he demanded, thankful that Miss Gregory was a few steps ahead of them and blissfully unaware of his sister's words.

Lucy grinned. "Hope for you and Hannah, of course. Though 'tis a pity you two have gotten off on such testy footing. She told me she called you a turnip. But then you should not have made that tasteless remark about her deafness."

Julian wondered if his own hearing had somehow been affected. He could not have heard his sister aright. "You cannot think that Miss Gregory and I—"

"Not yet," Lucy replied calmly. "You scarcely know each other, after all. But she is staying in our house, and that should provide ample opportunity for you to deepen your acquaintance. Gifting him with a look of solemn sincerity, she added, "She is just the bride for you."

Julian's mouth fell open. "You cannot be serious!"

"Hannah has great strength of character," Lucy continued. "She is strong, independent, and forthright—just the sort of woman you need to jolt you from that offputting shell of yours."

She rubbed her hands together in anticipation. "Just wait until you see the wardrobe I have chosen for her. I have wonderful ideas for her hairstyle. She must wear it down, so that everyone can see how lovely she is."

If Lucy had not looked so earnest, Julian would have laughed aloud at the irony of his sister's promoting a prostitute as his bride. Women like Miss Gregory were fit for only one thing—and it was not being a duchess. Anyway, marriage for him was out of the question.

"Miss Gregory and I should not suit," he said tersely, hoping Lucy would be content to leave it at that.

Being Lucy, she was not.

"Nonsense. It is just that you have no experience with virgins."

Julian emitted a strangled sound that prevented an immediate reply. "This is an exceedingly improper topic to discuss with one's sister," he managed at last.

Lucy turned to him with a mischievous grin. "Hiding behind propriety does not suit you in the least, brother. I have seen the sort of women you cavort with, and they are nothing like Hannah."

"I'll have no more of this—" Julian began sternly, only to break off as Lucy patted his back sympathetically, as if he were a disgruntled puppydog.

"Hannah must find a husband, and I fear that you will have a great deal of competition if you do not act soon," Lucy warned. "It is too bad that she has not yet discovered that there is a very devastating man under her own roof."

"Devil take it! She is Charles's cousin!" Julian fairly shouted, stung by Lucy's blithe assumption that Hannah had not found him attractive. Had she not kissed him that time in the hunting box?

Perhaps—now that he thought on it—she had simply suffered his kiss because she had not wanted to offend her new employer. But only yesterday in the garden, something had passed between them, unspoken but powerful. Or had he just imagined the entire thing? Had it been just as elusive as last night's unsettling dream?

"Yes," Lucy agreed in a musing tone, "perhaps it will be difficult for her to see you as someone other than her cousin's best friend—especially since you have had words." She sighed. "You have always been your own worst enemy, Julian. Do you not think you could make yourself more amiable to Hannah? I think you will be happily surprised."

"A surprise?" Miss Gregory echoed, having turned in time to catch that last. "What are you planning, Lucy?" she asked pleasantly.

"Oh, 'tis nothing." Lucy waived a dismissive hand. "Nothing at all."

Julian followed the two women into his carriage, which was instantly filled with Lucy's gay laughter. He sat stiff and humorless the remainder of the ride, prompting a reproving look from his sister.

He congratulated himself on ignoring it.

Chapter Ten

Lady Huffington wore a pained expression, but it was impossible to tell whether it was the countess' usual demeanor or merely the result of seeing Hannah once more. Swathed in pink from head to toe, the countess reclined on a chaise longue in a flowing pink dressing gown, matching slippers, and a pink turban. She held a white lace handkerchief to her forehead with a mournful air. Though the woman looked to be in the throes of some dreadful illness, Hannah suspected that self-indulgence rather than genuine discomfort kept her off her feet.

For two days the countess had stayed in her rooms, refusing visitors. When Higgins informed Hannah that his employer had condescended to hear her apology, providing it could be accomplished in fewer than five minutes, Hannah had swallowed her pride and entered the lioness' den.

"Thank you for agreeing to see me, Lady Huffington," she began.

Higgins hovered at the countess' elbow, pouring tea which Lady Huffington waved weakly away. "I am far too ill for tea at the moment," she murmured.

Hannah looked questioningly at Higgins, but he merely shrugged, as if to say that he had not promised miracles. Hannah cleared her throat.

"I wish to say how deeply sorry I am for my words of the other night."

When the countess made no response, Hannah continued. "You stated my obvious shortcomings in realistic terms. Finding a husband for me will be quite a challenge. Please accept my apology for offending you."

Lady Huffington's eyes narrowed, and for the briefest moment Hannah was put in mind of the duke's steely gaze. The countess did not speak for some moments. Then she shifted herself to a sitting position.

"You may leave, Miss Gregory," she said coolly.

Hannah blinked. She was being dismissed without any acknowledgment of her apology or any indication as to whether the countess would continue to regard her as if she were a bit of offensive lint.

"Lady Huffington—" Hannah protested.

"I said that you may leave, girl," the countess repeated, eyeing her haughtily. "Do not belie your pretty words by further insolence."

No wonder the woman wore such a sour expression, Hannah thought. She was a termagant. Decades of dourness had ruined what must have been a rather comely face in her younger years. Even now, a smile would go a long way in lifting age from her features—she was probably no older than Hannah's mother might have been. But Lady Huffington apparently did not know how to smile, only to bully.

A slow burn crept up the back of Hannah's neck. Countess or no, the woman had no right to treat her so rudely.

"Lady Huffington, I assure you I do not intend to be a burden to this house," Hannah said, carefully modulating her voice. The last thing she wanted was to sound shrill. "Nor will my obvious drawbacks detract from Lady Lucille's season. Your niece has a kind and generous nature that even someone of limited vision must be forced to recognize."

"*Limited vision?*" The countess' brows arched skyward, and she drew herself up like a ruffled hen. "Do you refer to *me*, Miss Gregory?"

Out of the corner of her eye, Hannah saw Higgins close his eyes as if in pain. So much for her carefully orchestrated apology. She sighed. If only she could control her wicked tongue.

"I would not be so bold as to do so, ma'am," she replied, dropping a curtsy. "I believe my five minutes have expired. Good afternoon."

Rigid with rage, Lady Huffington did not speak until Hannah left the room. Then she turned to Higgins. "Insufferable chit," she pronounced, rubbing her temples and giving every sign of being on the verge of collapse.

Higgins shoved the rejected teacup into her hand, forcing her to forestall her relapse or risk spilling hot tea into her lap. Lady Huffington eyed him sharply, then took a bracing sip.

"That girl does not know her place," the countess complained. "Why she is but a poor relation of a mere baronet! How dare she expect to be treated as an equal?"

"Her connection seems respectable enough," Higgins offered in a neutral tone.

Lady Huffington sniffed. "I suppose you are thinking about your own background. I forget that you were a poor relation yourself."

Higgins stiffened. "My father was a member of the Commons and a right honorable gentleman."

"Yes, yes"—Lady Huffington waved one hand impatiently—"but you have always known your place. I would not have kept you on all these years if you had not."

Higgins did not reply.

"Miss Gregory, on the other hand, seems to think she is entitled to the same privileges as Lucille," the countess continued.

"Since the duke has given them to her," Higgins ventured, "perhaps it would be unworthy of you to continue to rebuff her."

"*Unworthy?*" The countess' graying brows rose sharply.

Higgins hesitated, then cleared his throat. "Lord Huffington was proud of his reputation as a philanthropist, was he not?"

Lady Huffington grew rigid. The name of her late husband was rarely mentioned in her presence. "My husband had a reputation for many things."

"Granted, madam," Higgins acknowledged, reddening, "but generosity was foremost among them."

"What of it?" Her mouth thinned into a bitter line.

"I have always thought you capable of great generosity, too, my lady," he said quietly, "given the right circumstances."

Lady Huffington stared at him, too stunned to speak. A flush spread over her face. "Truly, Higgins?" she asked in a small voice.

"Truly, madam."

The countess looked away, then stared wordlessly into the bottom of her teacup. Finally, she handed the cup to him without meeting his gaze. Higgins bowed and silently rolled the tea cart out of the room.

Sir Charles came to dinner that night. While he displayed great warmth toward Hannah—as if they were indeed close relations—his eyes were all for Lucy. Hannah wondered that Lucy could miss what was written in his gaze, but she treated him like a brother, without evincing any flirtatiousness or feminine interest.

Lucy had argued that if passion was to exist between a man and woman, it must be present from the very start. There was certainly nothing of the kind between her and Sir Charles. Poor man. How could he break through that barrier of cordiality without risking the sacrifice of the friendship he treasured with her?

Hannah knew herself no expert in matters of the heart. The encounters she had witnessed in Covent Garden were based entirely on lust. Perhaps passion turned to love if one gave it enough time, but she did not think those sordid meetings her friends had with their customers did. On the other hand, risking a friendship to see if passion might grow must be a terrifying gamble, for the friendship would never be the same. While Lucy remained blissfully ignorant, the baronet must be tormented by his dilemma.

To be sure, Sir Charles did not look tormented. Only an occasional flicker in his clear green eyes hinted of any feeling out of the ordinary. Since Lucy had refused him three times, Hannah assumed that he had long ago disciplined himself to dampen his passions, and she could scarcely blame him. Only a rare man indeed would brave that daunting gaiety and effortless ebullience with which Lucy Pembroke faced the world.

"I have the most wonderful idea," Lucy exclaimed when the men joined them in the drawing room following their after-dinner port. "Since Hannah is to attend her first ball soon, this is a perfect time to teach her the new dances." She clasped Hannah's hand and drew her toward the door to the adjacent music room.

Vehemently Hannah shook her head. "I cannot."

Undaunted, Lucy threw open the door. Hannah froze, for there in the music room was the most exquisite instrument she had ever seen. The case of the grand old clavichord looked to be of fine rosewood, which age had given a burnished patina the color of molten fire. On the open lid, onyx inlay framed a scene of such pastoral beauty that it nearly robbed her of breath. Fur trees rose in the foreground, tufts of dark green presiding over a mountain lake's serene beauty and the majestical peaks miles away. A true artist, one with a keen understanding of natural harmony, had adorned this wonderful instrument.

Her eyes burned as images of her mother's old clavichord sprang to mind and with it visions of the mountains of Wales beckoning over low-rise Cheshire hills remarkably like those the artist had painted. Would this clavichord sound as lovely as it looked? She swallowed a bitter taste at the knowledge that she would never know.

Vaguely, she was aware of someone nearby. She looked up, and discovered that the duke was speaking.

". . . admirable notion. Charles is accounted something of an expert on the dance floor. You will find him an able instructor."

As Lucy seated herself at another instrument, a pianoforte, the duke nudged Sir Charles toward Hannah, then promptly sat on the piano bench next to Lucy. The baronet's startled gaze filled with disappointment, and Hannah realized that he had hoped to turn the pages for Lucy.

In the face of his honest emotion, Hannah suddenly felt a thorough fraud. For all her fine new clothes, she was nothing more than a fallen women with a shocking amount of worldly experience, a sharp tongue, and not a prayer of winning redemption for this despicable masquerade. Was a chance to regain her hearing worth such deception?

With a rueful gaze, Sir Charles watched the couple at the piano. Gentlemanly politeness quickly covered his disappointment, however, as he turned to smile at Hannah and lead her out for what soon became a disastrous exercise in clumsiness. Trying to follow the figures, Hannah stumbled several times. She eyed him helplessly, but could not seem to do anything right. Finally, he drew her over to a corner to walk her slowly through the steps.

"I do not know if I can manage this, Sir Charles," she said unhappily.

"You must call me Charles," he admonished. "It would look odd if you did not."

Hannah flushed, knowing that he was right to remind her, however gently, of her role. "Yes, of course."

"You must not underestimate yourself," he continued, smiling encouragingly. "With a little practice and guidance from your partner, you can learn most of the dances."

"You are a very patient man if you think that," Hannah said with a sigh.

Involuntarily his gaze flew to the pianoforte, where Lucy was playing happily as the duke turned the pages. "Perhaps I am too patient."

Hannah regarded him thoughtfully. Though Charles seemed a most gentle and understanding man, there was an edginess about the way he eyed the duke and Lucy. A curious thought assailed her.

"Forgive me if I speak out of turn," she said hesitantly, "but I wondered whether the duke had some reason for maneuvering us into this dance lesson."

Wariness filled his gaze. "Maneuvering us? Why would he have done that?"

"To keep you from his sister."

He stilled, then shot her a rueful smile. "You are very perceptive, Miss Gregory."

"Hannah," she corrected. "And if I am perceptive, it is because I must be. Tell me: why does the duke oppose your suit?"

"He does not."

Hannah frowned. "But he maneuvered you away from what would otherwise have been a pleasant time at Lucy's side."

Charles's gaze grew hooded. "It is in Julian's interest to keep me at bay for the nonce."

"Why?"

"It pertains to a certain wager between us," he said, looking very uncomfortable.

"A wager?"

"Let us just say that for the moment it suits him to keep me from bringing Lucy around. Not that there is any chance of that in any case," he added morosely.

"But you cannot sit idle while the duke keeps you from your heart's desire," Hannah protested.

Amusement filled his gaze. "You are quite the fighter, are you not, Hannah? Save your indignation. It is not Julian who holds Lucy from me. It is the young lady herself."

"That is nonsense," Hannah replied with asperity. "She holds you in great regard."

He grimaced. "Rather like a comfortable old shoe."

Hannah stared. Charles was truly suffering. Yet, she suspected he would be a devoted husband to Lucy—and a passionate one. It was a pity that Lucy could not see it, a pity that her conniving brother was intent on inflicting such misery on his friend. The Duke of Claridge certainly had no understanding of true friendship.

An intriguing thought popped into her mind. Her own future might be bleak, but Charles and Lucy deserved every happiness they could claim. With a little luck, the duke could be persuaded to step out of the way of true love and Lucy could be persuaded to seek her grand passion in the arms of an old friend.

Hannah smiled. Perhaps redemption was not so foreign a notion after all.

The evening had been a splendid success. Miss Gregory's table manners had not disgraced her at dinner, and she had even managed to learn some of the new dances from Charles. She and Lucy were becoming fast friends. Only Aunt Eleanor's cooperation was lacking, and Julian had every faith in Higgins. His wager would soon be won.

Tossing off a celebratory glass of brandy, he congratulated himself on the night's greatest victory—not having to teach Miss Gregory those dances himself.

The memory of waltzing her around his hunting box was all too vivid. He had no desire to repeat the experience—his matchmaking sister's schemes notwithstanding. Happily, he had ensconced himself as Lucy's page-turner, although it meant being the target of Charles's murderous glare for the rest of the evening.

Julian savored the heat of the brandy as it trickled down his throat. After enduring Lucy's erratic playing, Charles's hostility, and the vision of Miss Gregory floating around in his friend's arms, there was a great deal to be said for fine brandy, a warm fire, and the peaceful solitude of his study. Leaning back in his chair, he stretched out his feet, enjoying a rare moment of quiet satisfaction.

"I beg your pardon, Your Grace." To his dismay, Miss Gregory stood at the threshold of his sanctuary.

"What is it?" he demanded.

"I wish to know why you are making things so difficult for Sir Charles."

Julian blinked. "What are you talking about?"

"You are discouraging his suit."

Julian could not suppress a bark of laughter. "I see that Charles has been playing you for sympathy."

"He said you had a wager." Her solemn gray eyes regarded him intently.

Julian stilled. With her rebellious temperament, it would be disastrous if she learned the terms of their bet. "What do you know of it?" he asked carefully.

"Only that his future with Lucy is somehow on hold until the wager is fulfilled."

Julian rose and poured himself another brandy. As an afterthought, he filled a second glass. When he offered it to her, she seemed surprised and took a tentative, almost suspicious sip.

"Charles is not one to allow someone else to make his decisions for him," he said coolly. "Perhaps you do not know your 'cousin' as well as you think."

She frowned. "But he did nothing tonight when you insinuated yourself as Lucy's page-turner. You took advantage of his gentlemanly nature. That was not well done."

"You need not lecture, Miss Gregory. There was nothing sinister about my actions tonight, I assure you."

Her brow furrowed in thought. She took another sip of brandy. "Do you not know that he is in love with her?"

"Tedious emotion." He yawned. "A veritable nuisance. Have some more brandy, Miss Gregory."

Her eyes grew wide as he added more of the soothing liquid to her glass. In the glow of the candles, she looked quite lovely, which surprised him. He realized that Lucy, curse her meddling ways, had done something to her hair.

Gone were the usual hideous hair coverings. Two combs caught her hair loosely off her face. The dancing had loosened them, allowing honey-colored tresses to spill over her shoulders like a silk curtain.

Julian shook his head to clear his mind of the sudden image of that hair gracing bare shoulders. Then he realized that she had spoken. "What did you say?"

"Why did you not allow Charles to sit with Lucy? You could have taught me those dances yourself."

"As I recall, the last time we danced together had rather unforeseen results."

Her cheeks blushed scarlet. To cover her confusion, she took a large gulp of brandy. As the full force of the liquid seared her throat, she gasped and began to cough.

Instantly, Julian took her glass. He patted her firmly on the back until her coughing passed. The contact was vaguely unsettling. He frowned and took his hand away.

"You need not look so stern," she managed, still sputtering. "I am not trying to insinuate myself into your affections."

"Nor could you, madam," he retorted. "You are but a woman I have purchased for a time, nothing more."

His shins felt something sharp and uncomfortable. He looked down and realized that she had just kicked him with the tip of her satin-covered slippers. Amazed, he stared at her.

"You have purchased my *services*—limited ones at that," she corrected, fury turning the gray of her eyes into shards of ice. "You own nothing of *me*, Your Grace. Nor should I ever allow a rake like yourself to possess my person or—heaven forbid—my heart."

Rubbing his leg, Julian scowled, stung more by her scathing denunciation than her ineffectual blow.

"For your information, Miss Gregory, I am considered something of a *reformed* rake," he said, neglecting to add that no one—least of all himself—had taken his reformation seriously. "I have become so worthy, in fact, as to have my sister consider me an eligible *parti* for one of her friends." He did not mention that it was she whom Lucy had so ridiculously selected.

All the fire seemed to leave her. She eyed him uncertainly, no longer the spitfire who had kicked him without a moment's hesitation. "I suppose that is gratifying," she ventured in a strangely subdued tone.

"Gratifying?" His mouth twisted wryly. "Oh, yes, indeed. You cannot imagine how gratifying it is to have Lucy decide that I am in need of a wife—"

"When you do not intend to marry?"

His gaze darkened. "I had forgotten that I told you that."

"One remembers when a man declares that he does not intend to wed," she said quietly. "But perhaps you will change your mind."

"No."

"You must want children," she persisted. "Or need them to secure the line."

"I do not care to secure the line." It might not even be his to secure. He eyed her coldly. "When Lucy has children, I will settle as much of my estate on them as possible." And if his solicitors could break the entail, Lucy would receive almost everything. At least *she* would not suffer for his father's crimes.

Miss Gregory blinked. "That is quite generous. I suppose that means Lucy may wed where she chooses."

"As long as her husband is a decent, honorable man, I will not oppose the match."

"Then why are you standing in Charles's way?" she asked, mystified.

"Back to that, are we?" Julian drained the last of his brandy. He was weary of this war of wills. Not for the first time, he wished he could take back that moment in Reverend McGougal's office when he had decided that she would be a diverting specimen to mold.

Suddenly, he realized the only molding he wanted to do at the moment involved her body and his in the kind of intimate congress that left no room for argument.

And why not? Any woman who had the temerity to declare herself utterly impervious to him deserved to be tested.

Lucy had said Miss Gregory did not see him as a potential lover, but what did she know about such things? A woman who had allowed herself to be kissed the way she had in his hunting box most certainly desired him. A black, dangerous mood swept through him.

He had had enough of her dissembling.

His dream had shown him the way. She would learn that he was not to be dismissed, that he would not tolerate her airs, that he would have her on whatever terms he chose. A clever prostitute was no match for a man who could fool the world into believing him a duke.

With every thought in his head racing toward one end, Julian calmly refilled her glass and held it out to her. When she hesitated, he gently wrapped her hand around the glass, allowing his own fingers to linger tantalizingly on hers. It was a technique that had never failed him, and it did not now.

Dutifully she took the glass and took a hasty sip to cover her awkwardness. Julian waited, allowing her discomfiture to fill the space between them and the brandy to do its work.

"Perhaps I have been inconsiderate," he said smoothly, wrinkling his brow in apparent concern. "What do you suggest I do about poor Charles?"

Quickly, he moved to the plump leather sofa near the fire and perched stiffly on the edge—as if distracted by troubling thoughts. "It is not easy for a man to admit that he may be wrong," he added, remembering to catch her gaze so that she would have no trouble reading his lips. "Perhaps . . . I hesitate to ask it, but perhaps you might . . ." He looked away and stared into the fire.

It worked. To his delight, she drew closer. He pretended not to notice. Hesitantly she bent down, touching his arm. "What, Your Grace? What is it?" Her gaze was filled with concern.

Suppressing a smile of satisfaction, Julian turned to her. "If we might simply talk for a while?" Women loved to talk, he knew, and the temptation to hear a tormented rake unburden himself was simply too much to most of them.

"Oh." She eyed the mantel clock. "Well, of course . . . if you do not think it is too late."

Julian's calculating gaze shot to the clock as well. "Miss Gregory," he assured her gravely, "it is never too late."

Chapter Eleven

She really ought to leave. But the duke's unexpected and compelling vulnerability turned her wavering will to mush. Moreover, the opportunity to further press the case for Lucy and Charles must not be lost. Gingerly, Hannah perched on the sofa next to him and took another bracing sip of brandy.

"No, I do not suppose it is too late," she replied, wondering why her spine suddenly tingled with a warning of danger when the duke was regarding her with such a benign, remorseful expression that anyone could tell he was as harmless as a lamb.

"Thank you," he said simply, before turning to study the fire.

Hannah could not imagine the tormented thoughts that made him clench his hands in anguish and stare sightlessly into the flickering flames. Guilt filled her. She had said some truly horrid things to him, assuming him to be an utter reprobate. Now she saw that she had failed to try to understand what was at the root of his cynicism.

His lips moved, but Hannah could not catch the words as he buried his head in his hands.

"Please, Your Grace," she said, gently touching his arm, "you must look at me."

Instantly his dark, soulful gaze impaled her. The sorrowful yearning there nearly took her breath away.

"If I have been inconsiderate of Charles and Lucy, it is because . . . because I myself have never believed in love," he said slowly. "There has never been a woman who has fully understood me."

Hannah lowered her gaze. "I suppose it is difficult for one person to fully understand another."

His finely tapered fingertips touched her chin, tilting it up so that she met his liquid gaze. "You see, I have always been a solitary sort," he said, his expression solemn. "My mother died when I was six, and I was raised by a childless aunt in a remote castle on the Dorset coast."

"Oh, my," Hannah murmured, her heart instantly going out to the lonely boy he must have been.

"I did not lay eyes on my father until I was fifteen." For a moment he appeared lost in thought. "He was a cold, embittered man. At the age of seventeen I attended him at his deathbed. His last words cursed me to the heavens."

"How awful," she murmured, filled with compassion. She had been lonely most of her life as well, but at least she had had loving parents. No wonder the duke had grown surly and scornful. No one had shown him sufficient affection on which to model his own life.

"I am terribly sorry," she said, instinctively reaching for his hand.

Absently he rubbed it between his own, generating a penetrating warmth that suddenly put her in mind of those nettlesome butterflies in her stomach. The duke did not seem to realize what he was doing. His eyes bore a far-off look before they once more focused on hers.

"I do not want your pity, Miss Gregory. Perhaps you can simply help me understand about Charles and Lucy. Though I possess more wealth than most men, I am woefully impoverished on the subject you have raised. What would you have me do about them?"

"Well," she began hesitantly, "I am mindful of the task you have set for me, that is, to keep Lucy out of trouble. But I do think that we must arrange for her to spend more time with Charles so that she can come to see him in a different way."

"What way is that?" he asked, his fingers moving in gentle circles over her palm.

Hannah took another sip of brandy. "As . . . as more than a friend. I believe she regards him like a brother rather than as a potential—" She broke off, suddenly quite tongue-tied.

"Lover?" the duke offered helpfully.

Hannah nodded, hurriedly taking another gulp of the amber liquid, which was beginning to taste quite nice. It certainly did the most amazing things for one's courage. "I believe the only way to change the course of their relationship is to throw them together."

"Charles is frequently here. They are together quite often as it is." Idly his fingers moved to the very sensitive part of her inner wrist. Hannah swallowed hard.

"But not alone," she pointed out. "Not as we are now, quite private and unchaperoned."

The duke arched a brow. "Are you suggesting that I place my sister in a position where she could be compromised?"

"Oh, no," Hannah assured him. "No more than I am in danger at this moment. I merely suggest that Charles be given the chance to show Lucy that she can form a grand passion for him."

"Grand passion?" The duke's fingers meandered up to the soft skin at the inside of her elbow.

"Lucy wishes to be swept away," she explained, finding it increasingly difficult to concentrate.

"That sounds quite dangerous."

When had his arm found its way to the back of the sofa just behind her shoulders? When had his fingertips begun to caress the skin on her neck? Hannah drained what was left of her brandy and fanned herself. It was warm in front of the fire. She was grateful when the duke, seeming to read her mind, gently pushed her shawl from her shoulders.

"I do not think Lucy could get into danger with Charles," she replied. "He loves her, after all. He means to marry her. And he is a thorough gentleman."

"No man is impervious to temptation, Miss Gregory."

The lips she had been reading so intently were suddenly on hers, caressing her mouth with exquisite gentleness. Somehow, this act seemed most natural, for the danger she had sensed earlier had vanished in the face of this tormented man's surprising and humble gentleness. Hannah sighed contentedly as the masculine arm behind her shoulders tightened reassuringly and his hand toyed shyly with the lace trim on her gown.

When the kiss moved from gentle to insistent, Hannah could only marvel at the way her body had grown so lethargic and heavy as to need the support of his arm. A mesmerizing passiveness swept over her, and she wanted only to relax against him and feel this closeness between them. She felt safe, trusting, in a way she never had before.

Only when his fingers slipped under the lace trim to push aside the shoulder of her gown did a troubling awareness begin to nag at her. Only when his lips abandoned hers to nibble at her earlobe, then to trail tantalizingly down the sensitive skin of her neck, did Hannah think vaguely that something was amiss.

But then he stroked her hair and murmured something she had not a prayer of catching. The warm breath against her ear reassured her befogged brain, and when the hand that had rested so carelessly at her waist moved to the curve of her breast, Hannah could only sigh in pleasure and marvel that anything could feel so absolutely right.

Was it the brandy or her new understanding of his loneliness that robbed her of all fight? It mattered not—not when the silence that imprisoned her no longer seemed so empty. Under his careful ministrations, other senses rushed to fill the vacuum.

His lips felt like roughened satin against her skin, his warm breath like the kiss of life itself. Heady scents of brandy and sandalwood held her captive, and the midnight of his eyes spoke of masculine secrets that made her tremble. Every nerve in her scalp tingled as he stroked her hair, freeing it from its encumbering combs.

When he clasped her face between his hands, covering her mouth with just a hint of violence, Hannah fairly shook in anticipation. He seemed to know that she yearned for more than just a gentle touch. His lips bruised hers, demanding her own passionate response in payment. His hands ran the length of her back, cupping her buttocks, settling her down on the sofa as he covered her with his body. The bodice of her gown slipped away.

Hannah knew she ought to have protested when his knee separated her legs through the skirt of her gown, but she was long past rational thought or deed. The storm of sensation that held her in its grip left her helpless with longing. In the deafening silence of this intimate touching, the Duke of Claridge had made her his slave.

When his lips moved against her ear once more, Hannah did not need to hear to know the question he asked. A small kernel of joy emerged from the dense web of her desire.

"Yes," she murmured recklessly. "Yes, my love."

Julian's hand turned to stone over the very soft orb of flesh that was her left breast. The passion boiling in his veins chilled to ice.

"I should not have said that." Her voice was strained. As she looked up at him with those impossibly intense gray eyes, Julian felt more like a bastard than he had in his nearly thirty years on the earth.

He did not understand why he felt like a heel. She had played right into his hands, bought his tale of loneliness and his inability to find a woman who understood him. She had been more than willing to admit him to the silky portals that scores of men had already sampled.

It was nothing to seduce a prostitute—it should not have been necessary to go to such lengths at all, but he had and he had enjoyed the game. Until now, when she had broken the rules and mentioned that word in her moment of surrender, turning it all to sand and dust.

"Forgive me," he said, more angry than apologetic as he pulled her up from the divan. He averted his gaze as she repaired her bodice.

"No, no. It was my fault," she said, speaking rapidly, nervously. "I did not mean *love*, exactly. I am not sure I know why I said it, Your Grace, but I would never—"

"Under the circumstance," he muttered dryly, "I believe you might call me Julian."

But she had not seen him speak and so went on chattering in a way that left him no doubt that she was mortified and miserable. Why a woman of her experience should feel so was another matter, but Julian had no desire to examine it. When a man bent on seduction has the tables turned on him, he is in no mood to reason it out. Julian had figured her for an easy conquest, and she proved herself that, but somewhere between his sympathetic tale of woe and the stroking of her silken tresses he had gotten caught up in something he did not fully understand.

Possessing Hannah Gregory had suddenly become the most important thing in the world.

"I am very confused." She was looking at him with eyes so deep with wonder that a man could lose himself in them.

"That makes two of us," he muttered.

Looking at the mantel clock, he discovered that it was one in the morning. Not an impossibly late hour, by any means, but one at which certain things had to be decided.

"Good night, Miss Gregory," he said, putting her shawl around her shoulders as if she were some delicate virgin and hustling her out of his study like a man trying to rid himself of the plague.

At the door she paused to look at him. Her lips were swollen from his kisses, and her hair tumbled across her shoulders in disarray. Her repaired bodice exposed rather more of her curves than it had before their activities on the sofa, and that infernal shawl provided entirely inadequate covering.

"I am sorry," she said.

"And I, Miss Gregory, am an idiot."

With that, he closed the door in her face.

"Miss Gregory plays the clavichord."

The book of sermons Lady Huffington had been reading fell from her lap onto the floor with a loud thump.

"No," she protested, her voice cracking. "It cannot be."

Higgins picked up the book and placed it on the table next to the chaise longue. "I heard her in the music room this morning. Her playing was tentative, as if she had not done so in a long time."

Lady Huffington scarcely seemed to breathe as she absorbed this information. "Perhaps she was only toying with the thing," she ventured at last. "Very few people truly know the clavichord these days."

"That is so," Higgins agreed. "But she plays like an angel."

The countess frowned. "You said she was tentative."

"At first. The longer she sat at the keys, the more confident she grew. The tone was pure, her *tremblement* exquisite."

"Truly?" Lady Huffington sighed. "How I have longed to hear—" She broke off suddenly, and made a great show of examining her book.

Higgins regarded her for a long time, and anyone who thought the dour lines etched permanently into his face would have been surprised to see the softening of those stony features.

"Perhaps Miss Gregory would play for you."

"What?" The countess looked up, horrified. "I would never allow that rude young woman to do such a thing. To give her the satisfaction . . ." Her voice trailed off as she saw something unsettling in Higgins's gaze.

"It has been a very long time, my lady." Both of them knew he was not referring to the three days in which the countess had been ensconced in her chamber.

"Too long," he added quietly.

Chapter Twelve

It was only a variation on a simple nursery rhyme, a folk song her mother had loved. Yet even her mother's old clavichord had eloquently conveyed the tune's wistful yearning. On this magnificent instrument, with its resonant rosewood and ivory and tortoiseshell keys, the song would have broken hearts.

The Mozart variation Hannah had discovered amid the volumes of music wove a brilliant contrast of passages. The andante possessed a spare simplicity articulated by long melodic lines and a subtle phrasing that demanded a performer's utmost skill.

Coaxing from the keys what must have been a splendid vibrato, Hannah vowed not to lapse into self-pity. It was enough to sit at this beautiful clavichord and do what she had never thought to do again—touch the keys and know that music resulted, whether she could hear it or not.

She was surprised at how much of her knowledge of the clavichord came back—the short octave with which piano makers had so disdainfully dispensed, the tremolo that imparted an insistent pathos in the slow movements. Above all, the delicacy of touch and constancy of pressure needed to prevent an alternation of pitch.

With the world of sound lost to her, other worlds had opened. Her fingers were more sensitive to the nuances of the keys. Her eye took in the composer's markings at a glance, hearing them in the part of her mind that remembered sound. Perhaps deafness had made her a better clavichordist, for nuance and technique were the keys to mining the instrument's deep expressiveness. But though she had been accounted quite excellent in her girlhood, Hannah did not delude herself that standards of excellence in a Cheshire village approached those of London.

Suddenly ashamed of her temerity in daring even to touch such a splendid instrument, Hannah allowed her hands to fall back into her lap. She did not know why she had come to the music room this morning, nor seated herself at the keys in search of what she had always found there—solace and clarity of thought.

Confusion from the events of last night cluttered her brain. She had been on the verge of the unthinkable—giving herself to the Duke of Claridge. But why? What about that scant hour in his study had touched her heart, when she had so defiantly girded her defenses against him?

Was it his loneliness? His moving tale of growing up a virtual orphan, rejected by the father who could not be troubled with fatherhood? Had pity been at the root of her capitulation?

Hannah did not think so. Indeed, she almost wondered whether she truly believed his sorrowful tale. A prudent woman would question why the duke had opened his budget to her when he had rarely shown her anything but disdain, when he was known to be a man who used women uncaringly. Perhaps seduction had been his intent all along—though why he would target her was a mystery, when he must have had access to all manner of beautiful and elegant females.

If there was one thing that deafness had given her, it was the ability to listen to the silence, to inner thoughts that could not be denied. Truth was all that mattered, and the truth of the matter was that she had not cooperated in her own seduction because of pity for the duke or naïveté at what might lie behind his words. There was only one reason: she had desired him.

She wanted this cynical duke who was miles above her in social standing and years beyond her in experience. The lust that she had thought beneath her when she encountered it on the streets was all too appealing amid the marble sculptures, polished oaken banisters, and gold leaf that abounded in this ducal household.

But it was not his riches that attracted her. It was the man himself and the dark and dangerous masculinity that, even as it stalked her, intrigued her more than anything ever had.

Fraud that she was, she had not been able to admit that fact to herself last night. She had dressed it up in compassion and told herself that he needed her, when the truth was that she needed him.

Wanted him, she corrected.

As for love—that awful word that she had uttered, repelling them both—she no more knew its meaning than he did. Her parents had given her love, but they were long gone. Certainly her father had not loved her enough to remain in this world after he disgraced himself. And no man in those terrible months with her cousins and the time in that Covent Garden boardinghouse had looked at her with anything that might have passed for true affection.

Hannah put her head in her hands, knowing that she was giving in to self-pity after all, but powerless to stop.

The tentative touch on her shoulder made her jump. Had someone actually witnessed her moment of weakness? Horrified, she turned.

"You play very well."

Lady Huffington stood before her, an air of resolve about her stern features. Though her eyes were unreadable, her lips trembled slightly. "I wonder if you might . . . continue for a while."

"What the devil are you about, Higgins?" Julian halted outside the music room door where his aunt's majordomo knelt, giving every impression of listening at the keyhole.

The man brought himself up stiffly. "I was enjoying the music, Your Grace."

Julian frowned. A faint, disturbing melody that sounded vaguely familiar wafted into the corridor. The sound was delicate and pure, too subtle to have come from his sister's artless banging.

Though he had been headed out for a morning gallop, Julian could not resist pushing the door open slightly to see what was afoot.

Miss Gregory was seated at the old clavichord his aunt had once owned and which she had inexplicably given to his father years ago. Aunt Eleanor herself sat stiffly in one of the straight chairs, staring straight ahead as Miss Gregory's hands moved over the keys.

"Good God," he murmured.

Julian stepped forward, but Higgins touched his sleeve. "I do not think it wise to intervene, Your Grace. Something momentous is occurring."

"Momentous?" He arched a skeptical brow. Certainly it was surprising that Miss Gregory could play the clavichord and that his aunt had deigned to listen, but surely "momentous" was too strong a word. "I am pleased that your efforts have resulted in my aunt's condescending to come downstairs, but I hardly think . . ."

Just then, the playing stopped. The countess rose quickly, and Miss Gregory looked up at her with an expression that could only be described as bemused.

"That instrument used to reside in my music room in Yorkshire," Aunt Eleanor declared. "I believe its tone has improved over the years."

Julian cast a jaundiced eye at his aunt. "I suppose that must pass as a compliment," he muttered dryly. "I wonder Miss Gregory does not swoon in shock."

Higgins pursed his lips but did not reply. Julian could read indignation in every dour line of the man's features, but as Aunt Eleanor turned to leave the room, that quickly changed. Higgins threw open the door and stepped back so that she might pass. The look on the man's face was almost worshipful.

Briefly Aunt Eleanor met Higgins's gaze. In that wordless moment, Julian realized that there was something odd going on here. In the instant that thought flew into his head, however, his own gaze met Miss Gregory's as she sat at the clavichord. All else receded in the startling impact of those intense gray eyes.

Quickly, she looked away.

"Good morning, Miss Gregory," he said with perfect aplomb, priding himself on his ability to pretend that everything was as usual between them, that he had not made a fool of himself last night trying to seduce her.

When she did not answer, he strode away from the music room, a silent curse pounding in his brain. Damned wench would ignore him, would she?

It was only later, after he had ridden through the park at breakneck speed, that Julian realized she had looked away and could not have heard his wonderfully composed greeting.

And why should he care? Disappointment shot through him. Somehow he did.

Aunt Eleanor appeared for nuncheon as if it was nothing out of the ordinary, as if she had not spent the last three days secluded in her room with a purported case of the megrims.

"There is no need to gape, Lucy. It is most unladylike. Julian, wipe that insolent smile off your face. Miss Gregory, your posture is abysmal."

And just like that, Lady Huffington restored herself to her usual position in the household. Julian suspected his bet was all but won. At his aunt's next pronouncement, he was sure of it.

"A young lady making her come-out must be a pattern card of posture and behavior, Miss Gregory. We have our work cut out for us, it seems."

"We—we have?" Miss Gregory stammered in surprise.

"Yes, indeed," his aunt replied, buttering a roll. "I am not yet certain that you are up to it, but let us assume for argument's sake that you are able to make a passable impression."

"Oh, very passable, I think," Lucy put in, amused.

Aunt Eleanor eyed her niece sharply before turning again to Miss Gregory. "We must see to the matter of your wardrobe."

The two young women exchanged glances. "I ordered quite a few gowns for her," Lucy said, "while you were indisposed."

"Oh?" Aunt Eleanor looked dubious. "I hope your tastes have improved since we commissioned *your* wardrobe," she said acidly. "If I had not been present to see to things, I daresay the modiste would have concocted all manner of outlandish creations."

"Julian escorted us." A steely glint flashed in his sister's eyes. "You can rely on his tastes."

His aunt looked appalled. "The tastes of a known libertine? No, that does not give me cause to rest easy, Lucy. I daresay Julian's preferences in ladies' garments do not coincide with mine. Why, he would dress her like some strumpet from Covent Garden."

Julian set his wineglass on the table with a loud thump. "Why do we not wait until we see Miss Gregory's gowns before passing judgment?"

"Procuring vouchers for Almack's will be easy enough," the countess continued, oblivious to the interruption. "Several of the patronesses are my particular friends, and in any event they would not dare refuse a woman of my position and wealth. And," she added, with a sour look at her nephew, "there is something to be said for being the aunt of a duke, I suppose."

"You are too kind, madam," he muttered.

She frowned at a sudden thought. "But what will she *do* there? I daresay dancing is out of the question."

A small but distinct wave of irritation swept Miss Gregory's features. "I can manage a credible waltz, and last night Charles taught me the quadrille."

"What?" Aunt Eleanor stared. "How can you dance when you cannot hear the music?"

"By being most particular in my choice of partners," she replied. "Charles says that a good partner should be able to guide me with little difficulty."

Aunt Eleanor eyed her dubiously. "Very well. Let us assume she will be able to manage a few rudimentary dances. She cannot dance all night, however. How will she entertain her suitors, assuming she has them?"

"In the time-honored way of all women," Julian replied sardonically, wondering how long his aunt would continue to speak about Miss Gregory as if she were not present. "By batting her lashes and murmuring a few words of agreement with the gentleman's witty remarks."

"But she cannot hear!" his aunt protested. "How can she appreciate the nuances of conversation—and flirtation, for that matter?"

Julian took a sip of wine. As it slid languidly down his throat, he pondered just how well they had compensated last night for any real or imagined difficulties in that area. Nuances proved no barrier for Miss Gregory's understanding. Was it his imagination, or was she even now looking at him quite presciently?

"In the same way that I do now," she said firmly. "By studying a person's demeanor and expression and, of course, by reading lips."

"How did you learn to do it so well?" Lucy asked.

"My speech and vocabulary were fully formed years before I became deaf," she replied. "I can easily recognize words, although it may take me a while to become familiar with each person's distinctive speaking patterns. As long as the person faces me and does not speak too fast, I have little difficulty."

Aunt Eleanor's eyes narrowed assessingly. "But you are bound to miss things here and there, are you not?"

"Less than you might imagine," Miss Gregory replied, and this time Julian knew he was not mistaken in reading the challenge as those gray eyes held his. As their gazes locked, an odd current leaped between them.

"You will report to my sitting room, Miss Gregory," his aunt was saying, "so that I can review certain requirements of behavior with you. We will also study the protocol for morning calls. Later I will examine every stitch of this much-vaunted wardrobe Lucy chose for you."

Julian's mouth curled into a lazy, amused smile. Miss Gregory had not the slightest inkling that his aunt had issued a volley of imperial commands. Her gaze remained locked with his, and a distinctly scarlet color had begun to creep over her features.

To his great annoyance, his pulse thundered an answering response, and he felt his own skin grow warm. Abruptly, he scraped back his chair. He was not an unfledged lad to be affected by a mere look from a woman, even one who last night had left him in the throes of unrequited lust.

As he turned to leave, Lucy caught his eye and shot him a knowing smile. "Do not forget you are to escort us tonight, Julian. Hannah will need your support for her first ball." Julian did not miss the hopeful note in her voice.

Whose support, he wondered, would see him through an evening of enduring his protégée's disconcerting gaze? For a moment, panic filled him. Then he remembered that Charles was to accompany them. He sighed in relief. It would be a simple matter to foist Miss Gregory off on Charles.

Thank God for good friends.

Chapter Thirteen

"'Tis a pity about Rose," said Reverend McGougal, failing to muster a credible impression of that quality himself. "She was not one of our successes."

Hannah looked at the frail woman who had once been saucy and vibrant, if unwise. Her teeth were gone, and she was blind. All that remained of her nose was an ugly black cavity. She would not live to enjoy the extra bedding, night rails, and dresses Hannah had brought over from Claridge House.

"Rose could never bring herself to reform that stubborn nature of hers," McGougal continued mournfully. "Unlike you, she did not have a prayer of being returned to society."

This last was uttered with something of a smile as he led Hannah away, Rose's dreadful plight all but forgotten. "We are very proud of you, Hannah."

Hannah said nothing. An ineffable sadness swept her. Rose Jenkins was the last of the Lock Hospital patients whom she had accompanied from Mrs. Simpson's boardinghouse in Covent Garden. The others had either died from disease or its treatment.

Outrage filled her. None of the women had wanted to die, to waste away as Rose was doing. None of them would have refused a decent job or a chance to better themselves in a life devoid of licentiousness and the threat of infection and disease. None of them had embraced their fate; it had embraced them.

Hannah had seen how women like Rose, who had seemed so gay and careless, had little real choice about their lifestyle. The options for women of a certain class who possessed neither money nor husband were slim. One had to survive, even if the price was terrible. And once they grew sick, there was no one to protect them from quacks trying out their latest "cures." Hannah had watched helplessly as one by one, her friends had succumbed to mercury poisoning.

"Rose might have lived if she had not been dosed with such a free hand," Hannah said grimly.

"Now, Hannah"—Reverend McGougal shook his head in reproach—"such criticism is unworthy of you. Look at what we did for you. You are living in a duke's house, by all appearances a respectable young lady. How can you doubt our success?"

Hannah stilled. "What do you mean, sir, 'by all appearances'?"

A knowing smile wafted over his pallid features. "Come, dear. The duke does not seem possessed of infinite patience. I saw the way he looked at you. If you are not his mistress by now, I would be shocked to the tips of my toes."

"Reverend!" Hannah gasped. "How could you think such a thing?"

"There is no need to put on airs here, my girl," he replied. "I know what you are—remember? To be sure, you always were one of the clean ones."

Hannah stared in disbelief, but he merely smiled. "I know what you are about. You want to play the lady, to leave us behind. Oh, you have brought all those gowns and blankets from the grand household, but the day will come when you will no longer think of us. You have found your fortune, and you will make the best of it. That bit of defiance you showed him in my office was quite effective."

"What?" She frowned.

"Otherwise, the duke might not have been interested," he continued. "You were very smart. A man is intrigued by the unattainable—even if she is a whore. Perhaps," he added reflectively, "*especially* if she is a whore."

"Dear Lord," Hannah murmured.

"Shocked?" A wistful smile played over the minister's thin lips. "I have always thought you a wonderful actress, Hannah, and look where your talent has got you. Further than a deaf prostitute has any right or reason to expect." He paused. "I would have taken care of you, you know. The Lord made it clear you would have been mine in time."

Hannah felt suddenly ill. She gripped her reticule tightly and rose. "Good day, Reverend," she managed.

Reverend McGougal eyed her sorrowfully. "Do not worry, Hannah. I will not hold it against you. Have I not always looked after your interests? Why, just the other day I told Dr. Itard that you—"

"*Dr. Itard?*" She froze.

The minister smiled. "Did you not think that I knew your secret? Remember, I was present during that first examination he gave you so long ago. You still hold out hope of regaining your hearing, do you not?"

"I do not know what you are talking about," Hannah said stiffly.

"Hope is not a bad thing, my dear," he assured her, "although acceptance is the more worthy lesson. But perhaps now that you have latched on to a wealthy protector, your hopes may be realized."

"The duke is not my protector," Hannah protested, but she knew she would never make Reverend McGougal understand. His eyes bore the slightly fanatical look she had come to recognize from the most intense moments of his sermons.

He shook his head. "It is all right, my dear. You do not need to pretend with me. The duke is your best and last chance of attaining that which you have wanted since the age of seventeen. I could not give you that, for I am not a wealthy man and Dr. Itard is very expensive." He waved a piece of paper at her.

"This is his direction. He has always been very interested in your case—not enough to reduce his fee, of course, but even men of science have financial concerns. He will be in London for a month before returning to France. His lectures have created quite the sensation, you know. Thanks to that episode with that wild boy, he is very famous."

Gingerly, Hannah accepted the paper. Staring at the minister's snakelike scrawl, she felt rather like a snake herself for coveting what she might never have. And yet, Reverend McGougal was right: this is what she yearned for.

"Thank you," she murmured, regarding that inelegantly scribbled name with a mixture of awe and loathing.

* * *

Aunt Eleanor stormed into a ballroom much the way she had taken over his household—with every expectation of being treated like the queen herself.

Julian eyed his aunt's fuchsia gown and matching turban with the dyed ostrich plume and decided that Lady Fairchild had not a prayer of regaining control of her own ball. Aunt Eleanor cut a magnificently intimidating figure, her lorgnette dangling from her begloved wrist like a sword to be wielded in the event anyone dared to challenge her judgment that the two young women at her side were themselves worthy of royal treatment.

A gentleman seeking to remain in the same firmament with the ravishing Lady Lucille and her quietly intriguing friend, Miss Gregory, must needs curry Aunt Eleanor's parsimonious favor with all of the skills at his command. A young society matron seeking to claim Aunt Eleanor's valued patronage was obliged to herald the two debutantes as the diamonds they clearly were. Any high-sticklers wishing to avoid alienating the extremely powerful and wealthy Countess of Huffington knew precisely what was called for when Aunt Eleanor presented Miss Gregory with an admonition to "Look directly at the girl, as she is quite deaf."

After a startled moment, the woman would smile carefully and murmur, "Ah, an Original."

Julian watched these proceedings with a detached amusement that had been strained only during the ride to Lady Fairchild's, when Aunt Eleanor had insisted on claiming Charles for her carriage, leaving him to escort the young ladies in his own vehicle. Lucy had spent the entire ride making flattering remarks about Miss Gregory's appearance until Julian had been forced to murmur his agreement.

He wondered whose idea it had been to put Miss Gregory in a gown with such a dramatic décolletage. To be sure, the color pink—not one of those bland, insipid shades but something deeper and a bit more complicated—might have been invented with her in mind. Her deep gray eyes had never looked so compelling or so filled with mystery.

The glittering ornament that caught her hair back over one ear drew his eye to the exposed part of her neck, while allowing the rest of her hair to fall gracefully over one shoulder. Julian had never been able to decide the color of her hair. When she tucked it away under those caps and bonnets, he had thought it a mousy brown. But tonight, in the glow of lamp and candlelight, it was honey and cinnamon swirled together in perfect harmony.

But it was that swath of creamy skin exposed by her gown that truly unsettled him. The small but distinct rise of her breasts dared him to forget the night in his study, when he had all but seduced her.

Damnation. He wanted her still—a whore who looked like the princess his aunt decreed her to be.

Where the devil was Charles? It was time for the opening set. His aunt expected him to partner Miss Gregory and put the finishing touches on her dazzling debut. Julian had intended to slip that particular noose and prevail upon Charles to perform the duty; his friend, however, was nowhere to be seen.

As the orchestra struck up the strains of the music, Julian moved toward her with a sinking feeling. He bowed gallantly, however, for it would not do for anyone to think that anything was amiss. She must succeed. A few more glittering successes like tonight and Charles would have to concede the wager.

"This is not necessary," she murmured as he scrawled his name on her dance card.

"On the contrary," he replied irritably. "It will proclaim you an unequivocal success and inform your admirers they will not offend you by requesting a dance."

She frowned. "Offend me? I do not understand."

"Come, Miss Gregory. You must give the gentlemen credit for possessing some sensibility. No one is fool enough to walk up to a young lady who cannot hear and ask whether she might take a turn with him on the dance floor—unless someone else has already eased the way."

"I see." She accepted the hand that he offered. "Then I suppose this is necessary, but I confess it is one thing to dance in the privacy of your music room and quite another to put myself on display for all these people."

"You are nervous?"

"I am scared out of my wits. I would much rather take the air on the terrace."

"If that is a request, consider it denied," he said curtly, pulling her onto the dance floor. "There is no need to poker up," he added as she stiffened. "I merely seek to protect you from your own ignorance. A dance with a duke, even a rakish one, will elevate your consequence enormously, whereas a quiet turn on the terrace with me is guaranteed to damage that newly respectable reputation of yours. Such are the ironies of our little society."

She eyed him curiously. "But I though you had reformed. That you were no longer viewed as a . . ." Her voice trailed off.

"Reprobate?" he supplied hopefully. "It takes more than a declaration of intent to change a tiger's stripes, Miss Gregory."

Her attention wavered as she was forced to concentrate on the steps. Under his guidance, she began to relax somewhat. Her expression grew thoughtful.

"I suppose," she said at last, "that means that you are entirely capable of orchestrating a clever seduction designed to prey on a woman's compassion under the pretext of demonstrating how your maligned nature has been so woefully misunderstood."

Julian missed a step. "What?"

"You have not reformed after all, have you?" Her gaze bored into his. "You are a libertine and a liar, and several more despicable things besides."

At that moment the music swelled to magnificent heights, underscoring her simple condemnation with grandly judgmental eloquence. She could not have known, of course, but it was almost as if she did, for her next words came in the pregnant pause between orchestral movements.

"What are you really, Your Grace?" she asked softly.

Something snapped deep inside him. "A bastard," he snarled. "You would do well to remember it."

She studied his features for a moment, as if deciding what to make of his declaration. "If that was meant to frighten me," she said calmly, "it did not."

"Then you are an idiot," Julian growled, "for it scares the hell out of me."

Those unsettling gray eyes merely held his.

Desperately, Julian looked around the room, feeling like a parched man in the desert seeking a life-giving drink. Where in thunderation had Charles got to?

Charles had pulled off a coup. The half hour spent catering to Lady Huffington in that creaky carriage of hers had produced her rather startling permission to take Lucy out on the terrace for a brief stroll during one of the two dances he had claimed with her.

"If you can persuade her to do so," she had added skeptically, studying him. "Perhaps this is a good time to see what you are made of, my boy."

Charles did not even pretend to understand what the countess meant by that cryptic remark. He was too stunned to discover that she would allow him a few moments with Lucy alone. A stickler like Lady Huffington must think a baronet unworthy of her niece; indeed, she had never shown him much goodwill in the past. Perhaps the woman had a mercurial disposition. After all, she had initially taken Hannah in dislike and now was virtually assuring that his putative cousin became one of the season's successes.

That meant he was about to lose his bet. Unless he could get Lucy to view him with other than sisterly regard he was probably doomed to see her married off to some wealthy earl when the season ended.

He ventured a sidelong glance at Lucy. She gave no sign of being in the least moved by a stroll alone with him under the stars.

"It is lovely out here," he murmured lamely.

"Oh, quite!" Lucy enthused. "I was happy to be spared the necessity of another dance. I declare, my feet have danced quite out of my shoes."

Charles eyed the stars twinkling in the heavens and thought that he had never seen a lovelier evening. It was a pity that the object of his desire had not spared them so much as a glance. He cleared his throat. "I was gratified that your aunt gave me permission to take you out here. I daresay many chaperons would not grant their charges a romantic a tête-à-tête under the stars."

Lucy frowned. "Romantic? But it is only you, Charles. Aunt Eleanor knows nothing untoward could happen."

Then she smiled, and while those delectable lips and sparkling teeth should have lit up his universe, they suddenly seemed remarkably cruel and unfeeling.

"Damn it, Lucy," he began, "I—"

"Did you see Hannah and Julian dancing?" Lucy interjected, oblivious to his mood. "They make a lovely couple. I mean for them to wed, you know."

"*Wed?*" he echoed, stunned. "That is quite impossible!"

"Do not look so thunderstruck, Charles. They are perfect for each other. Since Hannah is here to find a husband, I can think of no better a prospect than a duke who is rich as Croesus and very handsome besides."

Charles stared at her. "You cannot be serious!"

She patted his cheek reassuringly. "You are worried about Julian's well-earned reputation as a scapegrace. Still, he is a good man. He will not abuse her. If anyone can be the making of my brother, it is your cousin." Her expression grew somber. "He needs her, Charles. Hannah may very well be Julian's last chance for happiness."

"Good God. You *are* serious." Charles stared into the beautiful features of his beloved with a strong sense of impending disaster. There was no way to dissuade Lucy from trying to marry Hannah to Julian without telling her the truth—that his "cousin" was a prostitute he had found on a wager. The truth would put a decisive end to any hopes he had for winning Lucy. She would not forgive such a despicable scheme and one which—as Julian had so helpfully reminded him—had been *his* idea.

Standing there with Lucy looking innocently up at him, Charles felt like the biggest heel imaginable. He had wagered his future with her and was about to lose it.

On the other hand, he thought philosophically, if a man was about to die, he might as well take advantage of his last earthly moments. The poetry of heroic loss filled his desperate soul.

"'We who are about to die salute you,'" he murmured recklessly as he bent his face to Lucy's.

A startled little gasp filled the rapidly narrowing space between them. It was quickly muffled by a very unbrotherly kiss.

Chapter Fourteen

"I claim victory," Julian drawled with more than a touch of smugness as he propped his feet on an ottoman and eyed Charles over the rim of his glass.

"What? After one ball?" Charles scoffed, flopping onto the sofa in Julian's study. "I hardly think so."

Julian frowned. Damned if he would spend another evening like the one he had just endured. "Even Lady Jersey pronounced Hannah an Original. She is made."

"'There is many a slip 'twixt cup and lip,'" Charles declared morosely.

"What the devil is the matter with you?" Julian's eyes narrowed. "More to the point, where were you all evening?"

"Drowning my sorrows," his friend muttered.

"That was obvious enough when the carriages were brought round and you showed up thoroughly foxed. I wonder that Aunt Eleanor saw fit to spare you one of her lectures."

"I fell asleep in Lady Fairchild's card room," Charles muttered. "I daresay no one missed me."

Julian fought the urge to dump the contents of his glass on Charles's head. "On the contrary," he snarled. "Hannah could have used your support. Instead, it was left to me to lead her out and take her into supper. Damn it, Charles. I was depending on you."

"You should never depend on a man in love. He is an exceedingly irrational fellow."

Julian studied his friend, who looked as if the devil himself had paid him a visit this evening. His red-rimmed eyes bore a tormented expression, his clothing was askew, and his hair was a disheveled mop.

"What happened? Lucy refuse you again?"

"Worse than that," the baronet confided with a bedeviled sigh. "I kissed her."

Julian arched a brow, amused in spite of himself. "Am I to wish you happy, then? Did my sister fall helplessly into your arms?"

Charles cast him a murderous look. "She giggled."

Julian tried to frame a diplomatic reply but could not resist the one that came to mind. "Your, er, technique must leave a great deal to be desired."

"There is nothing wrong with *me*." Charles glared at him. "It is your sister who is wrong in the upper story. She thought I invited her out on the terrace to spare her the necessity of ruining her dancing slippers. She was so startled when I kissed her that she giggled like a ninny."

"Perhaps she was only nervous," Julian offered.

Charles shook his head. "A woman who has scores of admirers? Lucy does not have a nervous bone in her body. No, I imagine she thought I was pulling some great joke on her. She simply cannot bring herself to see me as anything other than an amiable companion."

"I will talk to her," Julian offered magnanimously. "*After* you concede the bet."

"I do not need your help in winning my bride," Charles growled.

Julian regarded him pityingly. "It is clear that you shall not do so otherwise, dear fellow. Why do you not simply concede and I will smooth the way for you with Lucy? Hannah passed muster tonight with flying colors, so you have no reason to refuse."

"One ball does not a success make," Charles said stubbornly. "Our wager was that she must last the season. There are routs and musicales and the opera to be mastered. And, there is always the outside chance that I will somehow win Lucy over and declare victory myself."

"True love is long-suffering indeed," Julian murmured.

Charles shot him a glare that consigned him to the devil. "One of these days, you will get your comeuppance," he muttered. "Did you know, by the bye, that Lucy is determined that you and Hannah shall wed?"

"As you said," Julian muttered darkly, "my sister is a bit wrong in the upper works."

But it was nearly dawn before Julian could stop seeing the penetrating gray eyes that had regarded him so intently all evening. He knew she thought he was joking when he called himself a bastard. What would she think if she knew the truth?

"That was splendid, Hannah," Lucy declared, as Hannah let her hands fall from the keyboard into her lap. "You are more than ready to play at Lady Greeley's musicale. Who would have guessed that you were such a musician?"

Hannah eyed the square piano uncertainly. "I have never felt comfortable on this instrument. I think I am better suited to the clavichord, or even the harpsichord."

"Lady Greeley possesses neither," Lucy said. "All of London has been taken by the pianoforte and will be enchanted to hear you play. How I wish that I had your dexterity, your expressiveness. The piano is made for an artist of your caliber."

Hannah eyed the instrument dubiously. "I have heard that the strings often snap and are quite unreliable."

Lucy laughed. "To be sure, the piano does not have the benefit of centuries of refinement, but you need not worry. Lady Greeley is sure to have a Broadwood, and they are reputed to be quite excellent."

Her friend's assurances gave Hannah little comfort. If something untoward did happen, she would not know until it was too late. In her ignorance, she would continue playing while the piano slipped in and out of tune or otherwise disgraced her. The prospect was unnerving.

"I do not like putting myself forward like this," Hannah persisted.

Lucy eyed her sympathetically. "It is I who am putting you forward, dear, and I see that I should not have done so. But you are quite the success of the season. Everyone is dying to hear you play. I should be so proud if you would. I will leave you to your practice now."

Hannah sighed as Lucy left the room. Ever since the night of Lady Fairchild's ball, she had been deluged with invitations of all sorts. Lady Greeley's request that she play at her musicale had come quite unexpectedly, and it had been her strong inclination to decline. But Lucy and Lady Huffington had approved the idea, and Hannah felt obliged to please them.

Although she did not doubt Lucy's sincerity, she suspected that other members of society were not interested purely in her music. For them, tonight's performance would provide a diverting novelty, the chance to see a deaf girl play. She would be talked about for days.

Hannah sighed. She was the talk of London as it was, according to Lucy. How ironic that she should be hailed as an Original, as if the years in Covent Garden and the Lock Hospital had not existed, as if she truly were a respectable young lady.

It had been seductively easy to slip into the role of innocent debutante. The dancing lessons upon which her aunt had insisted years ago, the dictums about fans and feathers and balls and not dancing more than twice with the same man—all of it had come back to her.

But she was not the innocent she had once been. Circumstances had intervened, changing what surely would have been a very ordinary life into something strange and isolating. Her father had died, she had lost her hearing, and her relatives had turned her out. Those events were written upon her as surely as the notes of Mozart's music.

Hannah knew she would never truly belong to the *ton*. When the countess and Lucy learned the truth about her—as they undoubtedly would one day—they would despise her. They would be right to do so. She was not proud of deceiving them. She was not proud of what she had become.

Even her scheme to bring Lucy and Charles together—the only ennobling part of this masquerade—had borne no fruit. To be sure, Lucy had taken the night air with Charles at Lady Fairchild's ball, but—save for the flush on her cheeks which Hannah attributed to the night breezes—she had returned looking unaffected by her tête-à-tête. Indeed, she had been laughing so gaily that Hannah had begun to wonder whether she and

Charles would ever find anything together as profound and serious as love.

Taking a deep breath, Hannah returned her attention to the Mozart variations she had chosen for tonight's performance. With a wistful look at the clavichord across the room, she began to play.

A hand on her shoulder brought her up short. She looked up to meet the duke's dark, brooding gaze. "What is that piece?" he demanded.

"Something my mother played for me as a child," she stammered in surprise. "I believe it was an old French nursery rhyme."

"My own mother used to sing that very song." To her amazement, he sat on the bench next to her. "She was French," he said after a pause. There was an odd pensiveness about him.

French. Hannah's eyes grew wide. The duke would have been a young boy during the Terror. But surely he and his mother had not been in France during that terrible time. In the next breath, he answered her unspoken question.

"We lived in Paris. After my mother's parents were executed, she took me to her old nurse's home in the country. We lived there until my mother grew ill and died."

That night in his study—when he revealed that he lost his mother at the age of six—Hannah had assumed that he had been living in England at the time. Now it appeared that he had been alone, save for an old nurse, in a country torn apart by bloodthirsty madmen. Yet he had not met his father until the age of fifteen. Why had the man not come for him earlier? Why had he left his motherless young son to the mercies of a bloody revolution? Hannah dared not ask, but the duke seemed to read her mind.

"Foolishly, my mother believed that he would send for us," he said, his eyes filled with the sardonic anger that seemed to be a permanent part of him. "But he had only married her for her dowry. When she lost everything, he no longer wanted her."

"But he was a duke," she protested. "Why would he need her wealth?"

A cynical brilliance shone in his eyes. "So as not to be dependent on his sister. Aunt Eleanor married a wealthy earl who could have bought and sold my father several times. When my father inherited the dukedom, the estate's financial circumstances were such that he was forced to apply to her for funds. He would have hated that."

"And so he needed a rich wife," Hannah said slowly.

"Yes. He met my mother on his Grand Tour. Her wealth and lineage went back centuries, to kings. And so he wanted her."

"But you were his son," Hannah protested, appalled. "How could he not want you?"

"Careful, Miss Gregory." His lips curled scornfully. "You will accuse me of playing upon your sympathies again."

Hannah flushed. "I did not mean—"

"It is unimportant." He ran his hands idly over the keys.

His long, tapered fingers easily spanned more than an octave. "I did not know you played," Hannah said.

"I had a few lessons as a child, but I am not quite in your universe."

The compliment brought a flush to her cheeks. "Did your mother teach you?" she asked. He shook his head.

"Her nurse did. But I had barely learned the scales when I was shipped off to my mother's sister at Sommersby Castle."

"Were there no instruments in the castle?"

He laughed. "The earls of Sommersby were notorious fighters. The only instruments in Sommersby Castle were those of war. Suffice it to say, they fired a small boy's imagination more than any clavichord."

"It sounds rather gruesome."

"There is nothing quite so exciting as learning to wield a sword that belonged to Charlemagne. My father was pleased, when at last he came to fetch me, to discover that I could fight with the best of them. It was the only time he took pleasure in my existence."

His bald assessment took her aback. "I am sorry."

"Do not be." He shrugged. "My father did not care a damn about me, nor I him. He simply needed an heir because Lucy's mother, the wife that at last brought him all the wealth he needed, died without producing one. I was all he had."

The ice in his gaze made Hannah shiver. "I did not then realize the depths of his dislike," he continued, a faraway look in his eyes. "I did not think to question my right to the title until he suggested on his deathbed that he had never married my mother and that he had not been the first to sample her charms—implying, of course, that I might not even be his."

Hannah blinked. "What?"

His smile held no mirth. "Shocking, is it not? I have spent not a little time trying to disprove his ugly assertion. As far as I can determine, there is no record in all of France of any lawful union between my mother and father."

"But many records belonging to the aristocrats must have been obliterated during the Terror," she pointed out.

He shrugged. "Perhaps. One would have thought that my father would have kept a set of documents himself."

Hannah brightened. "Perhaps they are here."

"I have looked—not only here, but at Sommersby Castle in the hope that my late aunt might have hidden them away for safekeeping. It they exist, they have vanished. All I found here was a collection of Aunt Eleanor's sermons, which I have not mustered the endurance to study."

Hannah shook her head. "How terrible for you."

His gaze glittered with unnatural brilliance. "My father granted me a dukedom and then made certain I would take no pleasure in it because of the dilemma he forced on me: Would I renounce the title and all its wealth, in the process branding my poor deceased mother as a whore? Or, since no one else knew my secret, would I simply continue to live a lie? As you can see, I chose the latter. I imagine he knew I would."

"And that it would make you miserable," she whispered, horrified at such paternal cruelty.

"I am not miserable, Miss Gregory, just bored. Although lately, less so." Amid the cynicism, his gaze held a reluctant amusement.

"How can you take so cavalier an attitude to such a thing?" she demanded.

"I imagine it is a bit like your profession. One learns not to notice the degrading part."

Eyes alit with irony, he gestured to the music. "May I assist you with the pages? I do wish you to excel at tonight's performance."

* * *

"Charles! We have not seen you for days. I thought you had absented yourself from town." Lucy quickly returned her attention to the scene in the music room, which she had been watching with great interest from the hall. "Julian and Hannah look so contented there on the piano bench. I do believe I hear love blooming amid the arpeggios."

"I did not come to discuss Julian's romantic prospects," he said tersely.

Lucy shot him a sidelong gaze. "Yes, of course. You are here to visit Julian. I suppose you mean to call him away from Hannah's side, but I hope you will not. They need time alone together."

"I did not come to see Julian. I came to see you."

"Me?" Lucy blinked.

"Is there somewhere we can be private?"

"I do not think there is anyone in the drawing room," she replied, eyeing him curiously.

Without a word, Charles took her hand and pulled her into the adjacent room. Then he took a deep breath. "I wish to apologize for my actions of the other night."

"The other night?" She toyed with the knots in the fringe of her shawl. "I do not know what you mean . . ."

"The kiss, by Jove," he said in exasperation. "I kissed you out on the terrace—or do you not recall?"

"Of course I recall," she said indignantly. "You need not shout."

Charles sighed heavily. "I am sorry—" he began.

"Do not apologize," she said quickly. "I am not one of those silly girls who does not recognize a joke. I know you were just trying to put me in my place, just like you used to pull my braids when I would show off years ago. It is what I deserved for prattling on about how many dances I had danced. My vanity was showing, even though I did not mean—"

"There. I knew it," he said morosely. "You thought I was joking."

"But of course," she replied brightly. "Why else would you do such a thing?"

Charles gritted his teeth. "Tell me, Lucy: Was there something funny about my kiss? Did it greatly amuse you? Did it *feel* like a joke?"

Lucy furrowed her brow. "I do not know," she said slowly. "I have little experience along those lines. Lord Haversham kissed me once in the Lady Evelyn's maze, and the Marquess of Devonshire bestowed a rather wet kiss on me during Lord Peterson's scavenger hunt. Then there was the occasion of Lady Jersey's masquerade, when I stumbled into a darkened pantry on the way to the ladies' retiring room and some gentleman followed me inside so that he could kiss me anonymously in the darkness. Now that I think on it, I never discovered who he was."

Her recitation brought a look of appalled horror to Charles's face. "You are quite free with your kisses, it would seem."

"Oh, no," she assured him. "I have never kissed anyone *back*, you see. Well, perhaps that gentleman in the pantry. There was something rather exciting about not knowing who it was kissing me. I am afraid I got carried away."

"I stand in awe of your vast experience."

Lucy frowned. "I do not like your tone. Are you accusing me of loose behavior? It was nothing, really—only a few kisses."

"As mine was nothing."

She stared at him. "Pray, what did you wish it to be?"

"Anything but an occasion for giggling."

"I do not understand."

Charles put his hands on her shoulders. "Sometimes I wish to shake you until all of the foolishness is gone. Have I not asked you to marry me three times?"

"Yes, but—"

"But I was only joking, I suppose. Being kind or polite." His voice bore a dangerous edge. "Or did you think I was after your fortune?"

"Oh, no!" Lucy protested, horrified. "You would never do that. You are a dear friend."

"The precise root of the problem, as I see it," Charles muttered.

Lucy frowned. "But I should never wish to lose your friendship."

"It is Julian and I who are friends, Lucy."

"I know." She sighed. "I have always been the pesky little sister underfoot. I did not think you minded. All those times you helped me learn to fish and to ride, when Julian was holed up in his study learning the business of the estate. Do you remember the time you helped me bury Peaches?"

Charles frowned. "That yappy little dog?"

"She was my pet," Lucy replied indignantly. "I thought you cared about her as much as I did. Otherwise, why would you bother to help me with her funeral?"

"I cared about *you*, Lucy. Not that damned dog." He touched her chin, tilting it upward so that she must look into his eyes and see the message there.

"Oh." Lucy blinked, flushing. "Then you were never truly my friend?" Her voice cracked, and Charles suddenly realized how lonely her childhood must have been without a mother and father. And how important a friendship with her brother's friend must have been. His expression softened.

"I have always been your friend, Lucy," he said gently. "But I have always wanted to be more."

A single tear rolled down her cheek. "I am afraid, Charles."

"Of what?"

"Of what 'more' you speak of. Of venturing beyond the boundaries of friendship and discovering that I cannot go back and reclaim what was left behind."

"You are thinking too much, Lucy."

"You see?" She shook her head. "That is the difficulty with us. Love should not involve so much thinking and talking. It should be right from the outset. It should sweep one away and make thinking quite impossible. That is what I want."

"And you do not think you could come to view me in such a light?"

Her eyes were sorrowful. "You are the only man besides Julian with whom I can be myself. I treasure your friendship. I cannot risk losing it."

For a long moment he stared at her. "You just have."

"What? What do you mean?" she demanded as he turned away.

"Only that I am not going to hang around like your yappy little puppy anymore, Lucy. That I have had enough."

She reached for him, but he shook off her arm. "You are welcome to your fantasies about the lover who will someday sweep you off your feet. I am just an ordinary man. I cannot compete with your fertile imagination." He strode briskly to the door, his shoulders rigid.

"Charles!" Lucy cried. "Please, do not go."

At last he turned, but there was no softening of his gaze. "As a child you were quite daring, Lucy. I used to admire the way you baited your own hook, set your horse at any jump, and brazened your way through life. I suppose you took those risks to get some much needed attention. Now that you are grown, you have all the attention any young woman could want. And you are utterly afraid."

"I am not!" Lucy cried.

Charles regarded her sadly. "Yes, you are. The risk has gone out of you. You want to gain all by venturing nothing. I wish you good luck." He turned his back on her and left the room.

Lucy stared at the door for a long time, then burst into tears. With her lace handkerchief covering her face, she fled to her own room.

From the shadows, a figure rose from a grandly upholstered wing chair. Lady Huffington, who had been listening to Hannah's music until Charles and Lucy had invaded her sanctuary, emitted a long and sorrowful sigh. Then her brows furrowed in thought.

Higgins would know what to do.

Chapter Fifteen

The audience in Lady Greeley's vast music room smiled encouragingly. With a deep breath, Hannah settled herself on the bench and eyed the polished mahogany case and elaborate music desk of Mr. Broadwood's very fine creation. The brass fittings and ivory inlay gave the pianoforte an august elegance, and the trestle stand resembled that of the harpsichord. But none of its lovely features disguised the instrument's exotic unfamiliarity.

As her hands poised over the six-octave keyboard, Hannah felt Miss Greeley's friendly smile. She wished that Lucy, rather than the hostess' daughter, sat ready to turn the pages, but Lucy had felt ill tonight and did not come.

Flexing her fingers to release some of the tension, Hannah sent a silent prayer heavenward and began to play.

Only a light touch was required to depress the keys, and in that regard the piano was much like her beloved clavichord. As she moved through the familiar notes of the Mozart variation, Hannah began to relax a little.

To her relief, the piece went well. When she turned to the audience, she saw their applause, felt their goodwill. Smiling, she thanked Miss Greeley for her assistance.

The Beethoven sonata was next. Her fingers ran through the calmly sorrowful adagio, allowing the eighth-note triplets to fall like steady drops of rain on the keyboard as she immersed herself in Mr. Beethoven's wonderfully changeable moods.

All went well until the next movement. Then it went horribly wrong.

The allegretto, where it was so important to convey an invigorating spontaneity, did not feel right. The keys seemed to stick and grow sluggish, throwing her rhythm off. Hannah began to dread the coming presto, where sluggishness would mean disaster for the tumultuous finale. Still, she plunged valiantly ahead.

It was only when she nodded to Miss Greeley to turn the page that she caught the young lady's anguished expression and knew that disaster had struck.

With a sinking heart, Hannah lifted her hands from the keys and turned to the audience. The expressions on the faces of Lady Greeley's guests ranged from pity to horror to snickering amusement. Something indeed had gone terribly wrong—but what?

Hannah had never felt so helpless. Clearly, the piano was quite beyond her. She fought against the tears that welled in her eyes, determined not to give in to the overwhelming urge to sob in defeat. But her face was burning, and that odd ringing noise had begun in her ears. She felt dizzy, unable to move.

The light touch on her shoulder caught her by surprise. She looked over to see the duke standing slightly behind her, peering into the piano case in disapproval. He was the portrait of kingly elegance, without ostentation. His black superfine and striped marcella waistcoast bespoke the height of fashion, and his snowy cravat was tied to dazzling perfection. But his grandeur derived from more than mere clothing. The man himself radiated command, taking her weakness into himself and replacing it with his own strength. Just looking at him buoyed her.

"Some strings have broken." He arched a disdainful brow, as if to say that a decent instrument would never commit such a grave lapse. "The hammers are hopelessly entangled."

Lady Greeley rushed up, gushing horrified apologies and vowing to summon Mr. Broadwood to make amends this very night. Hannah smiled gamely, but all she could think was that she had made an utter spectacle of herself. How long had she continued playing, ignorant of the fact that the strings had broken? The guests must have been appalled by the great jumble of jarring, dissonant sounds.

But somehow, the haughty arch of that ducal brow and disdainful condemnation of the pianoforte's innards had worked wonders. Suddenly the guests were applauding as if Hannah had somehow committed an act of heroism. As one they rose and surged toward her.

A firm hand under her elbow helped her rise. Hannah did not have to look to know it was the duke who assisted her. Lifting her chin defiantly, she calmly met the gazes of Lady Greeley's guests.

"I imagine it was those triplets that caused all the mischief," she said with a ladylike shrug.

Relief showed on the face of her hostess, and everyone burst into good-natured laughter. The duke did not laugh, but his gaze was filled with something that might have been approval.

"Do you want to leave?" he said a few minutes later, after the crowd moved away from the pianoforte and onto other activities the hostess had hastily arranged.

"Yes," she confessed grimly, "but I am determined to remain for a while."

For the next hour, he did not leave her side. Hannah found his protective hovering reassuring, if rather curious. He held himself stiffly erect, with a soldier's watchfulness, almost as if he meant to spirit her to safety at any moment. Lady Huffington, meanwhile, did her best to dismiss the entire episode, mingling about to denounce the current fashion for "those awful new inventions, when the old ones are quite satisfactory."

Hannah sipped the punch the duke had brought her. Though most of the guests appeared to have forgotten the incident, she caught the occasional pointed look in her direction. Eventually, the pressure of trying to look unconcerned took its toll. Though the dizziness and ringing had vanished, she now had a splitting headache.

Watching her intently, as he had done all night, Julian did not miss the tiny, pained wrinkles at the corners of her eyes and the furrow in that otherwise smooth brow. He decided she had displayed her courage long enough.

"Come," he commanded, removing the cup from her hand. "I will summon the carriage."

"I cannot leave." Her voice lacked her usual conviction.

Julian steered her toward the door. "On the contrary. You have proven to one and all that you can face down disaster with aplomb. I see no point in remaining."

To his surprise, she gave no further argument. As they left, their hostess once more apologized profusely but seemed relieved that the very visible reminder of the unfortunate episode had decided to remove herself.

As he handed her into his carriage, she sighed gratefully then closed her eyes. She did not even protest when he seated himself next to her, instead of across.

Julian felt strangely protective of this woman who had displayed such valor in the face of ridicule. All evening he had been ready to kill anyone who dared to laugh at her. Amid her acute embarrassment, she had shown a simple, gracious dignity quite at odds with what might be expected of a woman of her background. Studying her, Julian knew why he had been so unwise as to tell her about his father's deathbed confession and the secret that—if she chose to disclose it—could bring down the dukedom. It was because blackmail seemed beneath that odd dignity of hers.

She put two fingers against her temples, her delicately tapered fingertips making healing circles over her skin. There was something immeasurably strong about this woman, even in her apparent fragility.

With a mind of its own, his arm slid across the back of her shoulders and his fingers moved to supplant hers. She stiffened slightly as he began to massage her temple. Then she leaned back against his arm as if to say that the protest on her lips was not worth the effort to utter it.

It was easy enough to provide her this small relief from her pain, Julian reflected as he smoothed her cool, dry skin. When those lines in her face began to relax, he knew a moment of great pleasure.

Coiling an errant tendril of her hair around his finger, he marveled at its sheen. At first, he toyed only with the wandering strands that had escaped the hairpins. But there was a restless tension within him, and soon his searching fingers began to remove the pins from the elaborate coiffure she had worn for the occasion.

He was sure she meant to object. But the fight had gone out of her. She simply sighed as he continued to run his hands through her hair until the tangle of honey-and-cinnamon curls tumbled down around her shoulders.

Slowly, he smoothed her hair into one glorious ribbon against her pale skin and delicate gown. She had worn that batiste confection he had bought her, with the profusion of tiny buttons up the back and the consistency of spun gossamer. Though it perfectly captured her grace and subtle femininity, he knew that were he to undo those tiny buttons, he would find a womanly strength beneath.

Without quite knowing why, Julian rapped gently on the roof. The signal was familiar to his coachman: he was to drive around a bit before reaching their destination. Julian had often found the privacy of a closed carriage perfect for seduction; the servant was accustomed to guiding the vehicle aimlessly through London streets at night.

Seduction was not his intent now, however. Though he had no compunction against using his wiles on the defiant wench from the Lock Hospital, he would not take advantage of this exhausted, troubled young lady who leaned into the crook of his arm so trustingly and who inspired such fierce protectiveness within him.

But neither could he bring himself to relinquish this mesmerizing moment so soon.

For many minutes, Julian smoothed her hair, delighting in her small sighs of pleasure, savoring the feel of the silken rope in his palm. He wondered whether her skin would feel as soft and could not prevent himself from trailing his hand over the sleeve of her gown until it met the bare part of her arm. Then he did so again, stroking from the crown of her head down the length of her arm.

Again and again his hand traveled that route, until once by sheerest accident his thumb grazed the outside curve of her breast. She made no sound or movement that might be interpreted as objection. As his loins stirred, Julian swallowed hard.

That night in his study he had been angry, vengeful, bent on using her. Now he simply wanted to comfort her, protect her, smooth away the memory of tonight's trials.

It was strange, then, that his fingers again brushed her breast. Strange that his hand snaked lower to rest lightly on her hip. Strangest still that his fingers had the audacity to curve over her abdomen, pressing ever so gently as they inscribed widening circles over the material of her gown.

Julian frowned, wondering why he could not seem to restrain his wandering hands. He had no intention of taking advantage of her condition. Tonight he had only noble intentions—if a man like him could possess such a thing.

Still, it would have been helpful if she had been her usual self, sitting up straight and briskly calling him to account.

Unfortunately, she did no such thing. When he lifted her gently into his lap, she simply curled against him, burrowing into his chest as if for warmth. And when his willful hand toyed with the hem of her gown, she merely sighed.

His restless fingers touched the raw silk of her stockings. Julian knew that if his hand wandered far enough afield it would find the ties that kept the stockings in place and shielded her bare calves from his touch. Scarcely daring to breathe, he willed his offending hand upward.

Still she made no objection, but continued to huddle against him as if for protection against the unsettling forces suddenly stirring around them.

At that moment, he hated the practiced seducer he had become. She would get no protection from him, after all. Apparently there was not a noble bone in his body. Deftly he untied the laces at her knees and knew himself for a true knave.

Strangely, touching her bare legs made him tremble. A helpless bewilderment swept him. This was not the carefully orchestrated seduction he had attempted in his study that night. This was beyond his control.

When his fingers crept unerringly upward to find the most delicate part of her, she grew very still—as if listening for something, though surely that was impossible.

Perhaps for a woman who could not hear, touch resonated as acutely as any sound. Julian pondered that thought, even as he began to stroke her softly, probing for the precise touch that would resonate for her.

In awe, he watched as she clung to him, hypnotized by his touch, lost in a world apart from the confines of his jostling carriage. His body ached to join her in that world, but his mind wanted only to drink in her trembling features as she took her pleasure.

When she arched into him with urgent abandon, he thought that he had never seen such a beautiful face as Hannah Gregory's in the moment of release.

Afterward, she did not say a word. Julian stared at the top of her head for a long time, savoring the feel of the smooth silk of her hair against his face. At last he rapped discreetly on the roof, signaling his coachman to take them home.

His loins ached. His nerves were taut with unslaked desire. But his mind was strangely at peace. In her silent passion, Hannah had done that for him, though he did not know how or why.

When the carriage rolled to a stop on the drive, Julian lifted her from the vehicle and carried her inside his house, past a gaping Higgins and up the stairs to her room. Gently he laid her on the bed. She stared up at him with solemn eyes as deep and wide as the moon.

As he held her gaze, the ridiculous observation floated through his brain that those little buttons up the back of her gown were still fastened tightly, as if nothing out of the ordinary had occurred.

Abruptly he pulled the quilt over her and left the room.

Out of the ethereal haze that surrounded her, Hannah caught a movement. Lucy stood at the door to her room, clad in a dressing gown.

"Are you all right?" Lucy asked, frowning. "You are home early. Where is Aunt Eleanor?"

Hannah cleared her throat. The second question was rather easier to answer than the first. "I believe the duke has returned to Lady Greeley's to fetch your aunt. He brought me home early because I had a headache."

Lucy advanced into the room, staring intently at Hannah, who lay under the quilt precisely as Julian had left her.

"Something went wrong, did it not?" Lucy bit her lip. "I knew it. I should have been there to turn the pages."

"Some of the piano strings broke and became entangled with the hammers," Hannah confessed.

Though she gave Lucy a reassuring smile, she did not feel like smiling. Something momentous had indeed occurred tonight, and it had nothing to do with Lady Greeley's piano strings. She ought to have been outraged at the liberties the duke had taken, ought to have fought him. But there was only this wondrous sense of pleasure, as if she had been given a new and precious gift. The silence had never contained such splendor and her heart such joy and wonder as during those few, precious moments in the carriage.

And now? Confusion, mortification, embarrassment filled her. Hannah knew she had been weak, turning to him for comfort against the vicissitudes of the evening. The duke was not a man to dispense such a precious commodity.

And yet, she had sensed a selflessness in him. It had made her feel cherished and—she almost would have said—loved.

Dear Lord. She could not fall victim to that fantasy. A woman like her did not believe in miracles.

"Can I help you out of your gown?" Lucy eyed her curiously. "I daresay you would sleep better if you got out of your clothes.

Hannah forced a laugh. "Yes, of course." She rose obediently, but she did not really want to let go of the gown or the memories connected with it. As long as she wore it, she could still sense his hands, still feel the way his probing fingers had shaken her world.

Lucy made short work of the buttons. When Hannah turned to thank her, Lucy bore a stricken expression and was chattering wildly.

". . . my fault . . . should have been there . . . all because of Charles."

Hannah frowned. "You were unwell. You were right to stay here."

"I am never unwell," Lucy replied, flopping into a chair and covering much of her face with her hands. Hannah caught only an occasional phrase. ". . . the wretch . . . never speak to me again . . . what shall I do?"

"Slow down, for one thing, or I shall never make sense of what you are saying." Hannah folded the batiste gown and placed it on a stool at the foot of the bed. She knew she would never wear it again.

Lucy pulled her hands away from her face. Her eyes were red. "I could not face Charles tonight."

"Charles? But he was not there," Hannah replied. "I thought it curious, but—"

"Not there! Then he must have meant it!" Lucy bit her lip until Hannah thought she would draw blood.

"What has happened, Lucy? What has Charles done?"

Tears rolled from Lucy's impossibly brilliant eyes and splashed onto her flawless cheeks. "He k-k-kissed me."

Heavens. If Lucy thought a kiss scandalous, what would she think about the activity that had taken place in her brother's carriage tonight? Fighting off her shame, Hannah studied her friend in concern.

"Charles does not strike me as the sort to take undue advantage of a woman." Unlike the duke, perhaps, who would readily take all sorts of liberties with a befuddled woman with a splitting headache. Doubtless she had deluded herself with notions of his selflessness. Given what she knew of the duke's character, he must be filled with smug satisfaction at what happened tonight. On the other hand, perhaps it had meant something to him. She wanted desperately to believe that it had . . .

"Oh, no! Charles did nothing untoward," Lucy assured her. "It is just that . . . I giggled when he kissed me, for I thought it was a joke."

"A joke?" Hannah echoed, uncomprehending.

"Absurd, is it not?" Lucy acknowledged. "Apparently he was quite serious. All those times he proposed to me . . . I am beginning to think that he meant it."

"Of course he meant it," Hannah declared. "Are you a complete ninny, Lucy? Charles is in love with you!"

Lucy covered her mouth in horror. "This is terrible!"

"Why? Because you do not feel the same for him? Because he has not lived up to those silly romantical notions in which you have indulged yourself?" Hannah's temper rose. Lucy had everything—wealth, beauty, intelligence—but she had made one man supremely miserable, laughing at his lovemaking and treating his proposals as insignificant without a care for his feelings.

"I do not know how I feel," Lucy confessed. "I only know that when he said I had lost his friendship, I was bereft."

"Lost his friendship? Whatever do you mean?"

"He said he wanted more than that. Oh, Hannah, what if we cross some invisible boundary and cannot get back to friendship again?"

"I would say that you already have."

Lucy's eyes grew wide. "You are right," she said, her lips trembling. "He has gone, Hannah. He said he had had enough."

"Bravo for him," Hannah retorted. "Did you think he would wait forever while you encouraged half of London's eligible bachelors to dance attendance on you? Did you think he would always be there when you felt the need for a little friendship?"

Lucy shook her head. "Pray, do not be so harsh, though I am certain I deserve it. I simply never allowed myself to think of Charles as anything but my friend. I was always so lonely. Until my father brought Julian into the household, I had no companions at all. But Julian has always had his own life . . . one that I could not really participate in."

Indeed, Hannah very much doubted that the sort of activities in which the duke engaged during his leisure hours were suitable for a young girl. "So Charles filled the void?"

"Yes. He was like a brother. His property marched with our estate in Devonshire. I welcomed his company, though I knew he had really come to see Julian. But perhaps I was wrong in assuming that. Perhaps . . ." Her voice trailed off.

"Perhaps he wanted you all along," Hannah finished. "He was waiting for you to grow up."

Lucy sighed. "It seems that I still have a lot of growing up to do."

Hannah eyed her curiously. "Tell me, Lucy. Did you enjoy Charles's kiss?"

A flush spread over Lucy's cheeks. "I do not know. I was more startled than anything. It was not like Charles at all. He was so, so . . . passionate. That is why I giggled."

"Then you were not . . . 'swept away'?" Hannah eyed her closely, thinking that if nothing else, the episode in the carriage had taught her what those words meant.

"No." Lucy looked suddenly shy. "But I would very much like to have a second chance."

A second chance. Did the Fates grant such a thing? Hannah thought of that moment when the duke had begun to fiddle with her hair. Had she only pulled away, she might have saved herself from the pain she felt now, the pain of wanting what could never be.

"So would I," Hannah said softly. "So would I."

Chapter Sixteen

Julian ran Charles to ground at White's. The baronet was slumped in a chair clutching a bottle of port and looking very much the worse for having consumed most of it.

"I wish to call off the wager," Julian said, signaling for a glass.

Red-rimmed eyes regarded him contemptuously. "What happened? Did your protégée finally show her true stripes—proposition Lord Greeley, p'rhaps? Hear he has a roving eye, you know. 'Tis said he is a regular customer of the Covent Garden set."

Julian made an effort to rein in his temper. "Hannah conducted herself superbly. If you had been at Lady Greeley's musicale, you would have seen for yourself."

"Not fond of musicales. Not fond of making a fool out of myself, either." Charles glowered into his glass.

"My little sister driving you a bit mad, eh?" Julian arched a sardonic brow.

"Oh, it is not funny. Not at all. But that is another story. At the moment I am more interested in why you are trying to weasel out of our bet. Mayhap you are finally showing *your* true stripes."

Julian's eyes narrowed. "If you were not foxed, I would be tempted to call you out."

"I am overcome with fear," Charles drawled.

Making an impatient sound, Julian rose. "You are past reasoning with. I will come round to see you in the afternoon."

"Good," Charles replied with a lopsided grin. "You will meet my splendid surprise."

"Surprise? What are you talking about?"

"It seems that my uncle has decided to visit."

"What uncle is that?"

"The old recluse you killed off when you decided to make him Hannah's father."

Julian stilled. "I see."

"Puts a different light on the subject, does it not?" Charles drained the last of his port. "Dropped in yesterday, he did. In town on business. Delighted to accept his only nephew's offer of bed and board."

He grinned, waiting for Julian's reaction. As none was immediately forthcoming, Charles continued. "I was thinking of taking him round to the parties tomorrow—just to make a few introductions, you understand."

"You promised not to sabotage my plan."

"True. But I did not promise to save you from your foolish mistakes," Charles retorted. "I warned you Uncle Erasmus had not gone aloft, but you would not listen. You think everything will go your way, simply because you wish it."

Charles did not seem to notice Julian's rigid features, or the sudden clenching of his jaw. "Uncle should be delighted to meet this daughter of his—especially since he never married," he continued in a goading voice. "Lady Huffington should be intrigued, as well."

"Do not forget Lucy," Julian added softly. "I imagine she will be especially interested."

Rising from his chair, Charles reeled slightly. "Lucy will not think well of me for cooperating with your lies, but you cannot scare me with that threat. I would far rather endure Lucy's anger than her giggles." He sighed forlornly.

"Whatever the reaction of my aunt and sister, the fact remains that Hannah has proven herself," Julian said, marshaling the last of his patience. "I do not care to continue with the wager."

"Ah, yes. The wager. You were about to tell me why you have had a change of heart."

"I intend to make Hannah my mistress."

Charles's mouth fell open. Then he burst into laughter. "That is rich!"

Balling his hands into fists at his side, Julian stared at him. "I fail to see anything amusing about it."

"Can you not? A duke who disdains whores decides to pass one off as a lady, then set her up as his light o' love. From Covent Garden to Mayfair to the demimonde—all in a few weeks! My little 'cousin' must be quite talented."

Julian fought against the growing urge to plant his friend a facer. "That is neither here nor there," he said evenly. "I have simply decided to keep her."

"'Simply decided to keep her,'" Charles echoed, nodding sagely. "How pleasant it must be to decide a woman will be yours and have your wish instantly gratified. Tell me, Julian, do you always get everything you wish for?"

"You know the answer to that," Julian said through gritted teeth.

"Yes, of course," Charles drawled in a tone of mock pity. "I must remember to feel sorry for the poor bastard who never had a true fath—"

A blazing uppercut to the jaw halted the baronet mid-sentence. Charles blinked in amazement, turned slowly around, and collapsed in a heap on the floor.

"You know, Higgins, I do like that girl. She has spunk and courage."

"Rather like you, madam."

Lady Huffington started. "I beg your pardon?"

Higgins poured out the countess' tea. "It took courage to ask Miss Gregory to play for you and to take her under your wing."

"I—I never thought of it like that," she stammered.

"She is good for you," Higgins said gently. "She has started a healing process that should have occurred years ago."

Bleakly, the countess stared into her teacup, seeing in the depths of the amber liquid other faces in other times. "I do not wish to talk about that," she murmured. "Let us speak of my niece instead."

"Lady Lucille?"

"It seems that Sir Charles is in love with her, but Lucy views him only as a trusted friend and confidant."

"I see." Higgins busied himself with the tea tray.

"He has little money," the countess continued. "I suppose many would cavil at marrying a duke's daughter to a man so far beneath her."

"Yes," Higgins replied gravely, "many would."

"Martin Luther tells us that a man determines his own worth," Lady Huffington said in a contemplative tone, "and Charles is possessed of a great deal of self-respect. Yet he is not one of those toplofty dandies, filled to excess with his own self-importance. Lucy needs a man like him."

Higgins considered this. "You are saying that Sir Charles is a worthy man, if not a wealthy one."

"Yes." The countess seemed pleased at his understanding. "Lucy has her own money and need not marry for wealth or title. Sir Charles is kind and decent, and the love he offers her seems strong and pure."

"You wish her to marry for love?"

The countess nodded. "No one in our family has ever done so. Octavius had to marry an heiress, and I . . ." Her gaze took on a faraway look. "Leon was good enough to marry me after I was with child, but he did not love me. He had so many mistresses that I knew he could not—"

"Please, madam," Higgins said, startled. "It is not necessary to—"

"In any case," the countess continued briskly, "our passion faded quickly."

Higgins was too tongue-tied to reply.

Lady Huffington sighed. "Well, that was long ago, so I suppose it does not matter." She eyed him consideringly. "It is easy to talk to you, Higgins. Perhaps that is because you are a trusted friend as well as my majordomo."

Higgins cleared his throat. "Thank you, my lady."

"As I was saying, I want Lucy to know something more than I had, something lasting. Charles can offer her respect, faithfulness, and a solid and abiding love that has developed over half a lifetime."

"But you said that she does not return his love," Higgins pointed out.

"I think she does, but does not yet know it," the countess replied, a speculative tone in her voice. "Deep friendship can be a strong foundation for love, you know."

Higgins did not speak.

"Unfortunately," she added, "Lucy fears altering their relationship and losing his friendship forever."

"There is much to risk in taking such a step," he agreed.

"But much to gain," she pointed out. "Sometimes in life we must take chances—embrace the unknown."

"Yes. Sometimes we must."

Unexpectedly, a tear trickled from her eye. Lady Huffington reached for her handkerchief. Higgins looked away.

"All this blathering about love and passion—it is not like me," the countess said, shaking her head. "Sometimes I wonder if I am coming apart at the seams. I do not know what has happened to me lately."

"It is the healing process," Higgins said gently. "You must give it time."

"My niece does not have time." She dabbed at her eyes. "Charles is weary of waiting for her to fall in love with him. I think we must do something, Higgins."

"*We*, madam?" he echoed in surprise.

"Yes, indeed," she replied. "I have given the matter some thought. In your younger days you must have been quite the ladies' man. I am depending upon you for ideas."

Higgins's mouth dropped open in amazement. "I assure you, madam, I was never—"

"Nonsense. Even at your age, you are still quite handsome. You have all of your hair, and you have not let yourself run to ruin as many men do in their upper years. Your eyes are quite the nicest shade of brown."

A coughing fit had Higgins grasping for the water pitcher. The countess shook her head. "Do not gammon me, Higgins. I imagine you know all of the tricks there are to know."

When at last he had himself under control, Higgins looked up to find the countess regarding him in wry amusement.

"I do believe I have embarrassed you, Higgins."

"Not at all, madam," he insisted.

"But you were quite the man about town, were you not?" she persisted mischievously. "I often wonder why you did not wed."

There was no frivolity in his gaze as it met hers. "Perhaps it is because that I, too, have come to believe that one must marry for love."

"And you have never loved?"

"Once." He paused. "But she was wed to another."

"Oh, dear. I am sorry." The countess smiled brightly. "I had no right to question you about something so personal. Let us turn our attention to the young people, shall we?"

Higgins bowed and poured his employer another cup of tea.

It just might be possible to get through the drive without looking at the Duke of Claridge. There were interesting sights in the park, people to greet and the brisk afternoon air to enjoy. One could sit right next to a person and never find reason to meet his gaze.

But that would be the coward's approach, and Hannah had never been a coward. And so, she looked the duke in the eye for the first time since last night, when he had tucked her under the quilt.

"I wish to thank you for your support at Lady Greeley's," she began. "But I also wish to say that I—I regret what happened in the carriage afterward." Her face flamed, but she held his gaze. It was important that they understand each other.

"You expect an apology?" His penetrating black eyes held a question that seemed rather deeper than the one he had spoken. He looked away only briefly, to direct the curricle toward an isolated area of trees.

"I do not expect anything," she said firmly. "I do not imagine you are the kind of man to make apologies."

"No," he agreed.

"But I do not want you to think that I am the sort of woman who"—Hannah took a deep breath—"who indulges in such behavior," she finished quickly.

His lips curled into a provocative smile, and he fixed her with a probing gaze. "Did you not enjoy my touch, Hannah? You seemed to—very much, I might add."

Hannah looked around, hoping no one had heard him—for there was no doubting his meaning. But he had driven the carriage into a cove of trees that shielded them from any curious eyes or ears.

"You know that I did." She closed her eyes in humiliation. It was typical of him to reduce those breathtaking moments in the carriage to one of simple physical enjoyment. For her it had been much, much more. That foolish kernel of joy inside her that had been planted that night in his study had found nourishment and even now was straining to send out roots.

When he covered her gloved hand with his, she opened her eyes, surprised to see a pensive look on his face. "Let us have done with these games, Hannah," he said. "Your body told me more last night than any words. You want me. We want each other. It is very simple."

"No." She shook her head in denial.

"I will take good care of you," he said, impatiently pushing that unruly shock of hair back off his forehead. "I imagine you are used to a very different, cruder sort of protector, one who does not care for your pleasure. But I am not unkind. I will not hold your previous life against you. I will set you up in a fine house and clothe you in fine gowns, and you will never want for anything again."

Hannah eyed him blankly.

"You will be safe," he continued, leaning close, his breath warming her earlobe. "You will be mine alone. You will never have to sell yourself again."

The import of his words suddenly became brilliantly, humiliatingly clear. "You are offering me carte blanche?" she demanded in amazement.

He smiled. "It is more than you could have hoped for, is it not? But it is what I want. We will enjoy each other, Hannah."

Hannah tried to remain calm. "No, sir, we will not."

"What?" He frowned. "Perhaps you do not understand, my dear. I am offering you every advantage to which the mistress of a duke is entitled. You will have a splendid house, many servants, and all the money you need."

"I understand perfectly, Your Grace," Hannah replied grimly. "It is you who are having difficulty. I will not be your mistress."

Those midnight eyes flashed like lightning amid gathering storm clouds. The scar on his cheek seemed to redden. "If you are holding out for a better offer," he said, his posture stiff with anger, "you will not get it."

"What I am holding out for," Hannah said distinctly, "is a husband. Failing that, I will be quite satisfied as a spinster."

"*Husband?*" He looked at her as if she had lost her mind. "What hope does a woman like you have of securing a husband? In a few short weeks you will collect your five hundred pounds and be on your way. None of the men who gather around you so eagerly now will know your name this time next month."

"I know what I am," Hannah retorted. "I know that I have no hope of finding a husband among your class. But that is not the point. The point is I do not intend to give myself to anyone other than the man I love."

"Damnation, woman!" he thundered. "You are a *prostitute*!"

Hannah drew herself up with as much dignity as she could muster. "Since I lack the ability to tell whether you just shouted those words to the heavens, I cannot judge whether anyone else heard. But if you expect me to continue playing the part of a lady, Your Grace, I advise you to refrain from such public utterances in the future."

She turned to stare fixedly at the leaves of a bay laurel. For a long time she felt his eyes on her, though he made no move to catch her attention. At last, she could take it no more. "Perhaps you will be good enough to take me back," she said stiffly.

Immediately, the curricle jerked forward. Hannah gripped the seat to avoid falling against him. They drove the rest of the way without speaking. Hannah could feel the anger emanating from him.

Finally, they rolled to a stop in front of the duke's town house. Several footmen rushed toward the carriage, but the duke waved them away. He placed his hand on her chin, forcing her to look at him. The wind had blown his hair every which way, giving him a wild, satanic air.

"Your bluntspokenness has always intrigued me." His black gaze bored into hers. "I did not realize you were at heart a hypocrite."

Hannah flinched.

"I will not be played for a fool," he continued, scowling as he brought his face closer, letting her see the masculine sensuality in his brooding gaze. "You want me. I could feel it last night. I can feel it now."

"Yes," she whispered, unable to deny the truth.

His fingers touched her jaw, and she wondered if he were about to kiss her, here on the drive in front of his servants and passersby.

But that was not his intent. His gaze filled with wrathful promise as it held hers.

"Your false virtue notwithstanding," he said, speaking slowly so that every word burned into her, "I will have you, Hannah. I will indeed."

With a curt nod at the footmen, who quickly came scurrying to do his bidding, he leaped from his seat. As one servant assisted Hannah, the duke tossed his whip to another. Then he swept past her into the house.

Rage radiated from him like smoke from an angry volcano.

Chapter Seventeen

"I am glad you came to me, Hannah. You are a physician's dream."

When Jean-Marc Itard smiled, his protruding chin and long, hooklike nose almost met over his thin lips. Twin warts under his lower lip stood out like little rubber balls. The hollows under his prominent cheekbones gave him a saturnine air that did not go with the bristly mop of hair curling wildly at the top of his high forehead.

Hannah suppressed a shiver. Though she was determined not to be affected by Dr. Itard's formidable appearance, she felt uneasy every time she met his penetrating gaze.

She forced herself to remember that many people viewed this man as a god for his work with a deaf–mute savage from the woods of southern France. The fact that Itard never managed to bring the wild boy up to the standards by which society accorded a human being civilized had not eroded his reputation as one of the physicians most knowledgeable about the deaf. In his present association with a famed French school for the deaf, he was said to work miracles.

A miracle was what she was hoping for.

"Do you think you can help me?" she asked, hoping her voice did not sound pleading.

He regarded her with a vaguely predatory look and stroked his chin. "It would be fun to try. The fact that you were not born deaf is reason to hope for the best."

"But Mr. Goya was not born deaf, nor Mr. Beethoven," Hannah pointed out, "and neither of them has regained their hearing."

"Neither of them is my patient." He smiled with a confidence born of years of fame. "We have had successes at the school, Hannah. The electrical prod was no good, nor the leeches. But one student responded to eardrum piercing, and I am working on a new method that requires inserting a probe into the eustachian tube."

Some of his words were unfamiliar, but Hannah understood enough to gain a picture of the discomfort involved. She swallowed hard. "Are there less invasive methods?"

"I do have a concoction of ginger, horseradish, glasswort, and rose of Provence that, when put into the ears in the form of drops, is thought to have some effect. But it does not produce consistent results, and in any case is not a cure. I have also used a purgative that blisters the skin of the ear. There is an old Chinese remedy that involves heating a cylinder filled with dried leaves of mugwort and burning the skin with it from the back of the neck to the chin. I have even tried fracturing the skull of a few pupils, to rather interesting effect . . ."

"Dear Lord," Hannah murmured. "Are these measures successful?"

Dr. Itard tilted his head. "To be quite frank, medicine has offered very little benefit to the deaf–mute—though one day I may hit upon a cure." He bent closer, and it seemed to Hannah that his eyes fairly glowed. "But you are not a deaf–mute, my dear. You speak wonderfully. You read lips perfectly. If I did not know it, I would never guess that you are deaf. You are very lucky."

"*Lucky?*" Hannah eyed him incredulously. "I do not feel lucky. That is why I have come to you." Tears sprang to her eyes. "I have known the song of the lark and the beauty of a symphony, Dr. Itard. I have heard the magic of voices united in song. I have heard how one man's voice is different from the next, how a child's laughter can delight the heavens. I cannot bear to do without these joys for the rest of my life."

Dr. Itard's large hand clamped down on her shoulder, and she was forced to look at him once more. "Do not despair, my dear." She wondered whether his tone was kind or patronizing and suspected it was the latter. "The accident that robbed you of hearing may have caused an injury that can be reversed. I have many methods at my disposal. What did not work on those who have been deaf and mute for a lifetime may very well work on a young woman who simply fell out of a tree."

He seated himself at a writing table and began to take notes. "Now. You will tell me about this occasional ringing in your ears."

Hannah lost track of time as she submitted to his questions and then to his examination of her ears. When it was time to leave, she felt much better. After all, she was in the hands of one of the world's most famous physicians. The Duchess of Wellington and the Duke of Orleans, as well as members of both houses of Parliament, had flocked to his lectures at the Argyle Room, with the result that the demonstrations had been extended by several weeks. If anyone could help her, surely it would be Dr. Itard.

Still, she was not certain.

"I can see by your face that you still have doubts, my dear," he said as he escorted her to the door. "Perhaps you will attend one of my little demonstrations and see the results of my work firsthand. Here are some tickets. I look forward to seeing you."

Hannah left his office in a hopeful state of mind. Dr. Itard's treatments might be painful, but she was accustomed to hardship. A little pain in exchange for the return of her hearing was worth the price. Perhaps she could get Lucy to accompany her to the lectures. It would be nice to have a friend there.

The buoyant mood carried her into the evening and Lady Melbourne's ball, one of the premier events of the season. For the first time in a long while Hannah saw the future as ripe with promise, for in a few weeks the season would be over and she could collect the money to pay Dr. Itard.

To be sure, she had made a mess of things with the duke, but that would soon be in the past. The fact that she had lied to Lucy and to Lady Huffington would always distress her, but was not a troubled conscience a price worth paying to regain her hearing?

The answer to that question eluded her. Studying the faces of Lucy and Lady Huffington, who stood next to her waiting for the duke to bring them all punch, Hannah wondered whether she might have outstanding obligations too steep to walk away from.

Lucy, for example, looked miserable. Hannah knew her high color stemmed from the fact that Charles was nowhere in evidence tonight. Lady Huffington appeared preoccupied, almost troubled, and Hannah's heart went out to her, for in these few weeks their shared love of music had brought them closer. A lonely, sensitive woman lay behind the countess' formidable facade, and Hannah yearned to know her better.

As for the duke, a perpetual scowl had been glued to his face tonight. Except for offering to fetch the punch, he had studiously avoided her since accompanying them through Lady Melbourne's receiving line. Hannah thought about his offer to make her his mistress. It had been arrogantly delivered, but she sensed that in his own strange way he was perhaps a little fond of her.

For a few moments at Lady Greeley's, he had had only her interests in mind. He had supported her after that debacle and taken care of her. More than raw lust had held her in his thrall in the carriage that night. She had felt treasured, even cherished as he wrapped her in his arms and held her tight. Under that gruff, contemptuous exterior, the Duke of Claridge was capable of heart-stopping affection. She wondered whether he realized it.

Her mind had barely completed that thought when a group of four frantically waving people hailed her from several yards away. She recognized them instantly as they approached, and her heart sank. The man and woman were speaking rapidly, and she missed many words. But the phrases she picked up as her gaze met first one and then another set of beaming eyes made her heart sink.

"Hannah, *dear*!"

". . . child, how wonderful to see you again!"

". . . splendid you look! When we heard about the newest Original . . . deaf young lady . . . see for ourselves . . . our own, dear Hannah . . . gratified that our dearest hopes were realized!"

The Earl of Rottenham, Lady Rottenham, and their two daughters, Elspeth and Grielda, stood before her with broad smiles pasted on their faces.

"Uncle Gerald . . . Aunt Madeline." Thunderstruck, Hannah stared at her father's brother and his family. She had not seen them since her aunt turned her out in a rage three years ago, vowing that her daughters' chances on the Marriage Mart would not be jeopardized by a deaf relative. Evidently, neither Elspeth nor Grielda had yet found husbands, for they had no escorts and were dressed like the other debutantes, in pale pastels that did not suit them.

Lucy frowned, obviously trying to figure out where on Charles's family tree these relatives belonged. Lady Huffington held up her lorgnette and subjected the newcomers to prolonged scrutiny. Neither moved immediately to greet the earl and his family.

Unfazed, Lord Rottenham executed a courtly bow. Lady Rottenham curtsied, with a sharp look at her daughters to follow suit.

"Allow me to introduce myself, Lady Huffington," the earl said, smiling broadly. "I am Lord Rottenham, Hannah's uncle. Her father was my younger brother. We have not set eyes on our dear niece for nearly three years." He eyed her fondly.

Hannah felt positively ill, but she could do naught but curtsy in return. Lucy, meanwhile, looked even more confused. She turned to Hannah with a questioning look.

"I thought your father was Charles' uncle."

"Now that would be me, young lady," interjected a man whose sudden appearance at Lucy's elbow instantly caught Hannah's attention. "And as far as I know, I have sired no offspring."

Charles, who stood at the stranger's side, smiled pleasantly. "Lady Huffington, Lady Lucille, Miss Gregory, allow me to present my uncle, Erasmus Tremaine."

"Your father's brother?" Lucy frowned.

"The same," Charles replied.

Lucy stared. "But . . . I thought he was deceased."

"Certainly not!" Uncle Erasmus barked indignantly.

"*My* brother is deceased," Lord Rottenham replied indignantly, scowling at Erasmus Tremaine.

"*Your* brother . . ." Lucy repeated, baffled.

"Hannah's father," the earl confirmed. "*I* am her uncle—her *only* uncle."

"Her uncle." Lucy looked positively dazed.

"And very proud of it, I might add," the earl finished.

"Oh, yes," added Aunt Madeline. "When Hannah left us, we despaired of ever seeing her again, but we are so glad to find her making her debut with such a distinguished family . . . even if it is not our own."

Lady Huffington squinted through her lorgnette at one speaker, then another and another. "This is all very confusing," she observed with a censorious frown.

For a moment, everyone simply looked at each other. At last, Lucy spoke up. "I think we must ask Julian to help us. He is very good at straightening things out."

Charles rubbed his jaw and winced. "By all means, let us ask Julian," he said blandly.

"Do you refer to the duke?" asked Lord Rottenham, beaming. "Always wanted to meet him. Never ran in the same circles, of course, as he was reputed to be a bit of a rapscallion—"

"Hush!" His wife rapped his knuckles with her fan as her two daughters began to giggle.

Hannah took a deep breath, knowing that the hour of her greatest humiliation was upon her and that it was best to get it over with.

"As the duke is not here at present," she began, with a sense of deep resignation, "I believe I can explain—"

A hand touched her arm.

"But I *am* here, Miss Gregory." The duke's eyes held hers, and there was an intensity in those midnight depths that made her heart race. There was also a shard of regret.

When his gaze turned to the rest of the group, however, it was cool and impassive. "Explanations are perhaps in order, but now is not the time," he said, his air of command defying anyone to disagree. "Meanwhile, the dancing has resumed. Miss Gregory has promised me this set, so if you will excuse us . . ."

Thrusting punch cups into his sister and aunt's hands, and fairly tossing Hannah's to Lady Rottenham, he bowed deeply. With perfect aplomb, he led Hannah onto the dance floor, away from eight pairs of questioning eyes.

"The fat's in the fire, you know." Julian said, watching Hannah's face carefully as he pulled her into the figures of the waltz.

"For once, I agree with you," she replied, grimly following his lead.

"We will have to give them some explanation. What do you suggest?"

She regarded him curiously. "Why not simply the truth?"

"The truth?" Julian echoed, frowning. What Hannah took for truth—that he had hired her to watch over Lucy—was but another lie. And yet, he did not know if he could bring himself to tell her about the wager.

"Everyone will be scandalized to learn about my time at the Lock Hospital, I suppose," she added.

Julian cleared his throat. "Perhaps they need not be told." He wondered at the oddly protective feeling that filled him at the thought of her becoming the object of such revulsion.

With a mulish tilt of her chin, she met his gaze. "I do not shrink from my background. At least in the hospital and in Covent Garden, I was accepted. It was better than living with my aunt and uncle."

Julian nearly stumbled. What was it about dancing with this woman that destroyed his sense of timing? Then he realized what had given him pause, what had nearly knocked him off his feet.

Slowly, the truth began to dawn: the country home, the father's suicide, the difficult relatives who took her in. That wild story he thought he had invented to give her a respectable past was all of it fact—except that she was not related to Charles, but to the encroaching Lord and Lady Rottenham.

She had not always been a whore.

"Why did you not tell me who you were?" he demanded.

Her eyes flashed. "Tell me, Your Grace: would you have believed me if I had said I was wellborn?"

"No," he said bluntly.

"Then there was no point in telling you, was there?"

Julian did not reply. His brain filled with questions as he tried to piece together the details of her past. Hannah's gaze was a careful blank, and Julian sensed she was furious. He was scarcely less so. She had lied to him, after all. It would have been better to have known the truth from the beginning. Perhaps he would not have been so . . . cavalier in his attitude toward her, or so disdainful.

He turned to another question that had nagged at him ever since he had overheard Lord Rottenham introduce himself as Hannah's uncle. "How is it that you ended up in that horrible hospital instead of with your family?"

"I do not consider them my family," she said fiercely. "They took me in after my father killed himself because I had nowhere else to go. At first we got along—providing I kept out of sight when visitors came. When I lost my hearing they quickly discovered they did not want to be saddled with a deaf girl. My aunt said she despaired of making me respectable. One day she simply turned me out."

She had not chosen the life of a whore, then. It had been thrust upon her. She had had no other choice.

Julian was silent for a moment. "I suppose your relatives' remarkable change of heart is owing to the fact that you are one of the season's successes," he said dryly. "Reflected glory is better than no glory at all."

Preoccupied, she made no immediate reply. "I must leave Claridge House," she said finally. "Lady Huffington and Lucy will be angry at my duplicity—as they should be."

It was the only sensible course of action, but every fiber of him rebelled at letting Hannah leave. Yet he knew she was right: after his family learned the truth, leaving was the only honorable thing to do.

Honor? Truth? He did not know much about either of those virtues. But looking at her somber gray eyes and the determined set of her chin, Julian had the strangest feeling he was about to learn.

Chapter Eighteen

The residents of Claridge House did not make their way to their respective beds immediately after returning from Lady Melbourne's ball. Instead, as if in response to an unspoken command, they gathered in the duke's study.

Hannah did not seat herself as Lucy and Lady Huffington had done. With her hands clasped in front of her, she stood before them and explained that she was not Charles's cousin after all but had been hired by the duke to keep an eye on Lucy. Finally, she told them that she had come to them from the Lock Hospital.

At first, Lucy appeared shocked. Then she recovered sufficiently to coolly inform Julian that, since he had never concerned himself with her behavior in the past, he need not have gone to such lengths. Lady Huffington sat stiffly in her chair but gave no hint of her thoughts.

Julian merely steepled his hands and studied Hannah over his fingertips. He said not a word.

Charles, on the other hand, looked as if he was burning to speak. Taking in the stony faces around the room, he could contain himself no more.

"Hannah has given you the truth as she believes it," he told the ladies, "but there are facts to which she was not privy."

Hannah's gaze flew to Julian, who merely arched a brow, as if daring Charles to continue. The baronet returned him a scowl.

"There was a wager," Charles began, slanting a sidelong look at Lucy.

"A wager?" Hannah echoed uncertainly. She had all but forgotten the bet he had vaguely described the night he taught her the new dances. She knew it somehow involved his future with Lucy, but could not imagine what it had to do with her.

Charles looked a challenge at Julian. "Why do you not tell them?"

All eyes shot to Julian, whose face was an unreadable mask. "Are you quite certain, Charles?"

"I have nothing to lose," the baronet said grimly.

"Very well. Charles and I had a wager." Julian paused for a heartbeat, then added: "I believe it was Charles's idea." Charles glowered at him, then eyed Lucy forlornly.

Julian crossed the room and, with seeming insouciance, leaned against the mantelpiece. "Charles wagered that I could not transform a street wench into a lady for the season."

Holding Hannah's gaze, he allowed the words to register among his audience.

Lucy and Lady Huffington stared from Julian to Hannah and back again. Lucy gasped. Lady Huffington put her hand to her chest.

"Speechless?" Julian queried, a strange light in his eyes. "Yes, I can see that you are. By your expressions of surprise, I think it can be safely said that I won the wager." He turned to Charles. "You owe me your matched bays, do you not?"

"Good God!" This, from Lady Huffington, who eyed the two men in appalled horror.

Lucy's expression was one of utter revulsion. "How awful!"

Dazed, Hannah sank into the nearest chair. "I do not believe it," she murmured. She had known that the duke and Charles thought her beneath them, but she had also assumed that they saw her as a person of worth, however small. 'Else why would they have recruited her to help Lucy?

How naive she had been! It had been merely a game, an absurd wager between men so depraved that they had nothing better to do than toy with people's lives. To them, she was only an object of ridicule, the pawn in their little bet.

It was too much to absorb.

A hand touched her shoulder. Charles stood before her, his eyes filled with remorse. "I am sorry, Hannah. I have no excuse to offer, save the demented state of a desperate man. I was certain Julian could not succeed—that must sound terribly insulting, I know, but there it is."

"If he lost, you see," he continued, "then he was to allow me to . . ." He shot a desperate look at Lucy. "To elope with his sister," he finished resolutely.

"What!" Lucy jumped out of her chair. "How could you contemplate such a thing?" she sputtered.

Charles shook his head. "It was unforgivable. Please accept my deepest apologies, Lady Lucille." Bowing formally, he turned and abruptly strode from the room.

Hannah rose. She could not stay another night in this house where the duke had made her a laughingstock, where her very presence must offend the ladies. "I must see to my packing. If you will excuse me—"

"No," Lucy protested. "Where would you go?"

"To my aunt and uncle's," Hannah answered. "For a few days, anyway. I do not expect they will wish me to remain once they know the truth."

Lady Huffington stood, though she found it necessary to lean heavily on the arm of the chair. "You may say you have been with me in Yorkshire since last they saw you. *I* do not plan to inform them otherwise, nor will anyone else here."

Her stern gaze moved from Lucy to the duke, daring them to disagree. Satisfied at what she saw in their eyes, the countess turned to Hannah. "Tomorrow we will send a message around to Lady Rottenham informing her that you will accept their invitation to come and stay for a while. I imagine they will leap at the opportunity."

Hannah knew very well that her aunt and uncle had extended no such invitation, but she also knew that as long as they believed her under the sponsorship of Lady Huffington, they would be delighted to have her. She could not imagine why the countess was being so charitable, but she curtsied deeply and murmured her thanks. Then she fled, half stumbling up the grand staircase to the solitude of her room.

An hour later, her door was flung open. Lucy stood at the threshold, her clear blue eyes searching Hannah's. Hannah could barely bring herself to meet her gaze.

Lucy gave her a surprisingly gentle smile as she strode into the room. "Please do not think I blame you," she said, pressing something into her hand. "It is those horrid men who are responsible for all of this."

Hannah looked down to discover herself in possession of a sheaf of banknotes. "What is this?"

"I know you did it to escape that dreadful place. You must have been desperate for money. I want you to have this. It is a thousand pounds—not much, but all I have on hand at the moment."

Hannah recoiled. *A thousand pounds? Not much?* It was the world. "I cannot. I have lied to you. I am not deserving of such kindness."

"You deserve your independence." Lucy's determined gaze burned into Hannah's. "If things do not work out with Lord and Lady Rottenham, I do not want you to have to return to that hospital—or to be dependent on Julian," she added with a knowing gaze.

"Julian?"

Lucy sighed. "If he has not already offered to make you his mistress, I am sure he will soon. It is just the sort of thing he would do."

Hannah flushed. Lucy crossed her arms and began to pace the room with growing agitation.

". . . told him what I think of his high-handed ways . . . unforgivably insulting . . . demeaning . . . both of us . . ." She halted, belatedly remembering that Hannah could not possibly catch her words. "I told him that he wronged you terribly."

Hannah had to know. "What did he say?"

"Very little, as you might expect." Lucy made an expression of disgust. "But that is neither here nor there. What is important is that you use this money to keep you safe from men like Julian who would wager over your virtue and treat you as an object of disdain."

"My *virtue*?" Hannah wondered whether she had understood correctly, or whether Lucy was simply caught up in another of her fanciful notions. "You know where I was. The Lock Hospital is a place for—"

"For diseased prostitutes," Lucy finished. "You will not persuade me that you are anything like those women, Hannah."

Hannah put her head into her hands. "What does it matter what I am?" she said, unable to stop a tear from betraying her. "Whore or virgin, it is all the same to men like your brother."

Gently, Lucy pulled her hands away, forcing Hannah to look at her. "I have been thinking about that." Her expression was thoughtful. "Did you notice how Julian offered no apology tonight?"

"What of it?" Hannah accepted the handkerchief Lucy offered. "It is his way."

"He is insufferably arrogant," Lucy conceded cheerfully. "But all the while I was upbraiding him after you left, he sat there with a stoic expression, not even bothering to defend himself. It was almost as if I was but echoing his own thoughts. He would never have tolerated my tirade otherwise."

The duke reproaching himself? The notion was laughable. Hannah suspected that Lucy did not know her brother as well as she thought. She could not know, for example, how their father had nearly destroyed his only son. Julian's dark mood tonight doubtless had less to do with Hannah than with his own painful dilemma. Hannah decided to steer the conversation in a different direction.

"Charles seemed most contrite," she offered, watching Lucy closely.

Lucy flounced angrily into a chair. "That wretched man! All the while I thought he was my friend, he was plotting to ruin my reputation!"

"He was plotting to *marry* you," Hannah corrected gently. "Perhaps he thought that the only way to get you to take him seriously was to make off with you."

Bewilderment swept Lucy's lovely features. "But I was beginning to take him seriously—I think. And anyway, what kind of man would wager the reputation of a woman he claimed to love? What kind of man would subject a woman to such ridicule?"

Hannah sighed, thinking not of Charles's apologetic features, but about the duke's dark, enigmatic eyes—which had displayed not a shred of contrition as they held hers.

"I do not know."

"Oh, Hannah! I shall miss you so!" Lucy rose and threw her arms around Hannah.

"And I shall miss you," Hannah replied sincerely.

But it was Julian's brooding gaze that haunted her dreams all night long.

"Charles and Lucy are truly estranged," the countess said in a mournful tone. "Julian ought to be horsewhipped for agreeing to such a shameful wager. As for Hannah . . ." Her voice trailed off, and she gave a great sigh.

"You do not blame her." It was a statement, not a question.

"She did not even know of the wager. Doubtless she needed the money he was to pay her—she cannot have had any of her own. She did not say so, but it is clear that Lord and Lady Rottenham severed relations with her after she became deaf. They did not want the burden of her."

Higgins frowned. "That seems rather heartless."

"They are shallow, encroaching people," the countess declared. Her gaze took on a faraway look and she bowed her head. "I am scarcely any better, Higgins," she said softly, her mind lost in past sorrows.

"Now, madam . . ."

"Do you not see the parallels?" the countess demanded fiercely. "From the moment of my daughter's birth it was clear that she was . . . defective. I allowed no one outside of Leon, the doctors, and you to know of her existence. My behavior was despicable—just like Hannah's horrid relatives."

"You did not turn your daughter out," he observed quietly.

"No," Lady Huffington agreed. "But I locked her away in that institution." She put her head in her hands. "God help me. I was ashamed of her, when I should have been ashamed of myself."

Higgins placed a cup of bracing Darjeeling in front of her. "You thought it was for her own good."

"So the doctors said, but I was never truly persuaded of that. That is why I finally brought her away from that place."

Her watery blue gaze met his. "I treasured those few months we had together at home. She played like an angel, Higgins. She could not speak, or laugh, or cry, but when she played the clavichord, none of that was necessary. I thought that it would be all right—that, given time, we could be like any mother and daughter."

"It was beyond her, madam," he said softly. "Her music was a beautiful gift, but it was her only gift."

The countess bowed her head. "It should have been enough for me, but it was not. When she was killed with Leon in that horrible carriage accident, I actually thanked God—" Her voice broke on a sob.

"It is a heavy burden to carry all this time, madam," Higgins said gently. "Perhaps you can begin to let it go a little?"

Lady Huffington dabbed her eyes with the handkerchief he proffered. "When I look at Hannah, I see it all over again. She, too, is . . . different."

"Defective?"

The countess stilled. "No. She is simply Hannah." Her voice cracked. "Why, Higgins? Why did my blindness prevent me from seeing Gwendolyn the same way—as simply my daughter? Why did I view her as one of nature's horrid mistakes?"

Higgins's hand hovered helplessly above his employer's trembling shoulders but did not touch them.

"Do you not see?" She shook her head. "*I* was the defective one for not being able to accept my own daughter."

"You have now," he said quietly.

"Yes." She clutched the handkerchief in a tight ball. "Yes, I suppose so."

For a long moment, the countess was lost in thought. "Poor Hannah," she said finally. "On her own these last few years. Heaven knows what atrocities she has had to face."

"But she has faced them, madam, just as she faced up to her deception. She is not a weak woman. She will survive."

"God willing, her aunt and uncle will never learn of her whereabouts these last few years. Let them think that she has been with me all this time. They will not turn her out now."

"It was very fine of you to offer that, madam."

Lady Huffington waved off the compliment. "Nonsense. Hannah is a decent woman, regardless of what anyone might think."

Higgins arched a brow, but the countess' nimble brain had moved on to something else that had caught her attention during the tumultuous scene in the study. Her expression brightened. "Higgins?"

"Yes, madam?"

"All the while Hannah was speaking, Julian was regarding her most oddly. As if he was drinking in her words, her very essence." She wiped away the remnants of her tears. "What do you think that means?"

The majordomo frowned. "The duke obviously admires Miss Gregory, but I have never detected anything unusual about his demeanor toward her—"

"When was the last time that Julian admired any woman?"

Higgins coughed discreetly. "The duke is known to have had any number of female liaisons . . ."

"Yes, but how many of those women has he actually *admired*?" the countess demanded. "Precious few, I warrant. No, this is more than simple admiration, Higgins."

"It is?"

"It is quite possible that he is besotted."

Higgins looked shocked. "It is not like the duke to—"

"People are so thick about these things," the countess continued. "A man can be in love and not even know it. And some women cannot see what is under their very noses."

Higgins busied himself with the tea tray. "Do you think Miss Gregory returns his regard?"

She shrugged. "I suspect the poor girl does not have an inkling of her feelings. Even if she did, a woman of Hannah's discipline would never allow those feelings to grow. She knows that a union between them is inappropriate, given her background."

"What would it take, then?" Higgins asked quietly.

The countess looked at him in surprise. "Take? What do you mean, Higgins?"

"What would it take for a woman to allow herself to consider returning a man's regard, even though the liaison may be . . . inappropriate?"

Lady Huffington was taken aback. "Why, I do not know. Something outlandish, I suppose."

"Outlandish," he repeated, furrowing his brow in thought. "Something on the order of what you have planned for Lady Lucille and Sir Charles?"

The countess smiled. "Oh, yes. That might do very well. And it is not my plan but *yours*, Higgins. Do not forget that."

"No, madam. I have not forgotten." He sighed heavily.

Lady Huffington giggled. "I never imagined you had such a *rakish* mind."

Higgins merely bowed in acknowledgment.

What he needed was a whore. A bottle of brandy and a whore.

Julian stared at the nearly empty bottle and gave a bitter, drunken laugh. The brandy was right before him, and the whore was upstairs somewhere packing her bags. Both were in his house, and precious good it did him. The bottle had not soothed his mood, and his chances of having Hannah were slightly less than the odds of quenching the fires of hell with a few paltry snowflakes.

What had been the point of that stupid bet, anyway? To prove once more that he could fool the world, as he had done all these years? To pass a whore off as a lady, a bastard off as a duke—it was all the same, was it not?

Ironically, the whore had proved herself a far better specimen of humanity than the bastard. She was strong where he was weak. She could face what she was and confess it before all. She did not shrink from the truth.

But then, she knew the truth about her life. He did not know his and might never. He wanted desperately to disbelieve his father's deathbed declaration, but nothing had surfaced to allow him to do so. The honorable course would be to stand up before the world—as Hannah had done tonight—renounce his title, confess that he had lived a lie, and thereby cleanse his soul of the corrosive duplicity that had stalked him for a decade.

Yes, it was easier to face the truth when one knew for certain. A lifetime of uncertainty was pure hell.

The only thing he knew for certain now was that he had played with Hannah's life as if she were a puppet on a string. Not once had he bothered to consider her feelings, but then he had never done so with any woman. He had thought of women as weak creatures, to be used as it suited him.

His mother had been weak. If she had truly been Octavius's wife, why had she not stood up to him, forced his father to come for them? She could have blackmailed him into coming, threatened to tell the world that he had abandoned his sick and helpless bride. Octavius would have responded to blackmail.

But she had not thought of taking on a powerful English duke. Perhaps, Julian mused, she had not been weak so much as spent. Her own parents had lost their lives to a bloody mob. She barely had the strength left to take care of a young boy. But whatever the reason, she had given up and allowed Octavius to treat her as nothing more than a whore.

Julian could not imagine Hannah giving up. She was a fighter, through and through. It had stunned him to realize that she was of respectable birth. Just like his mother, a well-bred whore.

And yet, every time he heard that word in his brain, he winced. It did not seem right, applying it to her. She was better than that. Better than him.

To think that he had once tried to reform. No wonder he had failed. Virtue and respectability would never be his. A tiger did not change his stripes. A bastard did not suddenly acquire legitimacy. He could not be something that he was not. He accepted those truths.

But tonight he had learned something else, a new truth that had chilled him to the bone.

Whatever Hannah was—lady or whore—she was too good for him.

Chapter Nineteen

The hall was mobbed. From his position in the back of the room Julian could barely make out Hannah's erect form in the front row. Her attention was focused on the man on stage. He imagined her intent, somber eyes as she concentrated on every word that fell from that preening, overlarge mouth. She appeared to be unaccompanied. He hoped that Rottenham had at least given her a maid and the use of his carriage for her outing.

Julian did not care for the demeanor of the celebrated Dr. Itard—or the predatory way he regarded Hannah. His "demonstration" bore more than a passing resemblance to a circus act. The audience had been invited to submit written questions, which were shown to the deaf patients on stage, who would then answer orally—their speaking proficiency presumably testimony to Itard's skill.

One questioner wished to know if the deaf and dumb were unhappy in that state. An especially articulate patient, who had evidently fielded such idiotic queries before, showed himself something of a philosopher.

"He who never had anything has never lost anything; and he who never lost anything has no loss to regret," replied the man, known as Massieu. "He who has nothing to lament cannot be unhappy. Consequently, the deaf and dumb are not unhappy."

Appreciative applause followed this answer, which seemed reasonable in its logic but failed to acknowledge the plight of people like Hannah. Massieu's words bore unnatural inflections that indicated he had been born deaf and developed the faculty of speech late in life. What of Hannah, who had lived a lifetime with sound and speech, only to have it taken away?

Julian watched her, sitting so stiff and tall at the front. What of the music that had been taken from her? What of the family that had turned her out because she had suddenly lost her hearing? She had known loss—profound loss.

As far as he could tell, she had borne these tragedies without a shred of self-pity. Even so, she must have deep regrets, 'else she would not be so riveted by that bombastic Itard and his "cures."

Julian cringed at the ghastly methods Itard so proudly described—boiling oil poured into the ear, threading a string through the neck with a scalding needle. The ghastlier the procedure, the prouder of it he seemed—as if he thought the deaf deserved such punishment for having the temerity to defy the natural order of things.

At no time did Itard show sympathy for his patients or indicate that he had any idea what it was like to be deaf. He did not try to communicate with them in their language—the curious finger movements they used with each other when he lectured to the crowd. He seemed intent on teaching them *his* language, the language of the hearing world, as if their worth relied on becoming like everyone else.

But the deaf were not like everyone else—they were different. Itard gave no indication that he viewed that difference as anything other than a mistake of nature. Julian felt sorry for the man's patients. Those who could not be cured would be discarded as scientific failures. Itard had no interest in helping the deaf live with their deafness.

So why was Hannah there in the front row, hanging on his every word? An ominous suspicion formed in his mind. Did she mean to subject herself to Itard's torturous treatments?

Not if he had anything to do with it.

The crowd gave Itard a standing ovation. Many rushed the stage to further scrutinize his patients. By the time Julian caught up with Hannah, she was standing outside with a maid, evidently waiting for her uncle's carriage.

The sight of her so dignified in that plain blue dress he had bought her so long ago unnerved him. It had been a week since she left his house, a week of trying unsuccessfully to purge himself of her memory. Today he had finally resolved to see her, only to learn when he had called at Rottenham's that she had come here. Now that she was so close, a strange joy surged within him.

"Hannah!" he shouted, knowing the futility of his cry but wanting to claim her in whatever way he could. The maid heard him and pulled on her mistress' arm.

Slowly, Hannah turned. As she spied him, a veiled look shuttered those clear gray eyes, sending sudden despair knifing through his gut.

"Your Grace," she acknowledged formally as he reached her side, "why are you here?"

Julian frowned. "To see you, of course."

She tilted her head, as if his statement needed diligent consideration. "Why?"

Polite verbal fencing was not one of his skills, and patience not one of his few virtues. With an exasperated sigh, Julian flung his hands heavenward.

"Damn it, Hannah. I forbid you to subject yourself to this man's treatments. He is nothing but a charlatan."

She looked away from him toward the carriage that rolled to a stop in front of her. A footman jumped down, ready to assist her into the vehicle.

"Dr. Itard is widely respected," she replied. "As for submitting to his treatments, Your Grace no longer has any authority over me whatsoever. Such decisions are my own."

With that, she ascended the carriage steps. The maid hurried to follow, but Julian stepped in front of her and pushed his way into the carriage before the startled footman could close the door.

"What can I do to persuade you?" he demanded.

"Very little, I imagine." She eyed him calmly. The maid, who had hurried into the carriage to protect her mistress, stared at him with eyes as round as saucers.

Julian wanted to shake Hannah. "There is no shame in being deaf," he ground out.

"No, no shame in it," she readily agreed. "I have never been ashamed of my condition."

"Then why subject yourself to harsh, degrading measures that can have no result in the end?"

She looked away. "I am willing to endure pain if it means I may regain my hearing."

Julian slammed a fist into the carriage seat. He could tell by the resolute look in her eyes that there was little hope of changing her mind. Still, he had to try. Gently he touched her chin, bringing her face to his.

"You are an intelligent, courageous, beautiful woman," he rasped, wondering if that strange warmth on his face could be something as unheard of as a blush. He had never before sincerely complimented a woman. "You need nothing more. You are complete as it is."

She frowned, but said nothing. Recklessly, Julian plunged on. "Damn it, woman! You have learned to face the world on your own terms—you understand what is said to you and you make yourself understood. That should be enough for anyone. Why can you not accept your deafness?"

Her eyes closed, as if she wished to block out his words. Her mouth twisted in what might have been pain before she opened them again and fixed him with that steady, unnerving gaze.

"Perhaps for the same reason that you cannot accept your condition."

"*My* condition?" Julian eyed her blankly.

Her gaze shot to the maid, who seemed to be hanging on every word of the conversation. "Those papers that you lack," she said carefully. "Without them, you live with the uncertainty of not knowing."

Anger surged through him. He did not want to talk about his parents' marriage papers or the lack of them. He wanted to talk about her. "What of it?" he demanded.

"Not knowing has made you less than you could be," she explained. "That is how I feel also. I wish to know if it is possible to hear again. I wish to try. If I fail, then I shall live with failure."

"Deafness is *not* failure!" Desperately, he took her hand between his, as if his conviction could somehow flow into her. "You are all that any woman could be. I have never met a woman like you."

The carriage rolled to a stop before Lord Rottenham's town house. Before she could respond, the footman opened the carriage door. She paused before descending.

"Yes, I am different." Defiantly, she lifted her chin. "You have always viewed me as something of a novelty, have you not?" She stepped out of the carriage.

"Damnation, Hannah!" he shouted after her. "That is not what I meant."

She had her back to him and did not catch his cry. But the little maid fairly jumped from her seat, nearly tripping over him in her haste to exit the carriage.

"Oh, la! I have always enjoyed your playing, Hannah, dear. Pity you cannot hear a note of it, but rest assured that we all stand in admiration of your artistry."

Hannah lowered her gaze to the keyboard, shutting out her aunt's insulting compliments. It had been like this since she had moved into the earl's town house—all false gaiety as her relatives basked in the glow of having one of the season's Originals ensconced in their home.

If Hannah had forgotten her aunt's shrieking denunciation three years ago, she might have been fooled by the fawning politeness with which her presence was welcomed now. Her aunt and uncle had supplied a maid, offered to buy her gowns, showered her with effusive compliments. Even Grielda and Elspeth seemed in awe of her.

But she had not forgotten, nor did she feel terribly guilty lying to them about her whereabouts for the last few years. They had easily accepted her story of being with Lady Huffington in Yorkshire. To be sure, things could not go on like this forever, but tomorrow she would have her first treatment. She would be on her way to regaining her hearing. Then, with the money Lucy had given her, she could make a respectable life without her hypocritical relatives.

But what, a nagging voice demanded, if the duke was right? What if Dr. Itard could not help her?

Hannah pushed aside the doubts. The odious man had only meant to try to control her again, as he tried to control and manipulate everything. Had not the doctor himself said that she was a perfect candidate for treatment, that he was confident in succeeding? After all, she had only fallen out of a tree. She had not been born deaf. It could not be a permanent state—could it?

Beethoven, Goya—they had been unlucky, that was all. And at the moment, Hannah felt very lucky. Her fingers fairly raced over the keyboard of her aunt's square piano. It was not so fine an instrument as Lucy's, but her aunt had volumes of music to go with it—including a sizable collection of Mr. Beethoven's works, which Hannah adored.

She quickly worked out the development section of the first movement of his Sonata in E flat major. Obviously, the piece had been composed in a passionate state of mind, for it was filled with grand and startling moments.

Perhaps it was only logical to see the duke's stern, cynical gaze as she allowed Mr. Beethoven's moods to buffet her. From what she heard of the composer, he and Julian were not so very different. Both were temperamental, tormented men whose souls held a dark beauty. At least the composer's did, she mentally amended. She was not so certain about Julian's.

Seeing him outside the Argyle Room today had thrown her heart into a somersault. Silly wretch that she was, she had even thought for a moment that he had come for her. That he had missed her. That he cared for her.

His first words told her otherwise, however. He had come to berate her, to exert his compelling will, to manipulate that pitiable woman who was the subject of his disgraceful wager.

What made him think he could intrude on her life now that she was no longer under his roof?

Hannah took a deep, calming breath. He would not stop her from going to Dr. Itard. Nothing would, now that she had Lucy's money. Someday she would repay every penny, but for now, she would use it to regain her hearing and establish her independence.

For the first time in a long while, the future looked rosy. Plunging into the rondo like a driven woman, Hannah willed Julian's tormented gaze from her mind.

"It is a lovely afternoon for a drive, is it not, children?" As Lady Huffington's venerable traveling coach rolled over a particularly jarring bump, she gifted her two companions with a beatific smile.

Two dour gazes met over the tip of the countess' plumed turban.

"I should have thought it rather late to undertake an outing to Richmond." Lucy pressed rigidly against the back of the seat to steady herself.

"Quite," Charles agreed stonily.

Lucy had finally abandoned as futile the questions of why her aunt had to see the maze this afternoon, why she had dallied until they had gotten an impossibly late start, and why she had insisted that Charles accompany them.

Apparently oblivious to the strained silence between Lucy and Charles, Aunt Eleanor had filled the carriage trip with her usual moralizing homilies—this one about the necessity of appreciating nature. Lucy had barely listened. Charles merely glared out the window.

The awkward atmosphere in the carriage at last caused her aunt to halt her rambling monologue and fix them with a stern gaze. "I suppose you are wondering why I wanted both of you to accompany me on this expedition. 'Tis simple: I wish you to settle your grievances."

Lucy gasped. "There is no need—"

"There is every need," the countess corrected. "Charles has done you no real harm, you know."

"What!" Lucy eyed her aunt incredulously. "Have you forgotten that he made me the stakes of that insulting wager—as if I were a horse or some other inanimate possession? If that is not harm, I do not know what is."

"When did you become such a stuffy miss?" Aunt Eleanor demanded. "The only thing he injured was your pride, which has seethed and festered until it has made you miserable."

"I am perfectly happy, Aunt." Lucy crossed her arms over her chest.

No less pleased to be a member of Lady Huffington's captive audience, Charles glowered. "As your niece has chosen not to accept my apologies, there is really very little else to say, madam."

"How like a man to ignore the obvious," the countess retorted.

Charles frowned. "The obvious? I do not understand."

Lady Huffington regarded them both in disapproval. "I have never seen such stubbornness—or such faint hearts. You do not speak, you do not touch, you do not even look at each other, when it is very plain that you wish to do all of those things—and more. By Jove, Charles, if you really cared for Lucy, you would not let a little quarrel get in the way."

"*Little quarrel?*" Charles eyed her in amazement. "Your niece has made it clear she cannot stand the sight of me."

"Lucy's pride is hurt. That is all," the countess explained briskly. "You must get her to rise above it. It is obvious she truly wants that which pride has made it impossible to have. Women often do, you know."

"That is odd," Charles said in a musing tone. "Julian said much the same thing back when we made our wager."

"I wish both of you would not speak of me as if I am not here," Lucy snapped.

Lady Huffington ignored her. "Seize the moment, Charles," she said sternly. "Make her see that she loves you. This is no time to play the gentleman."

"I demand that we change the subject," Lucy said fiercely, her face flaming.

Charles seemed lost in thought. "I am not so much the gentleman as you believe, madam," he confessed. "I truly intended to take her to Scotland if Julian lost the wager. I thought if I could get her alone—truly alone—for a time, she would be mine forever." He paused. "I still believe that."

The countess eyed him sympathetically. "Poor man," she said. "Lucy has led you a merry dance, has she not?"

"I will *not* be talked about like this!" Lucy cried. "Please, may we speak of something else?"

"Certainly," the countess said easily. "Do you see that cove of trees up ahead? I believe we have almost reached our destination."

Suddenly, the carriage lurched to a halt.

"Stand and deliver!" came a raspy voice.

Lucy put her hand to her chest. "Oh, no! 'Tis a highwayman!"

Charles frowned. "But it is not even dark."

"What does that matter?" Lucy cried. "The bandit is here, is he not?"

Still puzzled, Charles turned to the countess. "Do you have a pistol hidden somewhere?"

"A pistol?" The countess looked horrified. "Certainly not! He merely wants to rob us. You cannot mean to shoot him!"

Charles stared at her. "How else do you propose that I deal with him, madam?"

Just then, the door flew open. A man dressed in black, a mask obscuring his features, stood before them. "I will take your jewelry, if you please, ladies," he said in a muffled voice.

Calmly, Lady Huffington unfastened the clasp on her gold-and-emerald bracelet. As she handed it over, the man suddenly reached out and yanked her from the carriage.

"Aunt Eleanor!" Lucy exclaimed, horrified.

"Do not worry, children," the countess called, as the carriage wheels suddenly jerked forward.

Charles had been on the point of dashing to the countess' rescue, but Lucy shrieked and pulled him backward onto the seat just as the carriage took off. Struggling to right himself, Charles rapped frantically on the roof to get the coachman's attention.

"Stop! Stop this vehicle, damn it!" he barked—to no effect. Indeed, the crack of a whip indicated the driver had spurred the team on.

"The man must be scared out of his wits," he muttered.

"What shall we do?" Lucy cried. "We must save Aunt Eleanor!"

As the enormous coach careened around a curve, Charles stuck his head out of the window to see if he could catch a glimpse of Lady Huffington and her fate. To his surprise, the countess was standing at the highwayman's side, waving good-bye to them with her handkerchief. The two figures on the road grew ever smaller as the carriage raced away, but Charles could distinctly see Lady Huffington's expression.

She was smiling.

"Do you think this will do the trick?" Lady Huffington asked. "John Coachman will not stop until the inn, but what happens then?"

"What will," Higgins said, ripping the mask off his face. "Deuced uncomfortable getup," he muttered.

"But what if Charles has an attack of conscience?" the countess persisted. "It will soon be dark. What is to stop him from turning the carriage around and driving them back? He is a gentleman, after all."

Higgins stared at the fading silhouette of the departing carriage, which was just making the next rise in the road. "From the look in that young man's eyes, I imagine he will not let that fact get in the way."

The countess smiled. "You are positively brilliant, Higgins."

Higgins sighed. "Not at all, my lady. But I do know the face of lust when I see it."

Startled, Lady Huffington stared at him. "I see."

"No, madam," Higgins corrected, his tone strangely aloof. "I do not believe that you do."

Chapter Twenty

Outwardly calm, Hannah sat on the treatment table in Dr. Itard's office in Little Argyle Street. The doctor pulled a large needle from a case and smiled.

"We will begin with the eardrum piercing. If there is a blockage, this should clear it." He hesitated. "There may be some pain."

Hannah took a deep breath. "I do not fear pain."

"Do you wish a sedative? That may lessen the discomfort."

She shook her head.

"Very well." Itard inserted the needle into a long, probelike instrument. When he finished, the thing looked like a huge knitting needle. As he turned toward her, the kerosene lantern flickered wildly.

Nervously, Hannah wondered whether the uneven lighting was sufficient for such a delicate procedure. An evening appointment had been all he could give her, as the days of such an important man were far too busy to see patients. She was glad that her aunt and uncle were attending a house party in the country, since she would probably be in no condition to see anyone after the procedure. Eyeing Dr. Itard's needle, Hannah forced herself to put her fears aside. To hear again, to once more know the song of the birds and the joy of Mozart, was worth any price.

"It is important not to move, no matter how uncomfortable the procedure may be," Dr. Itard cautioned, his features stern. "I should not wish to inflict unnecessary damage."

Mutely, Hannah nodded. As he moved closer, she willed herself to perfect stillness. His eyes gleamed in anticipation. "I feel very good about this, my dear."

"Yes," she murmured with a tremulous smile.

Slowly, he inserted the needle into the outer part of her ear. Its cold, sharp metal felt like ice against her skin. Hannah focused her gaze on a spot above the doorway. It was a technique she had learned in the hospital. If one concentrated all one's attention on a single unmoving spot, one could sometimes keep pain and discomfort at bay.

Just as Dr. Itard moved the probe deeper into her ear, the door swung open, breaking her concentration.

The Duke of Claridge stood at the threshold, arms crossed over his chest, like an arrogant king regarding a rebellious subject who had dared to displease.

"Your Grace!" Hannah exclaimed.

Startled, Dr. Itard dropped the instrument. It fell to the floor and rolled under the examining table. He whirled. "What is the meaning of this?"

Julian merely returned him a chilling gaze. In one fluid movement, he strode past Itard, snatched Hannah's bonnet from a chair, plopped it on her head, and lifted her into his arms.

"What are you doing?" Itard sputtered. He made a belated grab for her, but Julian stepped them deftly out of his reach. "You cannot take her!" Itard shrieked. "I will not allow it!" He reached out again, and this time his hand touched the ducal sleeve.

An icy gaze was Julian's only response. Cold, murderous rage lurked within those black depths, and the scar on his cheek seemed to pulse with a fury of its own. Instantly, the doctor withdrew his hand.

Without a moment's pause, Julian carried her out of the office and down two flights of stairs to the street. Tossing her into his waiting carriage, he climbed in beside her, barked an order to his coachman, and they were off.

Flung none too gently against the squabs, Hannah could scarcely catch her breath. It was not so much the force of her landing that robbed her of air as it was her own anger.

"How dare you!" she demanded when at last she could speak.

He turned, his face hard as stone.

"The issue is not my behavior, but yours. I forbade you to go to that charlatan. Yet tonight I find you calmly sitting on his bed in near darkness, waiting for him to mutilate your ear with a needle so enormous as to be absurd."

"I was *not* sitting on his bed!" Hannah eyed him indignantly.

His brows met ominously. "You disobeyed my order."

"It was not your order to give," she retorted. "I am no longer in your employ."

Suddenly his brow relaxed, as if the storm had somehow abruptly passed. "No," he agreed. "You are not."

Hannah eyed him uncertainly. "You admit that you have no authority over me? That you had no right to do what you did?"

"On the contrary. I had every right."

"On what basis?" she demanded.

He looked surprised. "Why, as your lover, of course."

"*Lover!*" Hannah stared at him, anger giving way to confusion. "You are mad. We are nothing to each other."

"As to that," he said, holding her gaze, "I must disagree."

"What?" Hannah blinked, then flushed deeply as she discerned his meaning. "Because of that time in your carriage?"

He appeared to consider the matter. "In part."

"In *part*? What do you mean?"

"I have not yet worked that out." A contemplative look softened his features. "I will inform you when I do."

Dazed, Hannah sank against the squabs. Discussing anything with this man was pointless. He merely did what he wished and ignored any questions. She supposed that was what came with being a duke.

Of course he might not be a duke, after all. Perhaps that was what he was trying to work out. Her heart skipped a beat. What if he were just an ordinary man, without the burdens and obligations of a dukedom? He would not care that she was nobody, without money or respectability. Perhaps they might even have a future together.

Then again, any man would want a respectable wife—not one who had lived among prostitutes. There was no future for her with this or any man. She had known that all along. Anyway, she had never wanted anything other than a chance to regain her hearing and to survive without selling herself on the streets as her friends had done.

Now he had robbed her of even that chance. She ought to be furious, but the fury had somehow drained out of her and all she felt was a profound fatigue that came from the sheer hopelessness of her plight.

"Where are we going?" she said at last.

"To my home."

"I live at my uncle's now. I would rather be taken there."

"We are going to Claridge House."

Hannah sighed. There was no reasoning with him, and she would not even try. Closing her eyes, she sank into the solace of silence, letting it keep everything else at bay.

At Claridge House, Julian lifted her from the carriage, crushing her possessively against his broad chest as he carried her inside. Hannah did not bother to struggle.

Higgins did not betray by so much as an eyelash that there was anything unusual about seeing her in the duke's arms. He merely handed Julian a missive, which forced him to set her on her feet so that he could read it.

Julian read the contents, crumpled the note, and tossed it back to Higgins. The majordomo looked alarmed at such treatment of what was evidently a very important piece of paper.

"I beg your pardon, Your Grace," he said, "but you intend to *do* something, do you not?"

Julian eyed him blandly. "Just what would you have me do, Higgins?"

"Why, go after them, sir. I am certain that is what Lady Huffington wishes. She has taken this very hard. Even at this moment she is confined to her bed . . ."

"With a case of the megrims," Julian finished. "Yes, yes, Higgins. I am certain she feels dreadful. But I have no intention of racing after my sister just because she took it into her head to elope with Charles. Best thing for them, anyway."

Hannah gasped. "Lucy and Charles have gone?"

"This afternoon," Julian confirmed. "Seems they persuaded my aunt to accompany them to Richmond, then put her out of the carriage and drove north." Arching a brow, he studied the majordomo. "My aunt must have been quite inconvenienced, Higgins. Just how did she manage to find her way back?"

"Her ladyship had requested that I follow along in another carriage with extra provisions," Higgins replied hastily. "Fortunately, I spied her on the side of the road and rescued her."

Hannah frowned. "It is not like either Lucy or Charles to take such a drastic step."

"On the contrary," Julian corrected. "Lucy has always been headstrong, and Charles is a man at the end of his rope." He turned to Higgins. "I assume that my aunt is indefinitely indisposed?"

The majordomo nodded. "That is why she left this note for you. No one knew when you would be home." Higgins eyed Hannah uncertainly.

"It is too late to do anything now," Julian said.

"Oh, no!" Hannah protested. "There will be a terrible scandal. Lucy's reputation will be ruined."

"I doubt that. Anyway, by the time I found them, they would have spent half the night together. There would be a scandal in any case."

Hannah hesitated. "Not if they had been accompanied," she said slowly.

Julian frowned. "What are you suggesting?"

"That I go with you."

He eyed her incredulously. "You propose that *we* serve as Lucy's chaperons? That will not fadge. You will only sully your own reputation by letting it be known that you spent the night gadding about the countryside with one of the realm's most notorious rakes."

"Perhaps," she conceded. "But people know you would never involve your sister in scandal. That is why they will believe that the four of us set out for Richmond in Lady Huffington's coach and had an accident—a broken wheel that could not be repaired until the morrow. We put up at an inn for the night—Lucy and I together and Charles and you together."

"But *two* carriages would return to London—mine and Aunt Eleanor's," he pointed out. "That would raise suspicions."

"You can say that you sent word to Claridge House to have your carriage brought to us as soon as possible, in the event that the countess's wheel could not be repaired in a timely fashion."

The stern set of his features told her that he thought her plan ludicrous. Hannah did not know how to persuade him, but she knew she had to try. Lucy and Charles belonged together, but not in this slapdash scandalous fashion.

Shyly, she touched his sleeve. "Please, Julian. We have to try."

He stilled. "What did you call me?"

Too late, she realized that she had breached a boundary between their stations that should never have been crossed. Mortified, she flushed deeply. "I am sorry, Your Grace. I had no right to use your Christian name."

Enigmatic black eyes held hers. "I do not mind."

Strange currents in those dark depths tugged at her, making her dizzy. "Do you not?" Hannah stammered, feeling like the veriest schoolgirl.

"No." He turned to Higgins. "Have a fresh team brought out. Miss Gregory and I travel tonight."

Higgins bowed deeply. "Very well, Your Grace."

Hannah saw a smile on Higgins's face and knew he was relieved to be able to tell Lady Huffington that her nephew had matters well in hand.

"Why do you say that Aunt Eleanor is in no danger?"

Grimly, Charles stared ahead, his arms folded over his chest, his mood blacker than the night that was rapidly overtaking them. "Higgins will take care of her."

"*Higgins?*" Lucy frowned. "But she is in the hands of that . . . that brigand!"

He arched a brow. "Did you not notice something familiar about that 'brigand'?"

"His voice was rather odd," she said slowly, "but I imagine one does get hoarse riding about in the night air robbing coaches." When Charles let out a derisive laugh, she frowned. "What is so amusing?"

"Did it occur to you that he might have been trying to disguise his voice so that we could not recognize it?"

"Not recognize it . . . You cannot think . . ." She paused, then gasped. "Oh, merciful heavens! Never say that *Higgins* was our highwayman?"

Charles's bland look was confirmation enough.

"Then . . . then Aunt Eleanor must have known!" Lucy shook her head. "But *why*?"

"For the same reason that our driver has seen fit to ignore my entreaties to stop this infernal antique and turn us around."

"I do not understand."

Charles made an expression of disgust. "For someone who is normally so intelligent, you are being remarkably obtuse."

"Obtuse?" Confusion etched two neat little lines over her nose. "What reason could my aunt and Higgins have to stage a holdup and send us barreling alone away from London? Why, it is nearly dark!"

"Just so." His pointed look was full of meaning.

Lucy blinked. "Oh," she said in a small voice.

"Do I take it that you object?" Charles's gaze was unreadable.

Lucy looked away.

"Come now, my dear." His voice filled with sarcasm. "Your aunt has gone to all this trouble to arrange your abduction. I am certain she has also seen to it that, whatever inn our driver is bound for, there is only one room available. How can you object to having your future arranged so neatly? Why, we might as well start picking names for our children."

"You need not talk as if the notion is so utterly abhorrent." Lucy looked resolutely out the window, though the encroaching darkness provided little passing scenery to appreciate.

Charles studied her rigid profile. "Lucy?"

When she did not reply, he touched her chin and brought her face gently around. He was shocked to see tears in her eyes. "What is wrong?"

"You act as if being with me is the worst of all possible fates." Her voice wobbled precariously.

He frowned. "You know that it is not."

She pulled a handkerchief out of her reticule and blew her nose. "How am I to know anything of your feelings, Charles? You have scarcely spoken to me lately."

Incredulous, he stared at her. "I have thrice offered you marriage and you have thrice refused me. I made an utter fool of myself with that bet in the futile belief that passion could do what my words had not. You cannot doubt my feelings. It is yours that have been at issue."

"P-p-passion?" Lucy's eyes grew wide. "What do you mean?"

Charles colored. "I was certain that after we spent a night in each other's arms, your feelings would alter. That you would see the truth."

"The truth?" Lucy eyed him speculatively. "Are you trying to say that you care for me, Charles?"

Exasperated, Charles threw out his hands. "Of course I care for you! Do you think I would have gone through this for anyone else?"

"Then . . . then your feelings are not so brotherly as all that?"

Charles scowled. "Why would I wish to marry my sister?"

"You never said why, Charles. That is the point."

"Never said—" Charles broke off, perplexed. "What the devil is there to say?"

"Why you wish to marry me, of course."

"Why I wish to—" He broke off. "You mean that was all that it would have taken . . . some flowery declaration?" He scoffed. "Balderdash, Lucy Pembroke!"

Lucy eyed him in surprise. "But that is how 'tis done, Charles. All my other—" Abruptly she halted, biting her lips.

"'All your other suitors'?" His eyes bored into her. "I am not like the others, Lucy. I am a simple baronet, whose cuffs are frayed and whose bills are rather numerous. I have little to offer a duke's daughter, so we might as well turn this ancient buggy around and have done."

"I do not wish to have done," she said quietly.

He cocked his head, studying her. "No?"

"No."

For a long moment their gazes held. Something wordless passed between them. Charles felt his palms grow sweaty, and the sensation that gripped him in his gut rippled down to the tip of his toes and back again.

"Lucy?" he said softly.

"Yes?" she prodded, when he did not continue.

He sighed. "I love you."

"And I love you, Charles." Her smile was positively radiant. He eyed her strangely, unable to trust the meaning of her words.

"Will you marry me?" Tension gave his voice a harsh, shaky rasp. "I warn you, this is my last offer."

"Yes, but only if you do not turn the carriage around."

He stared. "Is this some new game? Because if it is—"

"It is no game." Lucy met his gaze without blinking. "I want to find out about . . . about this passion of yours," she finished in a rush. "I know it is unseemly, but—"

With a muttered oath, Charles pulled her into his arms. The first taste of her lips nearly sent him over the edge.

"Please," she murmured breathlessly against his mouth. "Please do not turn the carriage around."

Charles looked down into brilliant blue eyes shaded with passion. "I would not dream of it," he said at last.

Chapter Twenty-one

Julian's carriage rolled to a stop at the Swan's Rest Inn. Aunt Eleanor's distinctive traveling coach was easily visible from the road, as it took up most of the stableyard. A man bent on eloping could do a sight better than her conspicuous equipage, Julian reflected wryly. Since no attempt had been made to hide the ancient contraption, Julian assumed that Charles had no illusions about the fate that awaited him.

Dawn had yet to struggle over the horizon, and he was not surprised that no one hurried to see to his team. Everyone was doubtless abed, as he longed to be. With the help of his own exhausted coachman, Julian unhitched the horses and settled them in the stable with fresh oats and hay next to Aunt Eleanor's dappled grays.

Hannah had fallen asleep about an hour ago. The sight of her curled up on the carriage seat like a babe touched an unfamiliar place inside him. She trusted him to take care of her, of Lucy, of whatever difficulties this night brought. Her faith awed him.

He hated to wake her. As he lifted her into his arms, she stirred slightly.

Julian allowed himself a smile. He was getting used to carrying her about. For such a feisty woman, she weighed next to nothing. Nestling her against her chest stirred that strangely protective spirit within him, and a number of other confusing feelings besides.

By the time he set her down inside the front door of the inn, she was awake, although groggy.

"Are they here, Julian?" she asked sleepily, looking around the empty hall. Julian had rung a bell, but no one had come. He rang again.

"Upstairs, I imagine," he replied, unable to tear his gaze from the lovely picture she made with her eyes half closed and her hair tumbling down around her shoulders.

It had been an exhausting night. They had traveled for hours, stopping frequently so that he could inquire at inns and public houses along the way. They had spoken very little, since darkness made it difficult for her to catch his words without bringing her face very close to his.

She no longer shied away from using his Christian name. In the confines of his darkened carriage, her softly modulated tone had wrapped around his name like a close-fitting glove. Her increasingly disheveled appearance had stirred his passions, and the long road before them had forced him into hours of teeth-gritting control.

Julian wondered if Hannah realized the consequences of this night. He held no illusion that Lucy's reputation could be salvaged without a marriage to Charles posthaste. That issue did not concern him.

What troubled him was the fact that by going off with him tonight, Hannah had put herself beyond the pale. With his reputation, no one would really believe that they were merely chaperoning Lucy and Charles. Her clever plan notwithstanding, Hannah would be viewed as a fallen woman.

He reminded himself that a scandal would mean nothing to her. A woman of her background would scarcely concern herself with appearances. She would simply return to her former life among the sordid streets of London.

That realization brought a scowl to his face, which he turned on the ruddy-faced innkeeper who finally came running down the hall. A quantity of gold forestalled the man's complaints and produced the interesting information that Charles and Lucy had arrived very late, registered as Sir Charles and Lady Tremaine, and taken one room.

"Idiot," Julian muttered. Registering Lucy as his wife was unforgivably indiscreet. He vowed that Charles would wed his sister this very day. For a moment he contemplated rousing them at once, but that would change nothing. Best to let

Charles rest up for his wedding night—although from the looks of things, he had already had it.

Scribbling a note, Julian instructed the innkeeper to slip it under the baronet's door. He scrawled his name in the register under Charles's and accepted the key for what the innkeeper said was the only vacant room.

Hannah was nearly asleep on her feet and so was he when they crossed the threshold into the tiny little attic room. Two small rope beds were slung alongside each other, and from the disheveled look of the bedding, Julian suspected that servants had been hastily ousted to make room for paying customers. He also suspected that the bedding was none too clean.

No matter. They would sleep in their clothes, grateful for a few hours' rest. Hannah had lain down on one of the beds. Already she was fast asleep. He tucked a blanket around her and marveled at the wild tenderness she evoked in him. He had never felt so protective toward a woman, yet so filled with desire. It was not the predictable, tidy lust he had felt with others, the kind that could be satiated by a few hot moments under the sheets.

With Hannah, a man would never get his fill. There were so many sides to her—the proud side that dared him to treat her any differently because of her deafness, the shy side that blushed furiously at the thought of that night in his carriage when she had dropped her guard long enough to let him please her.

And there was a dark side to Hannah he was just beginning to understand—the side that saw herself as imperfect, damaged, that yearned for what could never be. He felt a strange kinship with that side, for he, too, lived as an outsider.

But she was whole, where he was not. Deafness had not diminished her; it was simply part of her, as much as that stubborn disposition and that delightful rebellious streak.

Why could she not accept who she was?

Kicking off his boots, Julian tried to make himself comfortable on the other bed. He could not fight her battles for her; he could only fight his own—and today, perhaps, his sister's, though Lucy probably needed a champion as much as she needed another gown. He was not sure what they had accomplished by this mad dash north to rescue a woman who undoubtedly did not need rescuing and who would shortly wed the man they were rescuing her from.

With a heavy sigh, Julian closed his eyes. *He* was the one who needed rescuing—from this tantalizing woman at his side. He should have kept up his guard, but then he had not known what to guard against. He should have reined in these tender feelings, but they had caught him unawares.

And now, he had not the slightest idea what to do with this softness that flowed through him like warm honey.

All he knew was that when Hannah said his name, it felt as though an angel had granted him a small measure of grace.

"I did not seduce her," Charles insisted.

"Oh, no, Julian," Lucy agreed. "It was *I* who propositioned *him*."

"Now wait a minute, Lucy," Charles protested. "A man has his reputation to uphold."

"I have no complaints," she said with a shy smile, nestling into the fold of his arm.

"This is all very charming," Julian snapped, "but the only information I care to have at the moment is your wedding plans."

"Oh, we have no wedding plans," Lucy said calmly.

"No," Charles confirmed. "None at all."

Julian's fist slammed onto the table of the private parlor they were sharing for breakfast. "Enough of this nonsense," he growled at his sister. "Or I will call your lover out and happily wipe that smile from his face."

"You would not!" Lucy cried.

"He would indeed, my dear." Charles patted her hand reassuringly. "But I am passably handy with a pistol."

Lucy turned on her brother. "What a hypocrite! Everyone knows you have had more mistresses than a tree has leaves!"

"That is enough!" Julian glanced quickly at Hannah. Just his luck—by the looks of her reddening complexion, she had caught Lucy's words.

Undaunted, Lucy continued: "I always looked up to you, Julian—not for your careless womanizing, of course, but for your determination to be yourself, heedless of society's expectations. But now it seems you are just like everyone else—you wish us to appear respectable when we are not!"

"Not respectable! Coming it a bit too strong, Lucy," Charles warned.

Julian's gaze went from his sister to Charles, who was looking remarkably sanguine about the whole matter. Something was not quite right. "What exactly is afoot here?" he demanded.

Lucy merely bestowed an adoring look on her lover. As Charles met Julian's gaze, an oddly mirthful gleam lurked in his friend's eyes.

"I am probably the only man in England," Charles said mournfully, "who has carried a Special License in his pocket for the entire season." He sighed. "Hope springs eternal, or so Pope said."

"A Special License!" Julian stared. At last the man had shown some sense. "Then there is no impediment to your being wed today."

Lucy promptly burst into giggles.

"We were wed last night," Charles said quietly, "though I cannot say what would have happened if I had not had that piece of paper with me—"

"I can," Lucy interjected.

Charles silenced her with a glance. "We roused the local vicar just before midnight." He grinned at Julian. "Consequently, today you have the pleasure of addressing your sister's husband." He put his arm around his wife. "I am the luckiest man in all England."

Julian was too stunned to speak. But Hannah rose quickly and enveloped Lucy in a hug.

"I am so happy for you!" she cried. Julian found himself staring—not at his wayward sister, but at Hannah and the delighted smile on her face.

Lucy erupted in more giggles. Hannah joined her. Charles looked as pleased as he could be.

For some reason, Julian suddenly felt miserable. He shook Charles's hand, wished his sister well, downed the rest of his coffee, and wondered why the morning suddenly felt so empty. It might be small of him, but the sight of the two laughing women and Charles's self-satisfied smile plunged him into despair—as if he had suddenly come face-to-face with what he could never have.

He had to leave. He rose abruptly, but just as his hand found the door, Charles's words brought him to a halt.

"Hold, Julian," he said softly. "You cannot go without informing us of your intentions toward Hannah."

Julian frowned. "My intentions?"

"You have compromised her as surely as I would have compromised your sister had we not been wed," Charles said quietly.

Julian heard Hannah's shocked gasp.

"Nothing happened," she protested. "We simply came to find you and—"

"And spent the evening in a closed carriage and the waning hours of the night in the same bedchamber," Charles pointed out. "You are not to blame, Hannah," he assured her. "But Julian knows what is what."

Julian scowled at Charles. "Nothing improper occurred. And even if it did, it is none of your concern."

"On the contrary, my friend. You are speaking of my cousin."

Julian stared. "You know that's a lie."

Charles regarded him calmly. "*I* know, as does everyone in this room. But the world thinks Hannah is my relative. If her reputation is destroyed, it is I who must see to it. And I will, make no mistake about it."

"Oh, no!" Lucy looked appalled. "You will not fight a duel! I cannot bear it!"

"There will be no duel," Hannah said firmly. Her chin was set in that determined look Julian had come to know so well. "Julian is right. There was no harm done. I will not allow you to fight over a reputation that never existed in the first place."

"Now wait a minute, Hannah," Charles protested. "This is not your concern."

"It is every bit my concern," she declared. "I do not care a fig about my reputation. A woman in my position cannot afford to." Her gaze moved from one to the other. "I appreciate your assistance, but I have my own life to live. I will decide my fate, not any of you."

Then she walked swiftly from the room. All eyes promptly turned to Julian. He shook his head. "Stubborn woman," he muttered.

"What are you going to do?" Lucy demanded.

Hannah could not disappear from his life. He would not allow it. "Go after her," he said grimly.

"And then?" Charles inquired with a mischievous grin.

Julian merely glowered.

The mail was due in a hour, the innkeeper informed her. Hannah purchased a ticket with some of the money she had intended to give Dr. Itard last night.

Had it only been last night that Julian had swept her out of the doctor's office and into his carriage? Had it only been this morning that she had wakened to find those dark, brooding eyes staring down at her?

So much had happened in so short a time. Was it possible that he cared for her just a little?

She had seen the way he had looked at her in the carriage last night. Not just with lust—although there had been that—but with the eyes of that motherless boy of six who wanted badly to believe in feelings that endured. And with the eyes of a man who had taught himself to be strong even when they did not.

There was kindness in him, no matter that he tried to hide it. It was as if that part of him had been unused for so long he had forgotten it existed. His contemptuous veneer was meant to repel the faint of heart, but her own heart had been strengthened by hardship and she knew that veneer for what it was: armor that existed in the unspoken hope that it would one day be unnecessary.

Only a man of character would die a little inside when he knew himself helpless to resolve the dilemma of his birth. Only a man with the courage to face the truth would torment himself when the truth proved elusive.

And only a man capable of great tenderness would take care of her with such gentle strength, as he had done over and over again—from the moment he rescued her in the forest to his behavior during the debacle at Lady Greeley's and in the carriage afterward. Even last night, when he had swept her away from Dr. Itard's needle, she had sensed that his anger stemmed from concern as much as outrage over her defiance. And just this morning, he had gently tucked the covers around her as sleep overtook her.

Yes, she thought, perhaps he cared just a little. His touch betrayed him. And, foolish woman that she was, she wanted to be with him for the rest of her days.

Hannah shook her head. She did not belong with Julian. She would return to London and, with the help of Lucy's money, live on her own until she found work. That was the lonely life that stretched out before her—not some coddled existence with Julian.

She sat stiffly on a small bench to wait for the mail, careful to make her face a blank so as not to invite unwanted attention. She was grateful for the cocoon of silence that shielded her from the bustling of the stableyard. If any of the ostlers thought a solitary female an inviting target for their rude comments, she would never know. There was comfort, at least, in that.

Suddenly a shadow loomed over her. She did not need to look up to know who stood there. Julian's hand touched her shoulder. Against her will, she met his gaze.

"Hannah."

Just once, Hannah wished she could hear how her name sounded on his lips. Hating that self-pitying thought, she forced a smile. "Your Grace," she acknowledged politely.

"I thought we were at 'Julian.'" He sat beside her, his gaze probing hers. "Can you not say it?"

Hannah swallowed hard. "Julian," she repeated.

"Are you traveling somewhere?"

"I am returning to London." To her surprise, he did not take her to task. Instead, he stared at the ground, seeming to find something riveting there in an ant's struggle to move a seed ten times its size.

Gradually, Hannah became aware that his lips were moving. She touched his sleeve. "I am sorry. I did not catch your words."

Now he looked directly at her, and Hannah was surprised at the bleakness in his eyes. "I wish to explain—" He broke off and muttered something she could not make out. Then he took a deep breath and began again.

"Unlike Charles, I have never been given to honorable intentions," he said grimly. "The closest I have ever come to marriage was with a certain woman—a respectable lady, one of many I tried to seduce. Her uncle caught us in a compromising situation."

"Oh." Hannah did not know what to say.

"In the normal course of things, she and I would be long wed by now."

Of course. He would marry this respectable lady he had compromised. Perhaps this was the friend that Lucy had hoped he would wed. Hannah waited, holding her breath.

"She would not have me."

"What?" Hannah eyed him indignantly. "Why ever not?"

His mouth twisted bitterly. "Because I was deemed so beyond redemption that even a compromised woman would not take me on as a husband."

"Oh."

He gestured to his scar. "I had the temerity to cross swords with the man she would eventually marry, one of the finest swordsmen in England. Though I gave as good as I got, you can see the result."

Hannah stared at the jagged bolt of lightning that bisected his cheek. "I see."

"I am not proud of my reputation or my past, Hannah. Any woman would be insane to link her name to mine."

Hannah did not speak.

"But that is not why I do not marry," he continued, his expression hooded. "It is because of the cloud over my own lineage. I do not know whether the title I possess is mine by right. What if I can never prove my legitimacy? What would that mean for my wife, for our children?"

"I suppose it would be difficult for them." Hannah looked away.

She felt the bench move as he rose. He was leaving. A wave of sadness engulfed her, but she girded herself against the tears that threatened. There was, after all, nothing else to do.

His hand touched her chin, forcing her to look up at him. She eyed him resentfully. Must he prolong this ordeal?

"Will you marry me, Hannah?"

Hannah blinked. "*What?*"

"Will you marry me?"

"I . . . you just explained why that is impossible." She stared at him.

He just stood there, looking down at her with an unreadable gaze.

"B-b-besides, we are so different," she stammered. "I am nothing and you are . . . you are a duke!"

He shrugged. "And perhaps I am not."

"I lived among prostitutes."

"And I may be a bastard," he returned.

A river of panic washed over her. He was toying with her, making her believe when she should not, must not. "I am deaf!"

"That," he replied, scowling, "is your feeblest argument yet. Do you suggest that your inability to hear has impaired your intelligence?"

"No, but—"

"Perhaps you would have me believe it affects something else—your desire for me?" He gave her a rueful smile. "I can safely assure you that mine is not affected one whit by whether or not you can hear."

Hannah blushed. "I did not mean—"

"Then what is left?"

"We come from two different worlds."

"And are outcasts from each of them. Marry me, Hannah. You have no choice."

Hannah started. "What do you mean?"

"Our night together thoroughly compromised you in a way no one will overlook." Amusement crept into his gaze. "You are bound to become my mistress or my wife, and since you have refused to do the former, it will have to be the latter."

"My reputation does not concern me," Hannah declared, her chin high.

"Ah. Now *that* is where we are different." He arched a brow. "For it does concern me. A great deal."

Hannah frowned. "This is all very baffling. Why should you care about my reputation? And why should you feel compelled to take such a drastic step?"

"Because any other course is simply unthinkable." He shook his head, as if to say he did not understand either.

Hannah took a deep breath. Marriage! Surely, it was impossible. And yet, there it was. But for the wrong reasons.

"I cannot, Julian," she said sadly. "I cannot marry you."

He did not immediately reply. That curious bleakness again swept his features. He stared at her. In that heartstopping moment, Hannah saw straight into the stark beauty of his soul.

And there in the stableyard in front of the ostlers and his own coachman, he got down on his knees in the dust before her. He spoke only one word, and if Hannah had not been so skilled at lipreading she would have doubted it herself.

"Please."

Chapter Twenty-two

"Everything has turned out splendidly." Lady Huffington positively beamed in the glow of countless candles that had been set to burning at Claridge House for Julian's wedding to Hannah.

"It would seem so, my lady," Higgins agreed tonelessly.

"I always say that what is meant to be, will. One cannot thwart the Fates."

"One does feel compelled at times to give them a bit of a hand," he noted grimly.

The countess bestowed a dazzling smile on him. "Are you not as happy as I, my friend? I declare, you seem a bit out of sorts."

"I was only thinking of my own state, madam."

Lady Huffington frowned. "What state is that?"

"A solitary one."

Her face fell. "I am sorry, Higgins. Does all this wedding merriment remind you of a lost love?"

"No, madam. Only one that is not quite found."

"I do not understand."

"Nor do I expect you to, my lady. If you will excuse me, I have some duties to attend to."

Lady Huffington stared after him, a puzzled and slightly hurt expression on her face.

"Is something wrong, Aunt?" Lucy's radiant smile brought the countess out of her reverie.

"Higgins seems rather sad tonight," she said. "I wonder if he regrets going into service years ago rather than seeking his father's seat in Parliament. I fear it has meant a lonely life."

Lucy eyed her curiously. "I imagine his was a decision of necessity, rather than preference."

The countess sighed. "I sometimes forget that money is far more important to those who do not have it. It was that way with your father. He always resented the fact that I had married into more wealth than he did. Oh, I beg your pardon, Lucy. I did not mean to suggest—"

"It is all right, Aunt. I am well aware of why Octavius married my mother." Lucy smiled. "It is one of the reasons why the state of Charles's finances does not bother me. I have seen quite vividly that money does not guarantee a happy marriage."

"No." Lady Huffington's tone grew thoughtful. "I wonder if I have properly appreciated all that Higgins has done for me."

Lucy fell silent. After a moment, Lady Huffington smiled and shook her head. "I have been woolgathering, dear. Do not regard it. We are here to celebrate a wedding. *Two* weddings," she amended. "Julian and Hannah's nuptials were so hastily arranged that I never had the opportunity to give you and Charles a proper party."

"And I never had the opportunity to thank you for arranging my elopement." Lucy smiled mischievously.

Lady Huffington looked shocked. "I do not know what you mean."

"I know that you do," her niece said, laughing. "What is more, I have my suspicions about Julian and Hannah, too. You schemed to get all of us together, did you not? And you succeeded splendidly."

"Not at all," Lady Huffington replied modestly. "Oh, I admit to some connivance, but Julian would never have allowed himself to be led into such a drastic state as marriage if he had no wish to go there himself."

Lucy grinned. "I have never seen him look happier."

Julian felt their gazes from across the room. Cursed matchmaking females—no doubt congratulating themselves on their cleverness. But no one had manipulated him into the marital state. He had walked into it with his eyes open, fully aware of his crime.

Looking at Hannah, he tried to banish his doubts about the future and his guilt at saddling her with a title that might not be his to give. In the moment that he had knelt in the dirt and pleaded for her hand, doubt and guilt had given way to the blinding need to keep her with him. He had known that his life hung in the balance; when she nodded, giving mute assent to his wildest dreams, his heart had been so full that he wanted to shout his joy to the heavens.

Nevertheless, the doubts were real. He could not wish them away. What would become of their children if he did not resolve the issue of his birth? Would they someday become objects of ridicule? And what of Hannah? How would she endure the scandal?

The sin he had committed weighed heavily. He had no right to marry until he discovered the truth. But with Hannah, there was only one truth—he had to have her. Once again, his selfishness had prevailed.

As he watched her chatting with their guests, some of his guilt began to give way to hope. How could any man look into those unflinching gray eyes and know anything but hope?

He frowned. He had not noticed the tiny lines of fatigue at the corners of those eyes. He had been too busy congratulating himself for finally possessing the only woman who had thoroughly enthralled him that he had not thought of her comfort. She must be exhausted. The week since they had returned with Lucy and Charles had been filled with arrangements for today's ceremony. She had been surrounded by a bevy of seamstresses, hairdressers, maids—not to mention his aunt and Lucy, both issuing commands. It was enough to strain the patience of a saint.

It was time to retire. The knowledge produced a self-satisfied grin. He would make her wedding night special. He would not be too demanding—he would see to her pleasure without a thought for his own. She would know that he could, for a time at least, set selfishness aside.

Most important, he would banish the memory of those other men she had known. Part of him wished that he was to be the first, but what mattered was that she was his now.

Julian smiled down at her and was delighted to see a blush steal over her features. Yes, he would give her something she had not had with the others. He would drive her wild with passion. He had it all planned.

But when at last he had her alone in their chamber, Julian had difficulty remembering just how he meant this moment to go. Impatience raced through him, and he could not bear to leave her to the ministrations of her maid.

Instead, as she watched him with wide eyes, he set himself to the task of removing the pins from her hair and brushing that flowing mane until it shone. Their gazes met in the mirror. His composure deserted him.

"Hannah," he rasped, stunned at the force of his need.

She could not hear the strangeness in his voice. Perhaps that is why her gaze did not flinch from his. Perhaps that is why her eyes held no fear, only shyness, as she turned into his embrace.

As quickly as that, he was undone.

Gone were his plans to set his own desire aside. Gone was his control, disintegrating in the flames that burned within as he fumbled with the infernal little pearl buttons the seamstress had seen fit to sew securely up the back of her gown. Gone were his good intentions, evaporating in the heat that caused his desperate hands to seek the cool smoothness of her bare shoulders as the gown fell away.

And gone was the confidence that came with having made love to countless women. As her nakedness unfolded under his hands, Julian felt utterly at sea.

Her breasts were small and beautifully formed. The thought of another man's having seen them thus, nipples proudly erect and the soft roundness waiting to fill his palm, knifed him with despair. With a savage growl, he lifted her into his arms and carried her to the bed.

Not once did her solemn eyes show anything but trust as he fumbled with the fabric at her waist, freeing her of the voluminous wedding gown and the thin lawn chemise underneath.

When her nakedness was complete and she reached out for him, Julian could only marvel at the conviction that burned in her eyes.

She did not speak. Julian had never made love to a woman in so complete a silence. It covered them like a blanket, co-

cooning them in a pleasure made all the more intense by the sudden acuity of the other senses.

The fresh, seductive scent of her hair tingled his nostrils. The rapid rhythm of her breathing spurred an answering breathlessness in his own chest. The faint salty taste of her skin pleasured his tongue with a cornucopia of delights no edible feast could hope to match.

And when he joined their bodies, her eyes gave him more than words, more than sound, more than all the other senses combined. Abandoning all hope of restraint, he accepted the gift of the silence that enveloped them and the gift of her body that completed him at last.

It was only afterward, when he held her in his arms and mentally reproached himself for his lack of control, that he realized another truth he had banished in the wonder of fulfillment.

A truth he could scarcely dare to believe.

He stared at her. She was studying the canopy overhead, her gaze fixed on the intricate designs woven there but, he suspected, not really seeing them. Gently, he stroked her cheek. Instantly, she turned to him.

"Why did you not tell me you were a virgin?" he demanded, his voice raw with self-reproach.

"You would not have believed," she said simply.

Julian did not deny it. He could not believe he had been so blind. Hannah Gregory may have lived among whores, but only a completely self-absorbed idiot would think her anything like them. He groaned at his own insensitive stupidity. "You must be in pain."

"Some," she confessed. "It does not bother me."

Helpless to undo what had been done, he could only promise to do better. "I will never allow you to be hurt again," he vowed.

"I have learned in my life that one must take responsibility for one's own pain," she said calmly. "I do not shirk from that duty."

Julian stilled. "Our lovemaking was a . . . a duty?"

"Not at all." She flushed. "I only mean to say that you need not treat me any differently from anyone else. I am not fragile, despite my infirmity."

"Good God, woman! You are not anyone else—you are my wife!" Incredulous, he stared at her. "How I made love to you had nothing to do with your deafness. But had I had known you were a virgin, it would have been different."

Her expression grew curious. "In what way?"

Something in those intent gray eyes sent his heart to his throat. His pulse began to gallop, and suddenly he felt like an untried youth marveling at the sensual possibilities unfolding before him.

"Do you remember that night in the carriage?" he asked softly.

Her face grew scarlet. Part of him wondered that she could blush after what they had just shared; the other part felt as if he were a virgin himself. There was a newness here so delicate and fragile it filled him with awe.

"It would be impossible to forget," she confessed.

"Perhaps," he murmured, nibbling at her earlobe, "you will permit me to create a new memory or two."

Her brow furrowed. "I did not catch your words," she said with a little smile of apology.

Carefully, almost reverentially, Julian began to stroke her, his hands seeking new places along with the special ones he had found that night in the carriage.

"They were not important," he murmured, as she gave a breathless little moan.

But she missed his reply. Her eyes were closed in helpless pleasure.

Beethoven had not accepted his fate. Why should she?

Hannah's graceful fingers called forth the slow introduction to the composer's piano sonata *Pathétique*, an elegy for the world of sounds that had begun to desert him.

Sadness and futility dominated the piece, written two decades ago as his hearing deteriorated. The agitated E flat minor theme spoke of fears and restless denial. How deep must be his sorrow now, with music and sound only distant memories?

Yet his later works were even more breathtaking, more radical in their beauty. How had he moved from denial to despair to even greater creativity? How had he learned to accept his loss, yet to defy it?

A tear rolled down her cheek as she began the grand adagio cantabile. It fell onto the clavichord's luminous ivory keys, which for all her artistry remained resolutely silent to her ears.

As in Beethoven's music, despair and joy warred within her. A week of marriage had brought laughter to her face, blushes to her cheeks, and an embarrassing need to bask in the glow of delicious sensuality Julian had given her. Almost, she could believe that she was like any other new bride, marveling in the joys of married life.

But she was not like other women. He said her deafness was not important, but he was wrong. She could not put it aside as if it was some ordinary flaw, like a tendency to put on weight or to snore at night. She wanted to hear again. And that want would burden her marriage forever.

She had spent the last three years in the hope that one day she would find a cure. She wanted to be whole, like the woman he saw at night, when their bodies spoke more effectively than any words.

Julian might feel affection for her, but it was not the profound love that burned within her. One day he would tire of always having to look at her to speak, of compensating in a thousand other ways for her deficiency.

It was not his fault. He was just not a man to settle for second-best. She could not saddle him with a lifelong burden.

Her fingers moved into the classic rondo, coming to rest after the last, soundless notes of the coda. She sat for a moment, studying the music she had just played in useless pantomime. The *Pathétique* was filled with tragedy, despair, hope, defiance. Beethoven had understood.

Her chin high, Hannah rose from the clavichord and walked over to a small writing table. She pulled out a sheet of paper, dipped the pen into the inkwell, and began to compose a note to Dr. Itard.

Chapter Twenty-three

He thumbed the fragile pages, but the Bible's record of the family's unions and births was as barren as ever. A perverse desire for punishment must run deep in him, Julian thought bitterly, 'else why sit here like a fool seeking answers from a book that had previously failed him?

Because a week of marriage to Hannah had made him desperate for answers. She had given him her all, but what did he have to give? A dubious title and a lifetime of uncertainty. He could not encumber her with that burden for the rest of their days. Sooner or later it would eat away at that very precious thing that was beginning to blossom between them, that thing so fragile he scarcely knew what to call it.

One word caught his eye as he flipped through the pages. *Forgiveness.* It bothered him, that word, nagged at him like an obligation that would not go away.

Forgiveness. Octavius had not forgiven his mother for losing her fortune, and Julian had never forgiven Octavius for his cruelty. But the past was done, after all; he could not change what had gone before. The future lay ahead, and it was a future that held Hannah.

Still, Julian knew he would never, ever forgive himself if he saddled Hannah with a bastard's progeny.

An answer had to be found. Somewhere. Somehow.

With a heavy sigh, Julian picked up the sermons. Though the writing had faded with the years, his aunt's bold hand was easily recognizable. He could well imagine Octavius consigning her letters to the topmost forgotten shelf between the pages of the book he read the least. Why his father had saved them at all remained a mystery, for they were filled with reproach.

"Abandoning Helene would be reprehensible," his aunt had written. Julian's mouth twisted into a bitter smile. His father would have been livid at that, for he believed it his right to do what he wished, when he wished to do it.

Abandoning Helene. It occurred to him that his aunt referred to that very time of utmost importance to him. He frowned. If his mother had been no more than Octavius's mistress, why would Aunt Eleanor have objected to his ending the liaison?

Fascinated, Julian read on—until he became aware of another presence in his library. He looked up to see Higgins in the doorway.

"What is it?" Julian demanded, irritated by the interruption.

"There is a person in the house, Your Grace." Higgins allowed a portentous pause. "I believe he calls himself a physician."

Julian arched a brow. "I gather you do not approve of our visitor."

"It is not my place to approve or disapprove, Your Grace," Higgins replied stiffly.

One day soon, his aunt would return to Yorkshire and take Higgins with her. For now, the man stood before him as immovable as a mountain. Julian sighed. "You wish me to rid the house of my aunt's latest quack, I suppose."

"The man is here to see the *duchess*," Higgins corrected in an ominous tone. "They have been secluded in Her Grace's sitting room for half an hour. I thought it best to bring the matter to Your Grace's attention."

A bolt of alarm shot through him. "Is something wrong with my wife?"

"I do not know." Higgins's expression plainly said that it was Julian's place, not his, to investigate such a matter.

Julian's pulse began to race. Hannah had seemed perfectly healthy this morning—and last night, and every other night since their wedding. But perhaps her passion had not matched his. Perhaps he had done her some injury during their lovemaking that she had, in characteristic fashion, kept to herself.

Tossing the sermons aside, he strode swiftly into the hall, taking the steps two at a time up to Hannah's sitting room. With a feeling of dread, he pushed the door open.

Hannah lay motionless on the divan, curled into a ball. Dr. Itard hovered over her. An oily substance dripped from his fingers. Fear knifed through Julian's gut.

"What in God's name have you done to my wife?" He grabbed Itard by the collar and ripped him away from her.

"There is no need to panic." Indignantly, Itard straightened his jacket. "I have but cut a small hole in her eardrum, into which I have poured boiling eucalyptus oil. It is a very promising method of treatment which I devised myself."

Julian knelt over Hannah's too-still form, his heart in his throat. "If you have harmed her, I shall kill you."

"Oh, no," Itard hastened to assure him. "She merely fainted from the . . . ah, small discomfort of the procedure."

There was much Julian had yet to learn about his bride, but he knew for certain that no "small discomfort" would make Hannah faint. She was made of sterner stuff. The procedure she had endured must have been excruciating. Fury filled him.

"I will slice you to ribbons, Itard," he growled, as Itard edged nervously toward the door. Julian rose and followed him. "I swear you will feel every cut—just as she felt that needle of yours."

"Now, Your Grace, there is no need—"

"Higgins!" Julian barked.

"Yes, Your Grace," came the breathless response. Higgins leaned heavily against the doorjamb, trying to recover from following Julian's mad dash up the staircase.

"Send for a doctor at once—a *real* doctor."

"Yes, Your Grace."

"But *I* am a doctor," Itard protested feebly. "And I tell you that Her Grace is in no danger."

Julian seized him by the lapels. "A pain sufficient to overwhelm her senses will linger, Itard. She will suffer the results of your folly long after you have departed. And what of the risk of infection? Can you guarantee she faces no danger?"

Itard tried to shrink inside his coat.

"Get out of my sight," Julian said softly, "before I forget that it is unlawful to wring a man's neck like a turkey at Michaelmas."

Itard paled. In the next instant he was gone.

Lifting Hannah into his arms, Julian carried her into their chamber and gently laid her down on the bed. He tucked the covers carefully around her. At that moment, he would have given anything to see those gray eyes regard him with their unsettling intensity. An unfamiliar moisture clouded his vision.

"Hannah," he murmured, his voice breaking on an anguished sob, "you foolish, foolish woman."

Pain, sharp and unforgiving, ripped through her. A hot stabbing needle danced through her dreams, taunting her. All her powers of concentration failed to control the agony it wielded like an invincible weapon.

Her head throbbed. Her body twitched restlessly. Every time her mind lured her toward wakefulness, pain drew her deeper into its embrace. Even sleep did not banish that searing pain or the icy chills that accompanied it.

Determined, she swam upward through layers of awareness and willed her eyes to open. Her husband sat at her bedside, his head in his hands.

"Julian?" Hannah felt her voice emerge from somewhere deep in her chest. He did not move. She tried again, expelling his name in what must have been an unsteady croak.

Instantly, his gaze met hers. His dark, brooding eyes searched hers relentlessly.

"How . . . do you feel?" he said slowly. Hannah was stunned to see fear in those midnight depths.

The pain receded to a faint throbbing in the vicinity of her left ear. "Better, I think." She hesitated. "Have I been ill long?"

"Ten days—an eternity." Harsh circles of fatigue rimmed his eyes. His face was pale, save for that angry, jagged scar. His mouth thinned into a bitter line. "An infection set in from the wound in your ear."

His grim, vengeful mask almost made her yearn for the tormented ignorance of sleep, but Hannah knew she must face the consequences of defying her husband.

"I am sorry," she said, lowering her gaze. "I had to try one last time. Will you ever forgive me?"

Strong fingers touched her chin, firmly bringing it up so that she must needs look at him. His gaze was as bleak as a moonless sky.

"I was afraid you were gone."

She stared, uncomprehending. His hand moved to her hair. With excruciating tenderness, he began to stroke it. Then, like a vengeful god, his brows drew together like thunderclouds.

"I would never have forgiven you for dying."

Hannah closed her eyes. She had lost him. Her foolish, selfish act had lost him forever.

His thumbs brushed her lids. Afraid of what she might see, Hannah nevertheless forced her eyes to open. His gaze bored into hers.

"I would not have forgiven you for dying," he said slowly, distinctly, so that she absorbed every word, "but I will forgive you anything else, Hannah. *Anything.*"

That slashing mouth curved into a tentative smile. In wonder, Hannah reached out to touch his lips. He caught her hand and softly kissed her fingertips.

For a breathless moment she studied him uncertainly. "I did not like to defy you," she said, willing him to understand, "but you deserve more than to suffer a deaf wife for the rest of your days."

With a helpless shake of his head, he gathered her into his arms. Hannah sighed as his comforting warmth stole over her. But even as she relaxed into his embrace, her lashes fluttered shut and sleep claimed her once more.

"What a horrid man!"

"Yes, madam."

"Julian has much to thank you for. If you had not come to him when you did, goodness knows what might have happened to Hannah."

Higgins did not speak.

Lady Huffington regarded him over the rim of her teacup. The majordomo was surveying the trunks and boxes that had been assembled for the return trip tomorrow. "Is something wrong, Higgins? You do not seem yourself today."

Higgins stiffened. "I am perfectly myself, madam."

"You need not poker up." Lady Huffington sniffed. "I was only concerned for your welfare. You have not said two words to me all morning."

"I have been thinking about our journey."

The countess smiled. "Yes, it will be good to be home in Yorkshire, will it not? Among our own things and friends."

"*Your* things, my lady."

"What? Oh, well . . ." Her voice trailed off. She eyed Higgins sharply. "What *is* it Higgins? I know you too well. Something is bothering you—I am sure of it."

Rigid as a stone, he faced her. "I am giving notice, madam."

Lady Huffington gasped. "What? But—you cannot!"

He arched a brow.

"That is, well . . . we have been together so long," the countess sputtered. "I have come to depend on you."

"Yes," he agreed, "rather like a faithful lapdog."

Frowning, the countess studied him. "I believe you *are* out of sorts, Higgins."

"Not at all."

"I have not sufficiently appreciated your work—is that it?" She brightened. "I will increase your wages, effective immediately."

"Thank you, but I still must give notice. I will see you home to Yorkshire and help you find a replacement, but I must leave your employ."

"Leave?" Lady Huffington looked stricken. "But Higgins, you cannot! I would not know what to do without you. You are . . . you are irreplaceable."

"Is that a fact?" He met her gaze.

Lady Huffington looked away.

Higgins returned his attention to the boxes.

"Have you . . . have you been unhappy, Higgins?" the countess asked in a small voice.

"Yes, madam. I fear I have."

"I am sorry," she said. "I know I am a difficult woman but I thought . . . you did not mind being with me."

He turned. "I have been privileged to serve you, madam. But there are times when a person must change the course of his life to save his own sanity."

"Sanity?" The countess looked bewildered. "Is there anything . . . anything I can do to persuade you to stay?"

Higgins regarded her for a moment, then shook his head. "My mind is made up."

"Oh, dear. I am sorry, Higgins."

"So am I." Without another word, he picked up a box and carried it from the room.

Sipping a restorative brandy, Julian mentally recounted this week's victories, small and large. Hannah had recovered her appetite, her color, and her indomitable spirit. Not bad for his first effort at nursing.

She was sleeping now. It was not the unnatural sleep that pain wrought, but the well-earned oblivion that came from a day of taking her first turn about the garden since her illness, bidding farewell to Aunt Eleanor and Higgins—who were, thank God, finally on their way to Yorkshire—and planning menus with the cook.

A strange peace had descended over his household that had nothing to do with his aunt's departure and everything to do with the wonder that was Hannah. Without any discernible reason, the weight on his shoulders had grown lighter. All that mattered now was that she regain her health. They would weather whatever else fate sent them.

Julian wished he understood what was happening to him. He wished he had words to describe the unfamiliar feeling that washed over him when he looked at her. He wished he did not fear that its fragile beauty would vanish, as everything he had ever counted on had vanished.

Long ago, he had taught himself not to care. Now, he knew he would care forever. The knowledge chilled him, even as it warmed the brittle edges of his frosty soul.

Idly, he glanced at the words that had leaped off the pages and across the decades at him in the moments before Higgins came to tell him of Itard's presence. They seemed unimportant now. Because of Hannah, the past had somehow lost its sting.

Still, he had nothing better to do while Hannah slept. He took another sip of brandy and tried to decipher his aunt's faded scrawl.

"You ought to have brought her here long ago. It is not Helene's fault that a group of insane Frenchmen deprived her family of their property and their heads. The Bible teaches that we must show compassion and mercy. Where is your compassion, Octavius?"

Again, that concern, wholly incongruous had Helene been Octavius's mistress. Julian skipped over several pages of his aunt's tirade, which consisted of passages of Scripture interposed with her own stern axioms. If his aunt had been born a male, he decided, she would have made a fine bishop.

On the last page, his gaze lurched to a halt on a paragraph that was sharp and direct:

"Know this: Octavius: You wed Helene for life before God. You must accept the consequences. I have therefore taken your marriage documents into my keeping to prevent you from destroying them should another woman catch your eye. And if you try to get a bill of divorcement through the Parliament, I will not send you another penny."

He must have been holding his breath, for suddenly it expelled in a great whoosh of air. His redoubtable aunt had taken the papers to Yorkshire. Doubtless it never occurred to her that he would care to have them, for Julian had never told her of his father's deathbed denunciation.

How Octavius must have hated the son who bound him to an unwanted wife and the sister who held his manhood hostage. How he must have hated the fact that the rich wife he eventually wed produced no heir. Long before they met, hate had poisoned the paternal bonds between Octavius and him; when his father at last claimed him, it was too late. Octavius had looked into his son's eyes and seen his own hate reflected back at him. To make certain Julian would never enjoy his legacy, he had told that vengeful lie.

The shame that had stalked Julian most of his life had been unnecessary. He was not a bastard.

Where was the boundless happiness he should feel?

For his entire adult life he had sought to prove his legitimacy, yet when proof came, it was nothing to the joy that Hannah had brought into his life—a gift more precious than any marriage papers. He did not understand: Why had a generous, strong, courageous, intelligent, talented woman married a man who had been selfish, ill-tempered, manipulative, and occasionally cruel?

Not to gain wealth and position, for she had known those things could have been ripped from a bastard duke. Not to save her reputation, for she had been immovable until he had dropped to the dirt and pleaded for her hand.

Suddenly, the truth cut like a blinding beacon of light through the lost years of dissipation and bitterness.

Love had somehow come to him, even though he had not dared to believe, even though he had spent a lifetime of creating a seamless veneer over his pitiable soul.

Abruptly, he cast his aunt's sermon aside. Precious, unspoken words haunted him as desperately as those taunting lies his father had spoken so easily from his deathbed.

His heart thundering in his chest, Julian jumped to his feet. And hoped Hannah would forgive him for interrupting her sleep.

Chapter Twenty-four

An inner power flowed through her hands to the keyboard. She was at one with Beethoven in this, one of his most introspective and noble works. The sonata's grandiose, contrapuntal allegro advanced to breathtaking dimensions. Then came the scherzo, with its brusque contrasts, and the long adagio, its somber melancholy interposed with moments of brightness and calm. Then the fugue. Fugues within fugues. And finally, Beethoven crashed the piece to a halt.

In her dream, Hannah heard every note. Her hands no longer depressed the keys in pantomime, but drew forth every grand theme Beethoven had written for this majestic key of B flat major.

His passion, his melancholy, his triumph were hers, and when the piece ended, Hannah's joy went on and on. She would always hear the music in that part of her that was beyond speech, beyond hearing. Perhaps it was time she accepted the music within—and the deafness without.

Gradually, Hannah became aware that someone was shaking her arm. She frowned. She was so tired. It had been such a busy day, and her night of sleep had only just begun. Burrowing deeper into the covers, she tried to shut out the distraction.

But the shaking grew more persistent, and she grabbed for her pillow, trying to cling to the last vestiges of sleep. "Go away," she murmured grumpily.

In answer, a pair of strong hands ripped the pillow from under her head and pulled her abruptly to a sitting position. Hannah's eyes shot open, flashing angrily.

"What in heaven's name . . . ?" Her voice trailed off as she saw Julian, his face illuminated by the light of a single candle. Fear, joy, determination filled his gaze, along with something else that jerked her heart to a halt.

"Are you fully awake?" he demanded.

Hannah rubbed her eyes. "Julian, what is it?"

"I want to make certain you are awake. I have never said this before." He put his hands on her shoulders. To her amazement, he was trembling.

She regarded him intently. "Whatever you have to say, be assured that you have my complete attention."

"I love you."

Hannah knew she could not have understood him correctly. "I did not . . ." Her voice trailed off. This brooding, cynical man was suddenly looking at her with all of the shy eagerness of a puppy, so perhaps she had. "Did—did you say 'love'?" she stammered.

"Yes. And I want to shout it to the skies." He pulled her into his arms. His lips moved against her skin, and Hannah felt his warm breath on her ear. Gently, she pushed him away.

"You must look at me when you speak," she pleaded, suddenly shy herself. "I want to understand why, why you—" She broke off, not daring to say the words.

"Why I suddenly realized that I love you, when the truth has been staring me in the face for who knows how long?" Julian grinned.

His wild exuberance caused the tender kernel of joy that had taken root inside her that long-ago night in his study to hope that it would be nourished at last.

"I have been so blind," he said, caressing her cheek.

For a long moment their gazes held. Then, almost as an afterthought, he added, "I am not a bastard, Hannah. My aunt has the marriage papers. I discovered the truth in one of her letters."

Hannah threw her arms around him. "That is wonderful, Julian. But your background never mattered to me."

"I know that now." He cocked his head. "The strange thing is, somewhere between our wedding and the aftermath of Itard's visit, it stopped mattering to me, too. You are all that I care about, Hannah."

She could only stare at him in wonder.

"Somehow I have managed to forgive the past. And to forgive myself for letting my father nearly destroy me." He studied her intently. "It is the same for you, is it not?"

"I think I understand," she said slowly. "I suppose I have finally forgiven myself for being deaf. I was afraid it would ruin things for us, but—"

"Never," he swore fiercely. "I love everything about you. Hannah, including the fact that your deafness forces me to face those lovely eyes of yours every time we speak. You brook no compromise, Hannah. You demand the truth. Now I demand it from you."

The loving power in that boundless gaze caused the little kernel inside her to throw joyous shoots heavenward. "I love you, Julian," she confessed, "so very much."

With a great whoop, he caught her to him. "Now *that* I shall certainly shout to the heavens," he declared. Before she could catch her breath, he carried her to the window, flung it open, and hurled the words into the night.

Years lifted from his face. Pure joy erased the harsh lines of cynicism. Eyes that had held deep pools of despair now reflected the glowing fires of love.

Looking up at that boldly planed face and the shock of unruly hair that would not be tamed, Hannah held her breath. Life burned within him. He had never looked more vibrant—like a fierce god waking from an endless sleep. It was as if she were witnessing a rebirth.

Again and again he shouted their love to the heavens, holding her up so the stars could witness his victory and hear his symphony of joy.

The music soared within her, too. The breathtaking allegro, the turbulent fugues, the song of the lark, the cry of the wind—all of them swelled within her. In Julian's pure, keening joy, she heard them anew.

Laughter bubbled up from deep inside, where that burgeoning kernel thrived and always would. Tears of happiness rolled down her cheeks. Overwhelmed, Hannah buried her face in his arms. Unable to speak, she simply shook her head and closed her eyes.

That was when he turned to the heavens and trumpeted his love once more.

And, to her boundless wonder, she heard every word.

Epilogue

"I am glad that Hannah is recovering nicely," Lady Huffington declared as the carriage lumbered over a particularly large bump in the road. "I could never have left Claridge House otherwise."

"No," Higgins agreed tersely. He sat across from her, having spent most of the journey staring silently out the window. There was an odd tenseness about him.

She shot him a sidelong glance. "I do wish you would think about your decision, Higgins. I—I will miss you."

"I have thought about it."

"Oh?" she asked hopefully.

"I must leave your employ."

Her face fell. "Then I suppose that is that." She glanced out the window. "It is wonderful to see the dear Yorkshire moors again," she said in a dull voice.

Higgins allowed his gaze to flick over the passing scenery. "I rather imagine"—he spoke carefully—"that you will enjoy the Scottish moors just as well."

Lady Huffington frowned. "Whatever do you mean?"

"Scotland, madam," he replied quietly.

"*Scotland?* But Huffington Manor is but a few miles away. I have no plans to go to Scotland."

"Nevertheless, we should be there shortly, despite the fact that this infernal coach has the speed of a turtle."

Lady Huffington put her lorgnette up to her nose and regarded the man who had been in her employ for so many years. "Higgins, have you lost your mind?"

"Not at all." He paused. "I am abducting you, madam."

The countess' mouth fell open. "*Abducting* me? You *have* lost your wits!"

Higgins sighed. "I suppose that comes of seeing so many happy lovers recently united in marriage."

Speechless, she could not reply.

His gaze was unreadable. "Once, you said that deep friendship can be a strong foundation for love. I wonder, madam: do you still believe that?"

She blinked. "I suppose . . . at least with Charles and Lucy that is how it happened. With Hannah and Julian, it was a bit more complicated."

"Lust."

"I beg your pardon?"

Higgins allowed his gaze to drift over the feather that swept from her turban. Then his steady brown eyes bored into hers. "We decided that theirs was a case of lust providing the initial attraction. Followed by love."

The countess tilted her head consideringly.

"What would it take?" he asked softly.

She eyed him blankly.

"What would it take," he repeated, "for a woman to allow herself to return a man's regard, even though the liaison may seem inappropriate? I asked you that once. Do you recall what you said?"

"Yes." Lady Huffington lowered her lashes. "Something . . . outlandish."

"Outlandish," he repeated, a gleam of satisfaction in his eyes.

Slowly, a pink glow suffused her features. "We also decided that sometimes in life one must take chances," she ventured. "Is . . . is that what this is, Higgins? A chance?"

Something warm and electric radiated from his gaze. "An *outlandish* chance, madam," he confessed.

A look of shy wonder crept into her gaze. "I fear I have been extremely slow-witted, Higgins. *Higgins?*" Her eyes grew wide as he crossed the space between their seats.

"And I, madam, have loved you for so long."

Lady Huffington expelled a great breath. "Then I . . . I was the woman you loved who—"

"Was wed to another," he confirmed.

"Why did you not speak up after Leon died?"

"You were so far above me that I dared not—"

"Your father was a member of Parliament," the countess interjected huffily. "I dare anyone to say a word against you. Why I recall—"

Higgins grinned, an event so rare that it halted Lady Huffington mid-sentence. When he reached for her hand, she blinked shyly.

"I confess I have wondered . . . even hoped," she said hesitantly, "but it seemed so . . ." Her voice trailed off as he brought her fingertips to his lips.

"Outlandish?" he queried with a mischievous arch of his brow.

"Oh, Higgins," she murmured, blushing furiously, "I declare, you have such a *rakish* mind." She did not look at all displeased.

Settling back against the squabs, Higgins tucked her hand under his arm. "I confess I am vastly looking forward to seeing Scotland—Eleanor."

"Oh, Higgins," she said, sighing happily.

And with that, the ancient traveling coach lumbered down the road toward Gretna Green.